HERCULE POIROT'S
SILENT NIGHT

Agatha Christie

Hercule Poirot's Silent Night

THE NEW HERCULE POIROT MYSTERY

SOPHIE HANNAH

HarperCollins*Publishers*

HarperCollins*Publishers*
1 London Bridge Street
London SE1 9GF
www.harpercollins.co.uk

HarperCollins*Publishers*
Macken House, 39/40 Mayor Street Upper
Dublin 1, D01 C9W8, Ireland

Published by HarperCollins*Publishers* 2023
1

'It Couldn't Be Done' from *The Path to Home* by Edgar Albert Guest
first published by The Reilly & Lee Co. 1919

Sophie Hannah asserts the moral right
to be identified as the author of this work.

A catalogue record for this book
is available from the British Library

ISBN 978-0-00-838079-3 HB
ISBN 978-0-00-838081-6 TPB

Set in Sabon LT STD by Palimpsest Book Production Ltd,
Falkirk, Stirlingshire.
Printed and bound in the UK using 100% renewable electricity at
CPI Group (UK) Ltd, Croydon CR0 4YY

MIX
Paper | Supporting
responsible forestry
FSC™ C007454

This book is produced from independently certified FSC™ paper
to ensure responsible forest management.

For more information visit: www.harpercollins.co.uk/green

For Kate Jones,
who is brilliant at everything and whose
editorial suggestions improved this book immensely.

Acknowledgements

Huge thanks as always to James and Mathew Prichard, Julia Wilde and all at Agatha Christie Ltd; to my incredible agent Peter Straus; to my amazing editor David Brawn (who came up with the perfect title) and to everyone at HarperCollins; also, to all my international publishers who have done such a wonderful job of helping my Poirot novels to reach so many readers all over the world.

Thank you to my family: Dan, Phoebe, Guy and Brewster, to my mum and sister; to Emily Winslow for the incomparable editorial feedback, as always; to Alex Michaelides, my 'book deadline twin', who kept me company on the breathless sprint to the deadline (and the next deadline, after we missed the first one), and to both Alex and Kemper Donovan for emergency consultation services!

Massive thanks to Kate, this book's dedicatee, for keeping the entire show on the road at all times; to Faith and Naomi, my brilliant website and newsletter gurus; and to all my

Dream Authors, with whom I discussed the development of this novel many times during the process of writing it.

Thank you to everyone who reads my books and writes to me to say you've enjoyed them. It means such a lot.

Last but not least, thank you to the Rightmove website for inspiration—specifically, for showing me a suspiciously cheap mansion on the Norfolk coast that turned out to be 'such a bargain' because it was definitely going to be falling into the sea within five years.

Contents

New Year's Eve 1931

My experiment was not working. I laid down my pen and considered tearing the sheet of paper into strips. In the end, I crushed it into a jagged ball, aimed it at the fire that was blazing in the grate, and missed.

Hercule Poirot, sitting across the room from me, looked up from the book he was reading. 'Your endeavour displeases you, *mon ami*?'

'Dismal failure.'

'Try placing an unmarked page in front of you. Immediately, your mind will produce better ideas.' His green eyes darted to and fro between the neat pile of paper on the corner of his desk and the crumpled ball of my failed project, which stood out prominently against the backdrop of his otherwise pristine London drawing room.

I knew what he was thinking: on my way to get more paper, I would surely take the opportunity to rectify the disorder that was entirely of my creation. Hercule Poirot is not a man who can tolerate anything in his immediate vicinity being in the wrong place for more than . . . how long? If I did nothing, would it be seconds or minutes before he asked me to tidy up the mess I had made?

Determined not to tarnish my record as an exemplary guest, I moved quickly. My second attempt landed the offending object in the fire where it belonged. I returned to my armchair without availing myself of a clean sheet of paper. 'You do not wish to try again?' said Poirot. 'You are giving up on your—what did you call it?—your "top hole" idea?'

'Some ideas are appealing only until one tries to make them a reality,' I said. My mistake had been to try to turn mine into after-dinner entertainment, when it was clear to me now that any species of fun was the very last thing it should be.

'Perhaps you could tell me what you had in mind, if it is no longer to be the great surprise—?'

'It was nothing, really.' I was too embarrassed to discuss it. 'I shall prepare a crossword puzzle instead.'

'Such secrecy.' Shaking his head, Poirot leaned back in his chair. 'Always, when I think about secrets, I shall remember the words of Miss Verity Hunt in her bright red evening gown. Do you recall them, Catchpool?'

'Unfortunately, yes.' I considered Miss Hunt's supposedly sage advice to be quite the most ludicrous bilge I had ever heard.

Predictably, Poirot repeated the irritating axiom, perhaps in the hope of provoking me: '"Whatever you most wish to keep hidden, steel yourself for the ordeal ahead and then tell it to the whole world. At once, you will be free." This is, I think, great wisdom.'

'It's codswallop,' I said. 'You will be free only from the secrecy—which you chose in the first place because you preferred it to all the things you *won't* be free of for very long if you reveal all: endless interference and pestering from every quarter, no doubt. And that is if you are not breaking the law. In the case of a criminal—let us say, a murderer—you would hardly be free from the hangman, would you, if you announced that you were the guilty party?'

Poirot nodded. 'I too am considering the case of a murderer.'

Neither of us spoke the name of the one who was still very much in our minds.

'It is true,' he said. 'Once the crimes were committed, subterfuge became necessary in order to evade justice. But I wonder . . . Without the determination to keep the terrible secret at all costs there would have been no motive to commit any murders at all.'

'Say that again, Poirot.' I thought I must have misheard.

'It is obvious: if the killer had not decided that it was worth committing two murders in order to keep the secret hidden—'

'That is quite wrong,' I interrupted, unable to contain my protest. His mistaken pronouncement was as intolerable to me as my paper ball on the floor had been to him. 'The motive for the murders was not a fear of other people finding out. That wasn't it at all.'

3

'What fit of delusion is this? Of course that was the reason!'

'No, it was not.'

Poirot looked alarmed. 'I do not understand your meaning, *mon ami*. Do you not recall hearing with your own ears when the killer confirmed—?'

'As clearly as you do.' It was little more than a week ago that Poirot had removed all need for further deception on the part of the murderer by revealing the full facts of the case himself, in his inimitable fashion. His deductions had been correct in every detail, and yet . . . how fascinating and frustrating that he was so wrong about the *why* of it all—and that his mistake should only now become apparent, eight days later.

I searched his face for signs that he was amusing himself by testing me, and found none; he meant every word of it. How extraordinary.

I fell silent for a while, assuming he must be right and I wrong. Traditionally, that was the way we did it. Could this be an unprecedented deviation from that general principle? The more I tossed the question around, the more certain I was: the Norfolk murders that Poirot had just solved so brilliantly were not committed in order to keep the killer's secret. To believe this was to misunderstand, profoundly, what had taken place at St Walstan's Hospital and at Frellingsloe House between 8 September and Christmas.

I hurried to Poirot's desk and took four sheets from the top of the stack of clean paper. I have written, so far, an account of every case that Poirot has solved with my (infinitely flawed but always devoted) help. I had not yet started on my retelling of the Norfolk murders, however. Until this moment, it had felt too soon to do so.

There were still a few hours before dinner. I would not normally embark upon something so important at the very end of a departing year but I was unwilling to wait a second longer. Silently, I said to myself, 'Let the wise reader be the judge of whether or not secrecy was the motive.' Then I picked up my pen, and went all the way back to the beginning . . .

19 DECEMBER 1931

CHAPTER 1

An Unwelcome Visitor

Poirot and I were debating the relative merits of turkey and duck, and which should feature in our Christmas luncheon, when there came a knock at the door of his Whitehaven Mansions drawing room. 'Enter!' he said.

I was grateful for the pause. It would give me time to consider whether I had done all I could and might now reasonably concede defeat. I had been making the case for turkey, but the truth was that I preferred duck. A strong belief in the importance of tradition had compelled me to argue against my own personal taste. Since Poirot was the one who would be hosting our Christmas festivities, he should probably be allowed to have his way—this was the conclusion I reached as George, Poirot's valet, leaned somewhat awkwardly into the room.

'I apologize for the interruption, sir, but a lady is here to see you. She has no appointment but says it is a matter of the utmost importance. She believes it cannot wait, not even until tomorrow.'

'I can leave—' I said, half out of my chair.

'No, no, Catchpool. Stay. I am not inclined to receive an unexpected visitor this afternoon. I have noticed that, since the American stock market unpleasantness, most people are unable to measure accurately the urgency of their predicament.'

We at Scotland Yard had noticed the same thing, I told him.

'They come to my door insisting that they must have the help of Hercule Poirot. *Eh bien*, I listen patiently, and usually there is nothing more than an easily resolvable misunderstanding—a trivial altercation with a business associate or something of that nature. Nothing to confound or delight the little grey cells.'

'Yes. Trifles are magnified and viewed as disasters,' I said, thinking of the woman who had barged into my office two weeks earlier, demanding that I investigate the 'robbery' of her spectacles. She telephoned the next day to tell me that the unknown miscreant had replaced them in the pocket of her gardening coat; in other words, she had deposited them there herself and forgotten all about it. 'Please consider the matter closed,' she had said briskly, unaware that this had been my resolution from the moment I first laid eyes upon her.

I felt satisfaction swell in my chest as it did each time I reminded myself that I was a mere two days into a two-week holiday from my job at Scotland Yard.

'What shall I tell Mrs Surtees?' George asked Poirot. 'That is the name of your visitor: Enid Surtees.'

As he repeated the name, I found myself wishing I were

elsewhere. Something inside my chest had tightened. *Enid Surtees*. How extraordinary: I had no idea who she was, but I was absolutely certain that I wanted George to give her her marching orders. Had I heard mention of her somewhere? A feeling of dread had come upon me. It was warm in Poirot's drawing room as it always was, yet the back of my neck was suddenly cold, as if something had breathed a chill over me.

I stayed in my chair. Nothing, after all, had happened. One thing was beyond doubt: I did not know a woman by the name of Enid Surtees.

'Show her in, Georges,' said Poirot. Once the valet had left the room, he said, 'It was your evident reluctance that decided the matter in her favour, Catchpool. She is known to you, *n'est-ce pas?*'

'No.'

'Ah. Now I am curious. Your face tells a different story. Well, we shall soon see. Perhaps you have broken another young woman's heart.' He chuckled.

'I have broken no women's hearts, ever.'

'*Mais ce n'est pas vrai.* What about Fee Spring? She—'

'Some women break their own hearts quite . . . unilaterally,' I said. 'If heart-breaking is an active pursuit, I can assure you that I have never deliberately engaged in it.'

'Ah. That is what you think, is it, my friend?'

'A few amiable chats with a waitress—nothing more, and unavoidable if one wishes to be served coffee in her establishment—and she takes it upon herself, without any encouragement, to—'

My summation for the defence was interrupted by a knock from George. The door opened and a woman walked in, wrapped in a navy blue woollen hat, coat and scarf. Efficiently, she began to divest herself of all three. George scooped them up from the arm of the sofa and retreated, closing the drawing-room door behind him.

My mouth must have dropped open. I could not help making an undignified noise that no letters of the alphabet can adequately convey.

Poirot rose to his feet and extended a hand, which was promptly shaken by the infuriating wretch of an intruder. (Did I know her? Oh, I knew her, all right!)

'Good afternoon, Madame Surtees.'

She was tall and bony, with gold-coloured hair, a square, pale face and piercingly bright blue eyes. She looked, to quote her own favoured refrain line, 'not a day older than sixty—because I have always avoided the sun, you see, Edward. You should think about doing the same, or your face and neck will be as leathery as your father's by the time you are forty.' In fact she was much closer to seventy than sixty. She would celebrate her seventieth birthday in March the following year.

Her name was not Enid Surtees.

'Hello, Mother,' I said.

'*Pardon?*' said Poirot. '*La mère?*' He turned from me to her. 'You are—?'

'My name is Cynthia Catchpool, Monsieur Poirot. I am Edward's mother, for my sins. I'm afraid I had to resort to dishonesty in order to secure an audience with you. Enid Surtees is an acquaintance of mine.'

Of course. That was where I had heard the name before. It was recited to me amid a flurry of others as part of Mother's lobbying for me to spend Christmas with her and a collection of complete strangers in a tiny village in Norfolk that 'really does feel as if it's beyond the end of the world, Edward. It's so charming.'

As far as I could see, there was no 'beyond' once one had reached the end of the world. It sounded appalling. Lately I had noticed that I was growing ever more reluctant to leave London. Life and vitality seemed to stop, or at least to struggle for breath, when one strayed too far outside that great city.

And life contained no greater struggle, for me at least, than time spent in the company of my mother. I was already trapped in the cast-iron tradition of joining her for a summer holiday in Great Yarmouth each summer. Nothing would induce me to add a winter ordeal to my filial burden. I knew that if I indulged her once, Mother would expect it to happen every year without fail. I had not spent a Christmas Day with either of my parents since I was eighteen years old and I had no wish to start now.

My first firm 'No, thank you' had apparently gone unheard. Eagerly, Mother had continued with her campaign, speaking loudly over my attempts to draw my dissent to her attention. She had listed the people who would be there, in Munby-on-Sea—Enid Surtees was one of them—and hooted about what a marvellous Christmas we would all spend together, playing games I had never heard of before ('Much more mischievous and provocative than anything

I could invent, I'm sure!') in what had to be the most beautiful mansion in England: 'Truly stunning. A jewel! A work of art, one might say. Frellingsloe House, known as Frelly to its friends—and soon you'll be one of them, Edward! Its position is at the very farthest tip of the Norfolk coast, on the edge of a rather dramatic cliff. There's a path that leads directly from the back door to steps that take you down to a little beach. Perfect for you! I know how you love to plunge yourself into icy cold water. Oh, and the views from the house are splendid. You can see all the way to . . . whichever country is over there, across the sea.' She had waved in a random direction. Then her face had contorted. 'This might be your last chance to see Frelly, darling.'

'Seeing a house I didn't know existed until a moment ago is not a particular ambition of mine,' I had told her.

'It's awfully sad,' Mother went on. 'Poor old Frelly is doomed, I'm afraid—though only because everybody is giving up far too easily. The coastal disintegration in that part of Norfolk is simply atrocious. It has something to do with the clay of the cliff. I can't think why no one has made it their mission to replace the faulty clay with a better kind. There must be some somewhere. It is surely not past the wit of man to find it and bring it to Munby. They all need to stop shilly-shallying and jolly well *do* something, or else poor Frelly will soon tumble into the water and be washed away. I would sort it out myself, except . . . well, it's hardly my place. Besides, I don't know the first thing about clay. And it's so hard to know how to raise the matter for a proper discussion when no one in the family ever mentions it. They're all thinking about it, though, every minute of the day. Dread of the approaching tragedy hovers over everything. The experts have said Frelly has three to four years left at most.'

Nothing she said had sounded remotely enticing—not the ill-fated house that was about to be swallowed up by the waves, nor the atmosphere of looming disaster that, according to Mother, pervaded the endangered building's every crevice and cubbyhole. Assuming I would find her dramatic descriptions as irresistible as she herself did (she contrived not to notice that I had my own mind and tastes and was not merely a younger, male replica of her), she went on to list every delectable, gruesome detail that she could think of in connection with Frellingsloe House and its inhabitants: one member of the family was dying of a rare kind of cancer; two sisters lived in the house who hated each other; their parents would never forgive the parents of their husbands (I did not ask why. Too many generations of too many clans seemed to be involved. One would have needed to be a genealogist to keep up.) And the local doctor, who had taken a room at Frellingsloe House, was probably in love with the matriarch of the family, 'or at least, he is evidently not in love with the woman to whom he is engaged to be married. It's very peculiar, Edward.' Meanwhile, the matriarch, whose name I could not recall (perhaps she was Enid Surtees) was 'definitely up to something' with the house's other lodger, a young curate.

Mother had also muttered something about a financial predicament, the cause of which was mysterious, she had implied—though it perhaps explained the presence in the house of two paying lodgers.

Listening in horror to the details of the venal-sounding muddle that she hoped to inflict upon me for the entirety of the Christmas holiday, I had quickly hatched a scheme to fend her off. I invented a prior arrangement that I hoped would act as an obstacle of immovable solidity: I had been invited to spend Christmas with Poirot, I told her. Furthermore, I had accepted. It was all arranged. (This became true soon afterwards, once I had dropped a hint or two.)

'If you will permit me to say, Madame Catchpool . . .' The hard edge in Poirot's voice brought me back to our present predicament. 'Many people would object to a visitor who gains entry under false pretences. I am one such person.'

'And for that I commend you.' Mother beamed her approval at him. 'I too would object most strongly.' She sat herself down in the chair nearest to the fire. 'I much prefer to tell the truth wherever possible, but . . . well, I know you understand how complicated life can be, Monsieur Poirot. You of all people! I've read every word Edward has written about your exploits together, so I know you're not above bending the truth if it furthers your cause. If I had given my real name, my son would have urged you to shoo me away. I'm sure you are unaware, but I have been asking to meet you for years. Edward has given me all manner of excuses as to why it cannot happen. He likes to keep everything separate. I imagine he thinks that you might find me a little . . . *de trop*, as you and your French compatriots would say.'

'I am not French, madame. I am—'

'Shall we arrange for your man to bring us some tea?' Mother rattled on. She turned and looked expectantly at the closed drawing-room door. 'And perhaps a little bite of something delicious? And then we can get down to business—for we must soon be on our way.'

'On our way where?' I said. 'What business?'

'Christmas. You can stamp your foot all you like, Edward, but there is nothing to be done about it: you and Monsieur Poirot will not, I am afraid, be able to spend Christmas together here in this . . . room.' She looked up at the ceiling, then over at the window. I wondered if she was comparing the size of Poirot's living quarters with the larger and grander Frellingsloe House, or perhaps with her own home: the vast, damp farmhouse in Kent where I spent my childhood, whose wooden beams might as well have been prison bars.

'Never mind,' she said brightly. 'There will be plenty of other Christmases when you will both be able to do as you please—Edward likes to suit himself and I expect you do too, Monsieur Poirot. This year, however, you shall spend Christmas with me in Munby-on-Sea.'

Out of the question, I said silently and forcefully to myself. Christmas with Poirot at Whitehaven Mansions was the part of my two-week holiday to which I was most looking forward.

17

'Do not bother to cavil, Edward,' said Mother. 'You will both come back with me this afternoon, once we have finished our tea and cakes. Monsieur Poirot will insist upon it, once he has heard my story.'

I wondered if she expected Poirot to conjure up a selection of cakes from a desk drawer.

'*Quelle histoire*, madame? What story?'

'The one about Stanley Niven,' Mother said pointedly, as if we ought to know who this was. As far as I could remember, his had not been one of the names on the list of those participating in the Norfolk Christmas ordeal. 'It is causing great distress to everybody, and I mean to put a stop to it,' she went on. 'What was I supposed to do? Sit and stare out of my window at the endless, crashing waves, knowing that in London my son was in the company of the very man—the only man in the world, I dare say—who is sure to be able to help us?'

From this, I gathered that Mother was already installed at Frellingsloe House well in advance of Christmas, since no waves were observable from her home in Kent. I wondered if she and my father had given up spending any time at all together under the same roof. I would not, I thought, blame either of them if that were the case.

'Who is Stanley Niven?' Poirot asked. 'Of what problem is he the cause?'

'Oh, the man himself is no longer bothering anyone— though he must have done so at one time or another, or he would not have been bashed about the head with a heavy vase,' said Mother.

'Monsieur Niven was attacked?'

'More than attacked. He was murdered. Now, Mr Niven himself is not important at all. He is a complete stranger, and neither here nor there. However, by getting himself murdered where he did—in that room on that ward—he has created a substantial problem for a very good friend of mine. For her whole family, in fact.'

How typical of Mother, I reflected, to believe that a man's murder only mattered if it adversely affected her and her friends.

'Monsieur Niven was murdered in a hospital?' asked Poirot.

'Yes, a little place just outside Munby-on-Sea: St Walstan's Cottage Hospital. Where lives are supposed to be saved,' Mother added pointedly, as if Stanley Niven's unfortunate fate proved the fundamental unsoundness of the whole institution. 'As far as I can tell, the staff at St Walstan's have come up with *no* ideas that might result in the catching of the murderer, and neither have the Norfolk constabulary.' She threw up her hands. 'Both are hoping the other lot will sort it out. Munby people are peculiar, Monsieur Poirot. They don't seem motivated to *do* anything about anything. I wonder if it's living so near to the sea that makes them that way. On the coast, one is constantly reminded that one can *go no further*.' She nodded, in full agreement with herself as usual. 'What could be more dispiriting? Human life is forced to stop where the land stops.'

'Unless one has a boat,' I said. 'If you hate the coast so much, why must we go to Great Yarmouth every year?'

'Oh, *summer* on the Norfolk coast is a completely different story,' she replied briskly. 'Will you kindly accompany me to Munby, Monsieur Poirot? You and Edward? You are so desperately needed there. Stanley Niven was murdered on 8 September, and the police don't know any more now than they did on that day. It is pitiful! The case has still not been solved, more than three months later. And my friend Vivienne has been subjected to intolerable anguish, which is most unfair given that, as I say, Mr Niven is a complete stranger to her and to all of us. If only he had been murdered elsewhere . . . but he was not.' Mother sighed. 'He was killed on Ward 6 of St Walstan's Hospital, and poor Vivienne is in a quite terrible state about it.'

'Why, if this Niven chap was a stranger to her?' I asked. 'Why is your friend so distressed by his having been murdered at this particular hospital?'

'If I explain now, we shall miss our train,' said Mother. 'We need to make haste. As soon as we have had our tea—' she glanced again at the closed drawing-room door, '—we must depart. That is, if you are in agreement, Monsieur Poirot? Do, please, assure me that I can count on your help in this matter.'

CHAPTER 2

An Unplanned Trip to Norfolk

Two hours and forty-five minutes later, Poirot, Mother and I were on a train bound for Norfolk. So much for my always suiting myself. Did she really believe that about me? It was precisely what I thought about her: she always got what she wanted—even, on this occasion, maddeningly, cakes, tea and the benefit of Poirot's finest china, thanks to his ever-resourceful valet, George.

I had been sure until the very last moment that Poirot was minded to decline her request. I knew only too well the expression that his face assumed when he was preparing to say no to somebody, being so often the person to whom he said it. At a certain juncture, however, Mother had said something that had aroused his interest. I watched it happen. The light in his eyes changed. I could not work out what had made the difference.

She had been talking about Stanley Niven, the murder victim, who, according to Mother, had possessed a sunny nature and a generous and delightful temperament. At the time of his death, he was sixty-eight years old and had a doting family and no enemies to speak of. He was the favourite patient of every doctor and every nurse at St Walstan's Cottage Hospital, always laughing and offering encouragement to others in spite of his own health troubles. His happiness was such that one could not help but feel jolly in his presence, no matter what mood one might have been in before encountering him. At sixty-eight, he was retired, but before that he had been a post office master in Cromer, where his customers and employees could not have been more devoted to him.

Mother had turned her stern gaze upon me at this point in her description of Mr Niven. 'A man like that is not supposed to get murdered, Edward: a cheerful, popular man who has worked hard his whole life and who endures poor health with great fortitude and a smile on his face. Really, you and your friends at Scotland Yard must deliver a clear message to the nation's rogues: if they insist on depriving people of their lives, they must choose more deserving candidates. Of course, taking another person's life is always wrong. You do not need to tell me that, Edward—I was the one who taught you about right and wrong, if you recall. But the fact is that not all crimes are equally heinous. What is this great nation coming to, really, when a man like Stanley Niven is not safe? Not that I care about him personally, you understand.'

'Yes, you have made that very clear,' I said. 'You care only insofar as it inconveniences your friend Vivienne.'

'Not only her,' said Mother. 'The whole family is affected.

And it goes far beyond inconvenience, Edward, so please do not be flippant. Vivienne is . . . why, in the three months since the murder, she has become a mere shell of a person. It is terrifying to observe. Of course Stanley Niven's death matters to *somebody somewhere*—I do not doubt that. I never intended to suggest otherwise. You are determined, as ever, to interpret everything I say in the most uncharitable manner possible.'

Poirot had asked her to explain the connection between the murder in the hospital and her friend's anguish: 'Why has your friend Vivienne become a shell in great distress?'

'Because if this crime is not solved before the start of the new year, then her husband might be murdered too—or at least, that is what Vivienne believes. And she herself will certainly go quite mad. Irretrievably so, I fear. Shall I explain, Monsieur Poirot? I might as well tell you a little of the story while we eat our cake.'

Poirot had not replied straight away. Instead, he had muttered to himself, 'One could not help but feel jolly in his presence.' Then he had smoothed down his moustaches with his fingers and stared fixedly at the china teapot on the small table between us. Shortly afterwards he said with a sigh, 'It appears that we must change our plans, Catchpool, and accompany your mother to Norfolk.'

Was it her reference to the jollity inspired by Stanley Niven that had made up his mind? If so, I could not see the relevance of it. No further explanations were offered—of anything, by anybody—and a flurry of preparations for travel followed. Now, as the train transported us to Norfolk,

I was still every bit as baffled as I had been in Poirot's drawing room about why Stanley Niven's unsolved murder was ruining the life of Mother's friend Vivienne and causing her to fear that her husband would be murdered too.

As a ruthless wind howled through our carriage, I clung to the one consolation that had been thrown to me: Poirot's declaration, as he had donned his hat and coat to depart for the railway station, that 'What the Norfolk constabulary has failed to achieve in three months and eleven days, I shall endeavour to bring to a close in . . . let us say, ten hours.' He smiled. 'Not counting the time that I am asleep, naturally. The murder was committed on a hospital ward? *Eh bien*, some questions asked of the nurses there, more at the police station . . . Some answers given—true ones, or lies, probably both. Then to sit quietly and let the little grey cells do their work. It might, from start to end, take me as many as fifteen hours to make sense of what has occurred. It is unlikely to take longer than that.'

To Mother he had said, 'Be in no doubt, madame: I shall solve the murder of Stanley Niven and return home in a matter of days. Catchpool and I will spend Christmas *chez Poirot*, as arranged.'

'No, no,' she had waved his words away. 'That won't do at all. You will stay until at least the day after Boxing Day.'

Now she took the opportunity to drive her message home: 'Boxing Day is the very soonest that you will be permitted to leave, Monsieur Poirot,' she said firmly. 'It is better that you know that from the outset. Oh, I have no doubt that you will make short work of solving the crime—but, you see, your visit to Munby has *two* purposes, and solving the murder at St Walstan's Cottage Hospital is only one of them. Both are equally important.'

'Catchpool, if you would be so kind as to close the window that is open in the next carriage?' said Poirot. 'This gale does its best to blow my moustaches from my face, all the way back to Whitehaven Mansions. There is certainly a window open somewhere, and since all the ones I can see are closed . . .'

I did as he asked; he was, of course, correct.

'So Stanley Niven had undergone surgery at St Walstan's Hospital immediately before he was killed?' Poirot was asking Mother when I returned.

'Yes,' she said. 'Though don't ask me what for. All I know is that he was expected to recover. His case was quite different from Arnold's.'

'Who is Arnold?' asked Poirot.

'Vivienne's husband. They will be our hosts in Munby: Arnold and Vivienne Laurier. Frellingsloe House belongs to them.'

'Arnold is also sick?' said Poirot.

'Dying,' I guessed aloud. Mother had certainly told me that a member of the Laurier family was terminally ill.

'Yes, the poor man has very little time left,' she confirmed. 'Dr Osgood—he is Arnold's doctor and also his and Vivienne's lodger—has said that Arnold has another three to six months at most.'

Even less time than his house has left, I reflected.

'And he is soon to be moved to St Walstan's, where he

will spend the remainder of his life,' said Mother. 'On Ward 6, in fact. That is why this is such a pressing problem.'

'The last thing this Arnold fellow must want is two more houseguests,' I said. 'Two strangers.'

'Oh, Hercule Poirot is anything but a stranger in Arnold's mind. That's why the two of you are going to stay until after Boxing—'

'*Non*, madame—'

'Until the day after Boxing Day. Yes, Monsieur Poirot. That will be Arnold's special treat, you see, to replace the one that you're about to deprive him of. But this new treat will be so much better: his last Christmas at his beloved Frelly, not only with his family but with his great *hero*.' She whispered the last word with especial reverence.

'What is Frelly?' Poirot asked.

'It's a ridiculous pet name for the house—Frellingsloe House—that you and I are under no obligation to use,' I told him.

'Oh, Edward, don't be such a sourpuss,' Mother snapped.

'Madame . . . you said that I am about to deprive Monsieur Laurier of a treat. What did you mean?'

'Oh, he will not mind at all! His new treat of spending Christmas with you—'

'Enough! I do not agree to the new treat.' Poirot spoke slowly and clearly. It amused me that he thought this approach might work with Mother. 'My question was about the old treat. You tell me I am to deprive Arnold Laurier of something that is important to him, when I have no wish to deprive a dying man, and no notion of what is the original treat he expects to receive. Please, madame, explain what you mean. Also: you will desist from telling me what I will and will not do, or I shall disembark at the next station and make my way home.'

'Goodness me, you men.' Mother shook her head. 'You carry on as if I am trying to keep you in the dark, Monsieur Poirot, when my only wish is to tell you all about it. The original treat, as you call it—the one Arnold is looking forward to with the eager anticipation of a schoolboy for a snowball fight—is the solving of Stanley Niven's murder. Solving it *himself*, I mean. That is what he proposes to do, as soon as he is admitted to St Walstan's in the new year.' The train juddered, apparently as shocked as I was by this latest twist in the story. I had assumed that Arnold Laurier was in a weak and feeble condition, as the imminently dying tend to be.

'The poor, foolish man wants to be the one to catch the killer,' said Mother. 'He will soon be "at the scene" as he keeps saying with great relish, and perfectly situated to do some sleuthing. You are his inspiration, Monsieur Poirot. He claims to be well versed in your methods and keeps telling everyone that he knows he can do it—he, Arnold Laurier, will succeed where Inspector Mackle and his men have failed. If the police haven't caught the culprit after three months of trying, then they probably never will—that is Arnold's contention. He has been your most devoted fan ever since he heard from me all about your and Edward's first case and how expertly you solved it. He is rather sweetly obsessed with you, I'm afraid. If there has ever been even the tiniest mention of you in a newspaper, I promise you, Arnold has cut it out and glued it into his scrapbook. And since he is due to move to St Walstan's immediately after the Christmas holidays . . . well, his argument is that lying around in a hospital bed waiting to die is nowhere near as much fun as getting one's teeth into a nice, juicy murder case—'

'There is nothing nice about murder,' I said.

'Well, quite, Edward.' Mother bestowed a rare, approving look upon me before returning her attention to Poirot. 'That is why dear Vivienne is beside herself. She and Arnold have been blissfully happily married for forty years. She was in full agreement with the plan to send Arnold to St Walstan's until there was a murder there. Now, of course, the prospect fills her with horror. She's terrified that, with a killer still at large in the hospital, Arnold might be the next victim— particularly if he announces to all and sundry that his mission is to find out the truth about who killed Stanley Niven. There is nothing subtle or understated about Arnold, and he will certainly tell all the doctors, all the other patients and anyone else who will listen that he's "playing Poirot", as he calls it. He claims not to be afraid and doesn't seem to understand Vivienne's fear at all. Quite the opposite: he chortles like a child having its tummy tickled and says, "I'm dying anyway, darling," as if it's all a big joke. "What's the harm?" he says. "I might as well die happy, with my brain working on something important, in the service of justice." He has always been too enthusiastic for his own good.'

'He is a happy man, Monsieur Laurier?' Poirot asked.

'Oh, yes,' said Mother. 'Even before Stanley Niven was murdered and he had his crime-solving project to look forward to, he could always find something to be full of beans about. Even when Dr Osgood told him that his time was running out. The first thing he said was, "Ah, but what a time I have had, Robert. What a time." Robert is Dr Osgood's Christian name,' Mother added unnecessarily. 'If anyone else had adopted such a cavalier attitude to their own demise, I should have disapproved most heartily, but . . . it is somehow impossible to disapprove of Arnold. It's his enthusiasm, you see.'

Poirot looked especially alert as he asked, 'Might those who know him describe Arnold Laurier as jolly?'

'The word could have been invented to describe him,' said Mother.

'This, then, is a quality he shares—shared—with Stanley Niven?'

So I had been right: it was the mention of Niven's cheerful character that had attracted Poirot's particular interest. Now he seemed equally fascinated to learn that Arnold Laurier was also a happy and exuberant sort. Why, for pity's sake?

'You are right,' said Mother. 'That had not occurred to me. Please, do not mention this . . . temperamental similarity to Vivienne. She is already beside herself with worry about the other one.'

'The other what?' I asked.

'The other thing that Arnold and Stanley Niven have in common: Ward 6 at St Walstan's. Stanley Niven had a private room there—the room in which he was murdered. And the very next room on the ward is the one reserved for Arnold, into which he plans to move at the beginning of January. The two are separated only by a wall,' she said, as if she believed that something more impressive or substantial ought to separate two hospital rooms. 'Of course, the hospital might agree to allocate Arnold a different room, but he will not hear of it. If he could, he would take the very room in which Mr Niven was murdered. Nothing better than being "at the scene", he would think. He also refuses to stay at home and live out the remainder of his days at Frelly, though Vivienne has begged him to reconsider. That is why your visit to Munby is so important, Monsieur Poirot. No other plan can work. Believe me, I would not have disturbed you if it were not absolutely necessary. This is the only way. Vivienne will be profoundly grateful to you if you deliver on both fronts, and so will I.'

'What are these fronts?' Poirot looked agitated. He hated not being able to understand things. 'What is it, precisely, that you wish me to deliver?'

'Have I not explained it all quite thoroughly?' said Mother. 'Task number one: spend Christmas at Frelly with poor Arnold. Nothing would give him greater joy—and you have so many more Christmases to look forward to, Monsieur Poirot. He does not. Don't spoil his very last one.'

'Mother, that is a monstrously unfair—'

'I have already told Vivienne that you have agreed to the plan,' Mother barrelled on. 'She will be busy preparing

Arnold for a wonderful surprise later today: the arrival of the most perfect Christmas guest!'

'Madame, how many times must I tell you that I cannot stay as long as—'

'And number two: solve the murder of Stanley Niven, so that the ne'er-do-well who killed him can be hauled off to the gallows—no longer a danger to Arnold or anyone else at St Walstan's. Then Vivienne will have nothing to fear. She will know that when Arnold moves into his room at the hospital, he will be safe from the killer.' Mother had it all neatly worked out. 'He must be deprived—by you, Monsieur Poirot—of the treat of solving Stanley Niven's murder. As compensation, he will get a different treat: spending his last Christmas at Frelly with you as his guest.'

'Madame—'

'Oh, and you might perhaps let him in on some of your crime-solving process. He would simply adore that—though he mustn't go anywhere near that hospital, not while the killer is still lurking. Still, as long as he is safe at home, there is absolutely no reason why you shouldn't confide in him a little as you go along.' Mother smiled. 'Consult him now and then, allow him to feel helpful. Rather like you do with Edward,' she said.

CHAPTER 3

We Arrive in Munby

The wind in Norfolk when we arrived that evening was severe enough to blow a man off his feet. It struck me as likely that, having once done battle with it, I would forever think of its London counterpart as an amateur. As soon as I stepped down from the train, tears started to stream from my eyes. Poirot dabbed at his with his handkerchief.

I planted my feet firmly on the solid ground. It would not do to be buffeted away in a landscape of this kind; there was almost nothing upright that one could grasp hold of, nothing but flat fields and the smell of wet earth for miles around.

We were met at the railway station by two men who introduced themselves as Robert Osgood and Felix Rawcliffe. Rawcliffe, the younger of the two by around thirty years, extended his hand and said, 'Monsieur Poirot, Inspector Catchpool. Welcome to Munby! What a delight to have you with us for Christmas!'

'*Merci, mais* . . . we intend to leave well before Christmas,' Poirot corrected him.

'Well before?' said Rawcliffe. 'You are rather late for that. Today is the nineteenth. Christmas is just around the corner.' He spoke in an inelegant manner; one had the sense that a struggle between words and teeth was taking place, with no clear winner emerging. Rawcliffe looked to be a little older than thirty. He had a lean, triangular face and a forward-tilting stance that suggested he might topple over. His green scarf, lumpy in some parts and distended in others, reached almost to his knees.

'It is Christmas already,' Mother declared. I told her that her position was at odds with the Christian calendar, to which she replied, 'I am speaking of the social calendar, Edward, and so was Felix. You are surely not accusing this exemplary young curate of heresy?'

'He meant to do nothing of the sort,' said Rawcliffe with good humour. 'Whatever the calendar, we could not be more delighted to welcome you both.' To me in particular he said, 'It warms my heart to meet a fellow who is willing to travel so far in such inclement weather to spend Christmas with his mother. I would have done the same for my dear late mama, God rest her soul.'

He would have been described as conventionally hand-some by a great many. His teeth neither protruded, nor were they too large or untidily arranged; it was simply that every word he spoke made one keenly aware of their presence.

Felix Rawcliffe, then, was the curate lodger at Frellingsloe

House. He introduced the older man, Dr Robert Osgood: a sturdy fellow of around sixty, with curly hair the colour of iron filings and a forehead slightly higher on one side than the other. He looked important—almost monumental. He was not wearing a hat, which, in this weather, made me question his sanity and added to his air of being, in the manner of a statue, immune to the elements. Dr Osgood, I recalled, was Arnold Laurier's doctor and also a lodger in his home.

It struck me as peculiar that these two gentlemen had been sent to collect us—almost rude, even. One did not send guests to fetch guests, though of course lodgers were not guests in the strictest sense. As far as I could recall, everyone else spending Christmas at Frellingsloe House, apart from Osgood and Rawcliffe, was either a Surtees or a Laurier. Now, what did I know about Mr and Mrs Surtees? They were not lodgers. They were guests, I thought, though not in the conventional sense. There was something about them . . .

I wished I had paid more attention to Mother's lengthy descriptions of everybody when she had first told me about them. How naïve I had been to assume I would never meet any of them. I was fairly sure she had said that the Surteeses were an elderly couple, and the parents of . . . somebody else in the house, could it be? Or was Mrs Surtees—Enid—the sister of Vivienne Laurier and sister-in-law of the dying Arnold? Somewhere in the picture were two sisters who had once been the best of friends but now loathed one another.

I had put it off for as long as I could, but the time had come for me to smile, shake hands with Osgood and Rawcliffe and comport myself as politeness required. It took some effort. I was aware that these two men had done me no harm; still, I viewed them as captor-collaborators, and Rawcliffe's remark about my travelling a great distance in order to spend Christmas with Mother had irked me. I was here because Poirot had set himself the task of solving the murder of Stanley Niven, and for that reason alone. Assisting him in his work had been the greatest honour of my life so far. Never would there come a day when I would refuse his request for my help, no matter what hardships it might entail. Christmas with Mother, far from being the purpose of my visit to Norfolk, was an unpleasant side effect that I was willing to endure if necessary but still very much hoped to avoid.

To my great relief, I was roundly ignored by everybody as soon as we were inside the motorcar. Mother, seated between Poirot and me, assailed him with more facts than he could ever need to know about the village of Munby-on-Sea: which houses had been in the same family for many generations, which smallholdings had recently sold off land, which streets had been graced briefly by the presence of people who sounded royal, of whom I had never heard.

Meanwhile, in lowered voices, Rawcliffe and Dr Osgood were discussing Rosaline from the Shakespeare play *Romeo and Juliet*. This must have been the continuation of a conversation that had started before Poirot and I alighted from the train, or else it made no sense. I had missed its first premise and was finding the second instalment unintelligible. Wasn't Rosaline Romeo's first love, the one he had dropped like a heavy stone the moment he had set eyes on Juliet? That seemed to be the point that Felix Rawcliffe was trying to make—that one could change one's love object if one so desired—though his teeth were doing their best to foil his effort.

Dr Osgood replied that Rawcliffe did not understand 'the way these things work' and that he ought to talk to somebody called Father Peter about it. Father Peter, apparently, was considerably older and had more experience than Rawcliffe. I pictured a wise, elderly priest of the parish with snow-white, windswept hair and a white beard clogged and stiffened by sea salt, who, in his spare time, proselytized about Shakespeare's tragedies.

Then it struck me: how had Dr Osgood and Rawcliffe known which train we would be on? Mother had made no telephone call between her first appearance in Poirot's drawing room and now. There was only one possibility, therefore: she had not doubted that we would fall in with her orders. She was quite the most enraging person I had ever known.

As an accompaniment to my resentment, I had a small anxiety to contend with as Rawcliffe drove us along tiny, winding roads and wind and rain assaulted the car windows. I could hardly raise the matter now, with two other conversations still in progress, but I was acutely aware that Poirot knew nothing of the imperilled status of Frellingsloe House, and I felt I ought to have told him. Surely he would wish to know that we were about to spend the night in a house that would soon be under the sea.

Dr Osgood turned in his seat and addressed Poirot. 'Mrs Catchpool has assured us that you will be able to solve the murder of Stanley Niven where the police have failed.'

'Oh, do please call me Cynthia, doctor,' said Mother. 'I keep reminding you and you keep forgetting.'

'I shall do my best to resolve the matter, monsieur. You have perhaps heard that my best is of the highest level of excellence?'

'I have.' Both disapproval and suspicion were present in Osgood's voice. I had tried several times to explain to Poirot that being quite so vocal about one's own prowess is not something that sits well with many of us English folk. But perhaps the doctor was not offended in the slightest by my Belgian friend's confidence; he had sounded equally stony when talking to Felix Rawcliffe about Romeo's rejected Rosaline.

'I hope you are as talented a detective as we have been led to believe,' he told Poirot. 'I have more faith in you than I do in our local police, but even so . . . I fear this will not be an easy case to solve, even for the most agile mind.'

'Why do you think so?' Poirot asked him.

'Only because of the facts of the case, which, were they not firmly established, I would call impossible,' said Osgood. 'Stanley Niven, the murder victim, was in his hospital bed in a private room on Ward 6. He was seen alive at two o'clock. Between then and twenty minutes after two, I was standing in the ward corridor talking to various people, and I can tell you for certain that no one entered or left Mr Niven's room. Even after that, I was in and out of the ward, and so were other doctors and nurses.'

I had the sense that Osgood had repeated these facts to himself many times, trying to make sense of them.

'No one noticed anything out of place or suspicious,' he continued. 'Nobody who should not have been there was seen. It therefore seems unlikely, verging on impossible, that an intruder could have entered Mr Niven's room, killed him, and exited again during the brief period of time in which all of that must have happened. Inspector Mackle is convinced the killer is a close relation of Niven's, but he has been unable to prove it and I for one think he is wrong. No one saw any of the family members on the ward that day—and they would have. I personally have met all four of the relatives whom Inspector Mackle suspects. To a man and a woman, they are good Christian people who loved Stanley Niven dearly and would not dream of murdering him nor anybody else. One cannot always say that of patients' relatives, incidentally. And . . . it is hard to convey this to those who did not know him, but Mr Niven was really such delightful company, and so considerate of others. I cannot believe that anyone would want him dead—yet plainly someone did, and nothing can be done about it.' The doctor sighed.

'Justice can be done,' said Poirot. 'I am here to ensure that it is.'

'I hope you have more luck than Inspector Mackle,' said Felix Rawcliffe.

'Fortunately, I do not need to rely on luck, monsieur. I have the little grey cells.' Poirot pointed to his head. 'They never let me down.'

'My main concern now is for the health and happiness of the living,' said Dr Osgood. 'I am talking about mental welfare as well as physical. What has Mrs Catchpool— Cynthia—told you about the condition of Vivienne Laurier?'

'I know only that her husband, Arnold Laurier, is gravely ill,' said Poirot.

'Arnold will be lucky if he lives to see another summer,' the doctor said. 'It is possible, but unlikely. However, his state of mind is substantially better than that of his wife. I am far more worried about her—which is why I implore you, Mr Poirot: please do everything you can to solve this murder expeditiously. Vivienne's future sanity depends upon your being able to do so.'

'Please tell me more,' said Poirot.

Mother was shaking her head. 'There is nothing wrong with Vivienne that would not be wrong with anyone in her position. She is as sane as you or I, doctor. She is merely grieving the impending loss of the man she has loved for forty years. Do you expect her to dance a jig? It is possible to grieve *before* a death, you know. I have seen several of my about-to-be-widowed friends do precisely that. The grief comes first, and at the most inconvenient time, while there is still serious illness and a rapid demise to contend with, and the back-breaking drudgery that accompanies all of that. The death, when it finally arrives, can be a relief.'

'That may be true,' said Dr Osgood, 'but—'

Mother did not let him finish. 'You are as bad as my friend Sunny,' she said. 'There was a horrid rift in our little group of Kent ladies for a while, after Sunny refused to try and understand why one might treat the loss of a husband after half a century as anything but a boon and a blessed liberation. I have met plenty like her, too. It is striking that those with that particular inclination do not have the wit to refrain from saying so to those with the opposite view. Sunny caused a thoroughly unpleasant dust-up—at the Chelsea Flower Show, too. Did she really have to do it in a public place? Even when she was given a good, hard shove and staggered backwards into some climbing Noisette roses, she kept going. I could scarcely credit it. I mean, we all know that some women of Sunny's age do rather want rid of their husbands and hope for a few years of freedom at the end of their lives—but is it necessary to say so, repeatedly, to a friend who would dearly have loved to retain her late beloved for the duration?' Mother shook her head. 'It fell to me to break up the scuffle, as the only person who could see both sides of the argument.'

Dr Osgood looked a little stunned. Recovering himself, he said to Poirot, 'It is not Vivienne's unhappiness that alarms me the most. A baffling irrationality has taken hold of her. She says she is afraid, but it is a fear that makes no sense.'

'Afraid of what?' I asked.

'She believes that someone will murder Arnold if he so much as sets foot in St Walstan's Hospital,' said Dr Osgood. 'Months ago, the family made the plan of moving him there, to Ward 6. It is a good plan. Undoubtedly, it is in Arnold's best interests. He will very soon need hospital staff in attendance at all times of the day and night. Vivienne has done sterling work caring for him until now, and of course it has helped that I have taken a room in the Laurier household, but I am not always able to be there. The time has come when, really, a hospital like St Walstan's is where Arnold needs to be. It was all agreed. The move would happen at the beginning of January. I advised that it should be sooner, but Arnold was quite determined to spend his last Christmas at Frellingsloe House.'

Dr Osgood, I noticed, did not refer to the place as Frelly. Good for him. I entertained myself with a fanciful notion: perhaps he and Felix Rawcliffe were the Poirot and Catchpool of yesteryear: compelled first to visit Frellingsloe House and then, later, to take up residence. I shivered at the idea that, once inside the Laurier family home, one was unable to escape.

Poirot and I would be escaping imminently, however. Two days at most: that was all it would take. This was far from the first time I had desperately looked forward to leaving a place before I had arrived; it was a state of mind I had inhabited almost daily, come to think of it, for most of my life. First boarding school, then more recently Scotland Yard . . . I wondered if anyone else shared my habit, or if I was the only fool in the world who regularly set off for destinations he had no desire to reach. There was only one thing I did habitually that I looked forward to: watching Poirot's brilliant mind in action. I would have found it a thoroughly stimulating prospect to observe his solving of the murder of Stanley Niven, had a generous helping of Mother not come as part of the bargain.

'So, Arnold got his way,' Osgood went on. 'It was agreed that this coming Christmas would be spent at his home, and he would proceed to St Walstan's thereafter. Then Stanley Niven was murdered on the ward: a complete stranger, with no connection whatsoever to the Lauriers— yet Vivienne immediately started to carry on as though Arnold were sure to be the hospital killer's next victim.'

'I do not find it surprising that Madame Laurier is reluctant to send her ailing husband to a place where a murder has occurred,' said Poirot.

'Neither would I, if that were all this was.' Dr Osgood had turned back around and was facing forward in his seat. I could not see his expression.

'What do you mean?' Poirot asked him.

'I spend half of my working week at St Walstan's. The relatives of many of the patients on Ward 6 have told me that they share Vivienne's worries about safety on the ward and at the hospital more generally. Some of the other doctors and nurses have said so too. St Walstan's no longer feels quite like the haven it was before. Yet most people have retained a sense of perspective. They understand that hatred of an individual is what leads to murder.'

'That is not always true,' said Poirot. 'Money, very often, is the reason.'

The doctor frowned. 'To inherit money, do you mean?'

'Sometimes that, assuredly. Sometimes blackmail is

involved. The blackmailed party exhausts his supply of funds—'

'You prove my point, Monsieur Poirot. Whether it is done for an inheritance, or after blackmail, or from a deep personal hatred, the motive always applies to an individual.'

'Ah!' Poirot nodded. 'I comprehend. You believe that those who happen to share a hospital ward with the victim are in no more danger than, let us say, people in hospitals a hundred miles away.'

'And those not in hospital at all,' said Osgood. 'Yes, indeed. If this killer has a motive that also applies to other patients at St Walstan's, why have there been no further murders since 8 September, more than three months ago? And why should the culprit kill anyone else, at the hospital or elsewhere? There is no good reason to believe that he will, it seems to me. No one knows his name, his circumstances or anything about him. He is just as likely, therefore—more likely, I should say—to have a motive that applied only to Stanley Niven and nobody else.'

'If Mother has briefed us correctly, Arnold Laurier has assigned himself the task of solving Stanley Niven's murder,' I said. 'Might that be what his wife is frightened of—that he will make himself an irresistible target for the killer?'

'No,' said Osgood. 'From the moment we learned that Stanley Niven had been murdered, Vivienne was terrified for Arnold. I was standing right beside her when she was given the news. Arnold had not yet announced his intention to meddle in the investigation. He had not at that point heard about the murder on Ward 6. I saw how Vivienne reacted, Monsieur Poirot: she was not merely concerned, not simply anxious as anyone would have been. She was immediately *in a state of terror*. As if—' Osgood stopped.

'Continue, please,' said Poirot.

'I was going to say: as if she knew exactly who the killer was, why he had killed Stanley Niven, and why he would be coming for Arnold next,' said the doctor.

CHAPTER 4

A State of Terror

Mother spent the next few seconds filling the air with exclamations that achieved nothing: 'Really, doctor, what nonsense!' 'Pure melodrama!' 'I am surprised at you—so fanciful for a man of science.' I had to concede that she made one good point: 'If Vivienne knew who Stanley Niven's killer was, and that he was intent on murdering Arnold, why the devil would she not tell the police?'

Dr Osgood muttered something inaudible under his breath. 'All I can tell you, Mrs Catchpool—'

'Cynthia.'

'—is that Vivienne clutched my arm and whispered, "Arnold will be murdered next." Those were the first words out of her mouth upon hearing of Stanley Niven's death. She almost collapsed, I tell you. When she and I were alone together soon afterwards, she grabbed me by the arms, wild with fear, and said, "What if the killer meant to kill Arnold all along?" Over and over, she said, "I won't send him to that hospital, Robert. I won't!" She begged me to help her persuade Arnold and the rest of the family to agree to him staying at home. Dying at home. So far, she has been unsuccessful. Certainly she has not persuaded the patient himself, who is eager to infiltrate Ward 6 and do some sleuthing.'

'This is most interesting,' said Poirot.

'She has been in that same state of heightened fear ever since,' Osgood told him. 'I think it might kill her if it lasts too much longer. This is why you must work quickly. Catch and remove this killer, and then Arnold will be safe at St Walstan's and Vivienne can stop torturing herself. Maybe then she will start to eat properly again. She is skin and bone—and on top of the terror, I believe she is causing herself additional strain by determinedly maintaining the pretence that she feels only a normal level of anxiety, one that would appear understandable to the rest of us.'

'I do not find Vivienne's fear to be mysterious or inexplicable in the least,' said Mother. 'For a lady of her age and background, an unsolved murder in such close proximity to oneself or a loved one would be reason enough for terror. I consider myself lucky to have a Scotland Yard inspector for a son; thanks to Edward, I am able to regard murder as an ordinary if unfortunate aspect of everyday life.'

'Perhaps,' said Poirot. 'Though, like Dr Osgood, I see no reason why Madame Laurier should have the specific fear that her husband will be the killer's next victim. And if that fear was expressed as a certainty—'

'It was,' said Osgood.

'Then that requires explanation.'

Mother laughed. 'You men really are determined to complicate matters, aren't you? Here I am—Vivienne's best friend in the whole world—and yet none of you has thought to ask *me*. Ah, well. You will ask Vivienne instead and you will get your explanation, Monsieur Poirot. She will tell you what she long ago confided to me: that she knows there is no logic to it. It is naïve to imagine our worst fears must have a rational basis. Often they have none whatever. At the risk of provoking you, Dr Osgood—' Mother fluttered her eyelashes, '—Vivienne does not put on a show in my presence as she does in yours. She admits that in her bones she is horribly afraid Arnold will be the killer's next victim *and* that it makes no sense. She knows of no reason why anyone should wish to kill Arnold, yet she is convinced it is the case—chiefly because the first murder happened when it did, on 8 September—'

'Mother,' I said. 'Do not refer to it as "the first murder", when—'

'—during the very hour that she was there, in the room next door. No more than a coincidence of course, but—'

'*Attendez!* What did you say, madame? Please repeat it.'

'I said that the timing of Stanley Niven's murder was merely a coincidence, and the two rooms being next to each other was also pure chance.'

'Vivienne Laurier was on Ward 6 of St Walstan's Hospital when Stanley Niven was killed?' said Poirot.

'Yes, they all were,' Mother said. 'Have I not already told you that? I thought I had.'

'*Non*, madame. Who are "they all"?'

'The Lauriers. Well, most of them.'

'What were they doing at the hospital on 8 September?' I asked. Arnold Laurier was not yet a patient at St Walstan's so they could not have been visiting him.

'They had been invited for a tour of the place,' said Mother. 'To meet the doctors and nurses, see the facilities—in particular the room that is to be Arnold's. Do not get excited, Monsieur Poirot. I see that you are, but it means nothing. That is probably why it did not occur to me to mention it. Like Vivienne, you are attributing profound significance to a mere coincidence. And none of the Lauriers could have killed Stanley Niven, in case you were thinking along those lines. All five of them were inside the room that has been reserved for Arnold, accompanied by a nurse and with the door closed, while Stanley Niven was being killed in the room next door. Besides, why should any of them wish to kill him? He was a complete stranger to them.'

Poirot and I exchanged a look. The motorcar engine struck a new note as we slowed down in front of two tall gateposts, each one a rectangular column topped by a round ball. We had arrived. There was a sign mounted on the gatepost closest to me but in the darkness I could not read the house's name. The windows of the vehicle were closed but I could hear, clearly, the sound of an agitated sea. A few seconds later I saw the dark shape of a large building ahead.

Frelly. No, I would never call it by that *soubriquet* nor think of it as that. It was infantile.

'Who was in the room?' Poirot asked Mother. 'Name them: "all five of them", you said. Vivienne Laurier, and a nurse. Who else from the Laurier family?'

'The nurse's name is Zillah Hunt,' said Dr Osgood. 'I too was at the hospital that day. Mrs Catchpool's account is accurate. I saw them all emerge from the room that will be Arnold's after Christmas. That was definitely *after* the murder had been committed. The police interviewed everybody, naturally, and all six of them—Zillah Hunt and the five Lauriers—they all said the same thing: no one entered or left Arnold's room at any point, until they all left together. No one opened the door until they were ready to make their exit as a party.'

'Who were the five Lauriers?' Poirot asked again.

Mother reeled them off: 'Vivienne; her and Arnold's two sons, Douglas and Jonathan; and their wives, Madeline and Janet.'

I don't know why hearing the two names again after not hearing them for weeks should have brought it back to me, but it did. *Madeline and Janet*. Memories are peculiar creatures; you think they've scarpered, and then suddenly they spring up, having been lurking in the shadows all along.

Madeline and Janet were the two sisters at Frellingsloe House who hated each other. And . . . had not Mother just said that each one was married to a son of Arnold and Vivienne Laurier? Yes, it was truly coming back to me now: Madeline and Janet Laurier were sisters who had been close, but then Janet had fallen in love with and married the younger Laurier son, several years after her sister had married the older one. Madeline had not taken kindly to her little sister following her into the Laurier family, Mother had said.

Suddenly, the full picture came to me. I knew who Enid Surtees was, also, and her husband, though I could not dredge up his Christian name. Mr and Mrs Surtees were the parents of Madeline and Janet Laurier, *nées* Surtees.

I was about to ask Mother to confirm I was right about all this when Poirot said, 'What about Arnold Laurier? He did not also go to the hospital that day, to see the room that was soon to be his?'

'No,' said Dr Osgood. 'He had very much hoped to go, but he was particularly unwell that afternoon, so he stayed at home.'

'So Nurse Zillah Hunt and five members of the Laurier family were close by when Stanley Niven was murdered,' Poirot said slowly. 'Who else?'

'Other doctors and nurses,' said Osgood. 'Nurse Olga Woodruff and Nurse Bee Haskins. Dr Wall. And all the patients on Ward 6, though I can assure you that none of them is the guilty party.'

There was one name he had not mentioned, perhaps because he thought it too obvious to be worth saying. Still, since he had added the ward's patients to his list in an apparent desire to be as thorough as possible, I found it interesting that he had not included himself. By his own account, Dr Robert Osgood had been in as close proximity to Stanley Niven's murder as all of the other people he had just named.

CHAPTER 5

At Frellingsloe House

Once inside Frellingsloe House, I saw that Mother's descrip-tion had been not so much an exaggeration as an outright lie. This was no stunning jewel of unparalleled beauty, though the stained-glass windows offered a pleasing pattern of circles with crosses inside them. The circles were blue glass, and the cross-shapes were composed of small green and pink flowers. There were cracks in two of the panes of glass nearest to the front door.

Poirot and I stood facing two ornate archways that looked as if they had been clumsily dropped into the middle of the wide entrance hall. One led to a staircase and the other to a corridor. They looked as if they had been placed incorrectly and should have been, respectively, further to the left and to the right.

This was a substantial building, but it did not feel to me like a mansion—another of Mother's lies. It lacked the sumptuous abundance that the word implies. Rather, it reminded me of a neglected old rectory. I could see no furniture at all from this vantage point, not even a small side table. A grand piano with a distinctly abandoned air stood to my left. Did it qualify as furniture? I did not think so. There was no stool in front of it, nor any chairs in sight. To my right was the tallest Christmas tree I had ever seen, but there was not a single decoration on it.

Mother, having ushered us in, had gone off in search of 'Darling Vivienne'. Dr Osgood and Felix Rawcliffe had not followed us into the house. The front door was slightly ajar, left in that position by Mother to enable the doctor and the curate to enter. I could hear no conversation from outside, however—only the roar and foam of waves that sounded close enough to crash in on us. Had the two men gone elsewhere? Did one of them have a cottage in the grounds?

'It is curious, *non*?' said Poirot. 'In this weather, to linger outside the house?'

'Osgood and Rawcliffe?'

He nodded. 'They are, I think, continuing their discussion from before. It is of great importance—to one if not to both of them.'

'Vivienne Laurier's fear that Arnold will be murdered?' I said.

'No, their earlier discussion.'

I laughed. 'You surely cannot think they are outside in a lashing gale talking about *Romeo and Juliet*?'

'Not Romeo and Juliet, my friend.' Poirot wagged his finger at me. 'You did not pay attention. They were discussing a different pair of lovers: Romeo and Rosaline.'

'I attended perfectly well,' I told him. 'I meant *Romeo and Juliet* the Shakespeare play. In which Romeo and Rosaline feature.'

'Ah, but it was not the play that our new friends were debating so fiercely,' he said. 'It was not an argument about a work of literature. They spoke of the characters Romeo and Rosaline as if they were real people who mattered.'

'I am not sure what you mean,' I told him.

'I caught the look that passed between them in the motorcar,' he said. 'It was one that sent the message very clearly, "We must speak no more of this now. Others are listening. Let us resume the conversation later." Then Dr Osgood started to talk to me about Madame Laurier. You did not notice?'

'The change of topic, yes, but not the look. If it is such a big secret, why did they refer to it at all in our presence?'

'They believed they were safe enough. Romeo and Rosaline are not the real names of those involved. Besides, they did not expect the conversation to become as impassioned as it did. But Dr Osgood grew agitated, and that, I think, was what made them decide it was not safe to carry on.'

'Poirot, there is something I need to tell you. It's about this house.'

'*Oui, mon ami?*'

'It is going to fall into the sea.'

'*Pardon?*'

'Not immediately. I mean, not tonight, or even tomorrow, so it hardly affects us—'

'What fantastical story do you tell me, Catchpool? And where is somebody to show us to our rooms? Where are our hosts?' He peered in the direction of the stairs, then looked over his shoulder at the open front door. Then he turned back to me. 'Continue, please.'

I told him about the coastal erosion problem and that it represented a death sentence for Frellingsloe House. I added some touches of absurdity for the sake of light relief: Mother's annoyance at the lack of initiative shown by Munby's inhabitants; their failure to track down superior clay and 'put it' in the cliffs here.

As I spoke, I wondered how, precisely, the house would meet its end. I pictured it tumbling off the cliff top, wholly intact, spinning round and round as it hurtled towards the ocean—but of course that was ludicrous. To Poirot, I emphasized that for one or two nights we would be perfectly safe here. The chances of us ending up underwater while in our pyjamas were minimal.

'That is sad for the Laurier family,' he said, 'but why do you tell me with such urgency?'

'I thought you might not want to stay here.'

'I do not. Neither do you wish to spend any more time than is necessary in Munby-*sur-la-mer*,' he reminded me. 'My preference has nothing to do with coastal erosion, however.'

'And everything to do with my mother?'

He chuckled. '*Pas du tout*. I have greatly enjoyed meeting Madame Catchpool. What an excellent mother for you to have, *mon ami*—the very one that you needed, I have no doubt.'

I was about to protest, but a tall, buxom young woman had appeared from the corridor and was striding towards us, carrying a cup and saucer in each hand. They clinked as she moved: one was curved and decorated with pink and gold details; the other was plain white. The person carrying them was dressed in the most astonishing miscellany of garments: muddy riding boots with a skirt that looked as if it was made of fine green silk, a lumpy maroon hat, and a pink blazer over a blue jumper. Around her neck she wore a thick black cord to which two brown shoes were tied by their laces. One knocked against a tea-cup as she strode towards us, splashing liquid on her clothes.

Next to my ear, Poirot said quietly, 'If only the most puzzling murders could be committed in the more fashionable districts of London—that would please me. Never mind. Let us hope at least that this personage will close the front door.'

'Hello,' she said. 'I'm Madeline Laurier, but please call me Maddie. Everyone does apart from my enemies, declared and covert, so if you address me as Madeline I shall know that you mean me harm. Haha!' She caught me scrutinizing her strange blazer, which had a greenish stain on one lapel. 'Oh, and please excuse my appearance,' she said. 'My real clothes are underneath. When you next see me, I shan't look anywhere near as strange as I do now. Blame this house! It is quite unreasonably large, and I am not prepared to trudge back and forth and up and down stairs all day long. I have had to devise some ingenious methods for transporting anything I want to carry. Everyone else around here is willing to make more than one trip, but I am not. All this lot is going in the rubbish.' She indicated her clothing. 'Apart from the shoes, which I'll be wearing as soon as I've chucked out these decaying boots. Oh, and I've brought you each a cup of tea. Cynthia said you'd want one. Drink them quickly. They're probably sepul- chrally cold already. The fancy cup is for you, Monsieur Poirot. French china, from some fancy-sounding shop in Paris, according to Cynthia. Though you are not French, are you? You're from Belgium. I have told Cynthia that, and so has Vivienne, but she doesn't seem to listen. I think she wants you to be French, for some reason. Now, has anybody told you that we are eating in twenty minutes?'

This was welcome news indeed.

'We delayed the evening meal in your honour.' Maddie smiled. 'That means everyone will be extra ravenous and bad tempered. You might as well see us at our worst on the first night, though, eh?'

I told her that we were very much looking forward to dinner. My stomach had been grumbling about its emptiness for some time.

'Don't look forward to it too much,' Maddie said. 'Enid is the cook. I did not use the word "dinner", did you spot that? If you are expecting what that word usually means, you will be disappointed. Enid is my mother. She is a terrible cook, as terrible as Terence is at gardening. Oh—Terence is Enid's husband, my father.'

It struck me then that Mother had said something about this when she first told me about her Norfolk Christmas plans. That was right: friends who were living at the house and paying nothing for the privilege, but instead contributing their labour to the running of the household. Mother had expressed disapproval. The Laurier family had plenty of money, apparently, but Arnold Laurier, the patriarch, no longer wished to spend any of it on employing the excellent cook who had worked for the family for many years.

Poirot took a sip of his tea, then another. He winced. 'This beverage is . . . I cannot drink it, I am afraid.'

'I warned you it would be cold.' Maddie looked over her shoulder, then lowered her voice to a whisper. 'Do not expect standards to be high here. It's barmy on the crumpet, the way things are done in this house. Sometimes I think Douglas and I are the only ones with a grip on reality. Douglas is my husband. And why is the front door open?' Maddie marched over and slammed it shut, then bolted it at the top and bottom. 'Has anyone shown you where your rooms are? Of course they have not. I shall point you in the right direction and you can find them yourselves. I would take you, but then all this rubbish I'm wearing would have to come upstairs with me and that is an intolerable prospect.'

She told us where to find our quarters, which, mercifully, were on a floor that contained no other bedrooms, the top floor of the house. The more distance I could keep between myself and any 'barmy on the crumpet' Laurier or Surtees family members, the better.

Maddie instructed us to discard our hats, coats and gloves on the hall floor—'Someone will find them soon and put them somewhere, probably'—and marched off to dispose of the unwanted items draped about her person.

'I shall certainly not discard my overcoat on the—' Poirot had started to say when we heard an exclamation, then footsteps.

Maddie reappeared. 'I forgot the most important thing of all,' she said. 'Has anyone told you about the Morality Game?'

'*Non,* madame.'

'It's a game we're going to play on Christmas Day—all my idea! I couldn't bear to spend another year playing Jonathan's ancient "Mansion of Happiness" game.'

'Poirot and I will have left before Chri—' I started to say.

Maddie spoke over me. 'As you unpack, think about villains from history,' she said. 'Who is the very worst person you can think of, from a moral point of view? Who is the absolute last word in evil? You will each need to choose a person.'

She hurried away without clarifying what we would need to do with or about whichever miscreant we picked.

'*Quelle femme extraordinaire,*' Poirot murmured.

I told him about the two Laurier sons' wives being sisters and, according to Mother, their hating one another. He did not seem to find it particularly interesting. I suspected he was disturbed by what Maddie Laurier had told us about the evening meal. An inadequate dinner was a fate that Poirot believed to be '*insupportable*', and even more so after a long journey.

To prevent his mood from deteriorating further, I offered to carry his suitcase up the stairs. We had made it no further than the first half landing when there was a loud banging on the front door, as if someone was throwing their entire body weight against it, followed by the sound of running feet, bolts being drawn back, and the door opening. 'Some fool locked us out!' a voice bellowed. I recognized it as belonging to Dr Osgood. A woman with a high-pitched voice that I had not heard before started to apologize to him. 'Was it you who locked us out?' Osgood demanded.

'No, no, it was not.' She sounded like a frightened mouse.

'Then why are you sorry? Don't be a fool, Janet!'

Ah, so the meek voice was Maddie's sister. She sounded nothing like her.

'Stop yelling at her, Robert,' came Felix Rawcliffe's voice. 'We are now inside, thanks to Janet.'

'*Le docteur*, he is not a happy man,' Poirot whispered.

'Speaking of your sudden interest in happy men—' I began, but got no further. It was as if my words had summoned an example of the very commodity I was describing. Down the stairs came bounding towards us a skeletally thin elderly man with a full head of reddish brown hair and a face so crumpled and lined that his features looked odd poking out from amid the creases. He seemed able to hop about with the agility of a mountain goat all the same. His eyes were large, grey and bright. 'Hercule Poirot? Is it really you? It is! It is the great, the *remarkable*, Poirot, here at Frelly! This truly is the greatest moment of my life. And—how rude of me, I'm so sorry—Inspector

Catchpool, the right-hand man of the greatest mind in the world. Welcome, welcome, gentlemen! I am Arnold Laurier. I could not be more thrilled to meet you both and to welcome you to my home.'

'It is most generous of you to accommodate us,' said Poirot. 'Especially in your state of health.'

'My state of lethal decrepitude, do you mean?' Laurier chuckled. Then he looked impatient suddenly, as if his fun had been spoiled by a triviality—a reminder that a dog needed walking or something of that nature. 'Shall we get the boring bit out of the way?' he said. 'You have been told that I am dying, which is true, but it is quite the least interesting thing about me and we need not discuss it further. Now, if there is time—' he produced a gold watch from his pocket. 'Ah, yes, we have a good few minutes. Excellent. Please follow me, gentlemen.'

He skipped off down the stairs at a surprisingly fast pace and without a backward glance. I looked at Poirot, who shrugged and said, 'Let us go. Leave *les valises* here on the landing. We can only pray that nobody will take the opportunity to dress up in our clothes or throw them away.'

'Gentlemen?' Arnold Laurier beamed up at us from the entrance hall. 'Hurry, or we might miss our chance. It is important that I speak to you both before supper-time—and before anyone else gets hold of you.'

CHAPTER 6

Arnold Offers a Deal

Arnold Laurier wasted no time once the three of us were in his study with the door closed. 'You will have been told by my wife, or by your mother, inspector—probably both— that a man by the name of Stanley Niven has been murdered. Vivienne will soon try to prevail upon you, if she has not done so already, to exert your influence in a particular direction that she considers prudent. She wants me to give up on my plan to solve Niven's murder—for my own good, she insists. Well, you needn't bother. It will be a waste of your efforts. My mind is made up. I am the patient, and ought therefore to have the primary say in what becomes of me, would you not agree?'

Poirot gave a small nod. I copied the gesture while trying not to shiver. It was uncomfortably cold in this high-ceilinged room, with an empty grate where a fire ought to have been. Each new onslaught of wind shook the glass panes as the icy air whistled in around the windows. Poirot must have been suffering, I thought; he was forever complaining about the inability of the English to heat their homes adequately.

The walls of Arnold Laurier's study were covered with shelves, into which leather-bound books were crammed, and framed portraits, mainly of men with the same red-brown hair as our host. Looking at them, I remembered something else I had heard from Mother: Arnold Laurier was born into great wealth. He need never have worked a day in his life, but he was passionate about . . . was it mathematics? Science? History? Whatever it was, he had taught the subject because he was passionate about it and felt strongly about making a valuable contribution to the world and leaving it a better place. And—another detail I recalled—he was reluctant to spend money on himself, but happy to spend it on anything that might benefit his two sons. He and his wife were both determined to bequeath to their children as much as possible, and lived very frugally in order that their sons should be able to do the opposite for the rest of their lives.

Like Frellingsloe House's entrance hall, this study contained a vertiginous Christmas tree, decorated minimally and only at the bottom, as if someone had been called away urgently after hanging the first few jewelled baubles.

'Gentlemen, I should like you to know . . . Wait.' Laurier arranged himself in a high-backed leather armchair the colour of my old school uniform. I'd always thought of it as 'dried blood'. 'I have felt a thousand times better since I started to apply my mind to this unsolved murder,' Laurier said. 'I have told Vivienne the same thing: if she wishes me to live for as long as possible, and she does, then the most sensible thing to do is let me pursue my investigation. There is only so much I can do from here, of course, but after Christmas I shall be admitted to St Walstan's and then I can properly get to work.'

Poirot said nothing. Again, I followed his lead.

Laurier, who had perhaps been hoping for an instant and resounding endorsement of his plan, looked rather put out. 'Poirot, tell me the truth. Do not hold back! Do I look to you like a person with nothing further to contribute to this world? Or do you see a man with a spring in his step?'

Apart from his creased and slightly yellow skin, Laurier seemed far more spirited and energetic than any dying person I had ever met before.

'All of this is not at all to say that I do not feel heartily sorry for poor Stanley Niven,' Laurier went on. 'I do. It is terrible, what happened to him. A horrible injustice. He was a lovely chap, too. A thoroughly decent fellow. That is what spurs me on, do you see? That, and—yes, I will admit it—the challenge of solving the puzzle in true Poirot fashion. Now, my wife would have you believe that it would be in my best interests if *you* were to solve Niven's murder instead of me—she and Cynthia have brought you here to do precisely that. They hope to prolong my life by an extra three weeks, or four or five, or some such pointlessness. I beg of you, Poirot: think of how you would feel in my situation. Would you choose to play it safe or to put yourself in harm's way in order to solve a murder in your usual brilliant fashion?'

This struck me as a tactic that might work with Poirot. I was fairly sure that, were he in Laurier's position, he would feel exactly as Laurier did.

'Allow me to have this one triumph before I die, Poirot. Please. I know I can do it. I have read about your cases, studied your methods. For some time I have thought of myself as your unknown apprentice, even before I had an unsolved murder to sink my teeth into. And with Niven's murder having happened at the very hospital that has been earmarked for me, and in the adjacent room, no less . . . This will sound fanciful, but I believe that Fate has marked this matter as being for my specific attention.' Laurier exhaled slowly. There was a rattling sound to his breath. He said, 'I would be immensely grateful if the two of us— the three of us—could make a bargain here in this room today.'

'What bargain, monsieur?'

'I am aware that it must go against your every instinct to leave a murder unsolved, particularly when my wife has summoned you to achieve the opposite result. And, you might be wondering, why should you stand aside for my sake? I have never before caught a killer. What if I fail? Poirot, Inspector Catchpool . . . I ask you for one month only. If within one month of my taking up residence at St Walstan's, I have not solved the crime, then it is all yours. Is that really so long to wait? It has already been more than three months since the murder occurred. How can another month make a difference one way or the other?'

'Monsieur—' Poirot tried to cut in.

'If you are inclined to refuse my request, and I am aware that it would not be unreasonable of you to do so, then I have another one for you. This is not my first choice but I could live with it: we work on the case together. I proceed to St Walstan's after Christmas as planned, and I act as your agent on the inside, as it were. The three of us—you, me and Catchpool here—put our heads together and work as a team of detectives.'

Suggesting one's second preference before one's first has been refused struck me as a poor tactic.

'Neither of the avenues you suggest will please your wife,' said Poirot. 'If you were my agent on the hospital's inside, her fear that you might attract the attention of Monsieur Niven's killer—'

'I am dying; that does not make me a fool,' Laurier interrupted. 'I shall be in hospital as a patient. That is all anyone will think I am. No one will suspect me of investigating anything.'

'It's difficult to find things out if you don't ask questions,' I told him.

'Ah, yes, but the way in which one asks a question makes all the difference.' Laurier smiled. 'You must know that, inspector. There's a knack to it. One can find out a lot simply by listening attentively, without asking anyone anything. It was by listening to Stanley Niven himself that I was able to pick up two excellent leads. I've told the police about both. They seem peculiarly uninterested.'

'You met Monsieur Niven?' said Poirot. 'When?'

'Yes, of course. I told you: a thoroughly amiable chap.'

'I assumed you were repeating what you had heard about him.'

'No, no. Second-hand reports tell you next to nothing about a chap. They are informative only about the opinions and beliefs of the second-hand reporters.'

'*C'est vrai*,' Poirot agreed.

I frowned. Had he not solved case after case as a direct result of people telling him at least some things that had turned out to be true? The skill was in judging when to trust and when to doubt.

'Please tell me about your meeting with Monsieur Niven,' Poirot said to Laurier. 'I was told that you did not accompany your family to the hospital on 8 September, the day of the murder.'

'No. I was supposed to, but I felt exceptionally unwell that day. I met Niven only once—in August. I am afraid I cannot remember what day it was. Vivienne might be able to tell you. I went to the hospital to see Dr Wall, a colleague of Dr Osgood. Wall knows more than anyone else at St Walstan's about my particular condition. Unfortunately he was delayed. Stanley Niven, who was taking his daily constitutional around the ward, noticed that I had been waiting for rather a long time and decided to keep me company. Jolly decent of him, it was, putting himself out to entertain a complete stranger.'

'You say you picked up two excellent leads while listening to him?' said Poirot.

'Well, they were not leads then, of course. Niven had not yet been murdered.'

'But they are leads now. What are they?'

'I will tell you, of course—though I should warn you, it might be a waste of your time. According to the police, they are not important enough to merit further consideration. It's frustrating, Poirot.' Laurier sighed. 'As a former schoolteacher, I cannot help wondering if schools these days are properly equipping children for adult life. Does anyone get a proper education any more? I am not convinced. Gerald Mackle looks about twelve years old—that's Inspector Mackle, the one in charge of the Niven murder. Nice enough fellow, but he doesn't seem able to think properly. My subject was Mathematics, but I also taught my pupils to use their brains effectively in all spheres of life. I have tried to encourage Inspector Mackle in that direction, but he seems remarkably resistant to instruction. He keeps trying to insist that one of four people must have killed Stanley Niven: his wife, his daughter, his son or his brother. Have you spoken to Mackle about the case, Poirot?'

'Not yet. I intend to do so first thing tomorrow. Please tell me about the two leads.'

'I will,' said Laurier enthusiastically. 'First, though, I must tell you why Mackle's four suspects cannot be guilty: they were not at the hospital when Niven was murdered. All of them were miles away. They were not even in Norfolk. Not a one of them!' He chuckled. 'You would think, would you not, that this bald fact might persuade Mackle to abandon his theory? Not a bit of it! He believes that one of their alibis must be false—oh yes, they can all prove they were elsewhere at the crucial moment. But Mackle doggedly clings to his belief that one of them has persuaded an associate to lie. Never mind that nobody—no doctor, no nurse, no patient—saw any of Niven's closest relatives on the ward that day. It is true that the hospital can be a little chaotic at times, but, really . . .' Laurier snorted with laughter.

'Monsieur,' said Poirot. 'The two leads, please.'

'Yes, yes. The all-important leads.' Laurier looked guarded suddenly. 'I trust we have an agreement in place, Poirot?'

'What exactly do you mean, Mr Laurier?'

I knew exactly what he meant, the cunning old cove. Well, he would need to be more straightforward about it.

'Will you give me the month I have asked for, before you take any steps to solve Stanley Niven's murder?' He looked first at Poirot, then at me.

'*Non*. This I cannot agree to do.'

'Then will you permit me to become a member of your investigative operation?' said Laurier. 'An equal partner with you and Inspector Catchpool here?'

I had to give full credit to Poirot: if he was shocked by the suggestion that I might be his equal, he hid it well.

'The first step will be to tell my wife that, in your expert opinion, I must go to St Walstan's after Christmas as planned,' said Laurier. 'I can hardly be your man on the inside if I'm twiddling my thumbs here at Frelly.'

'If you wish to be of any assistance to me at all, you must understand this, monsieur: whether they are on the inside or on the outside, my "men" do not withhold information from me in order to compel me to enter into agreements that, otherwise, I should not consider.'

Laurier's face seemed to fold in on itself. He was silent for a few seconds. Then he said, 'Yes, I can see how that might rub you up the wrong way. *Extremis malis, extrema remedia* and all that. Still, it is no excuse. I am sorry, Poirot. You are right: it was an unfair tactic. Please accept my apology.'

Poirot inclined his head graciously. 'It is forgotten, monsieur. I understand your predicament and I sympathize. I know, also, that your wife would not forgive me if I allowed you to place yourself in unnecessary danger—'

Once again, Laurier interrupted him. 'If Vivienne is right and I am next in line to be hit over the head with a large hospital-issue vase by Stanley Niven's murderer, then so be it. It is my life, my risk and my choice, and I choose to play an active part in trying to solve this crime. I believe this matter has crossed my path for a reason, and I simply wish to fulfil my God-given purpose on this earth before I leave it.'

'I see,' said Poirot.

'Nobody can stop me from going to St Walstan's after Christmas if I am set on it, and I am.' Laurier grinned, as if his declaration of defiance were bound to be a source of amusement and delight to all present. 'Surely you agree, Poirot: it makes sense that we should tackle this case together, does it not, rather than working on it separately?'

At that moment, the door of Arnold Laurier's study opened and in walked a woman who might have been anywhere between sixty and seventy. She had hollow cheeks, large green eyes, and seemed much too thin for her height—as if she ought to have had more padding on her bones.

She wore a long dress, I think, though I might be misremembering that detail; it was hard to focus on anything but her face, which was quite the most uncelebratory countenance I had ever seen: a mixture of disapproval, anger, sadness and dread. I could not tell if she was about to weep or punch each of us on the nose in turn; certainly nothing pleasant was going to happen. It was as if a heavy cloud of pain had filled the room. I wondered if Poirot felt it too.

'Vivienne!' Arnold seemed delighted by her arrival. 'I was just—'

'—disregarding all danger, and my feelings,' she finished his sentence for him in a voice much quieter and softer than I had expected. 'Telling Monsieur Poirot and Inspector Catchpool that you are quite happy to be murdered.'

She had been listening outside the door for some time, then.

'Must you be so dramatic, dear?' Laurier's tone was gentle. 'I want you to be able to enjoy my great achievement once I am gone. I want you to be able to say, "My husband solved a murder while at death's door," and feel proud.'

'I am not here to argue with you, Arnold,' said his wife. 'Did I not say this morning that I have given up? I meant it. I am here only to tell you that Enid has announced dinner as being ready. Which means it will be ready in about half an hour, I expect. Our guests have not yet been up to their rooms or unpacked. They will be grateful for a chance to settle in before we eat. You can speak to them later this evening. After dinner there will be plenty of time.'

'I do hope so,' said Laurier. 'There is another matter, very close to my heart, about which I am eager to consult you, Poirot. It has nothing at all to do with Stanley Niven or St Walstan's Hospital—it is about a life that might yet be saved.'

I was puzzled by this. Searching his wife's face for clues as to his possible meaning, I found none: she simply watched him with her big, sad, green eyes until he stopped speaking. Then, still without reacting in any way, she turned and left the room, closing the door quietly behind her.

Another person might have delivered her 'I have given up' speech as an attempt to manipulate their spouse, but she had sounded only sorrowful, as if she truly had dispensed with all hopeful feelings forever.

Poirot gave me a familiar order with his eyes: this was the one he reserved for occasions when he believed urgent action of the physical sort was required. His message was clear: 'Now, without delay.'

Naturally, I obeyed. Putting aside my reluctance to follow the pain-cloud to another part of the house, I stood up, excused myself and set off on in pursuit of Vivienne Laurier.

CHAPTER 7

A Conversation with Vivienne Laurier

'Mrs Laurier!'

Finally, I had caught up and could see her. She had reached the same half-landing on which Poirot and I had abandoned our suitcases a short while ago. They were no longer there. I hoped mine had been taken to my room, and wondered if I would have a chance to verify its where-abouts before dinner. No individual person nor any kind of generalized system seemed to be in charge at Frellingsloe House. It felt quite possible that my possessions had been spirited off somewhere, never to return.

Hearing me call out, Vivienne Laurier stopped and turned. 'Inspector Catchpool.'

'Edward, please.'

'Edward,' she agreed after a moment's pause. 'And you must call me Vivienne.'

I realized I did not know what Poirot would have me say to her next. Was he, at this moment, agreeing to appoint her husband as his right-hand man in the investigation of

72

Stanley Niven's murder, or was he explaining with great regret that it would not be possible? Ignorant of his preferred approach, I resolved to proceed as impartially as I could.

Vivienne Laurier reached out and touched my arm with no apparent purpose in mind: one light tap with the tips of her fingers. 'I am so sorry,' she said. 'So dreadfully sorry.' She looked distraught. 'What a reprehensible way for me to greet guests who have travelled all the way from London in this hellish weather. I should have said a proper hello and welcome to you and Monsieur Poirot. Sometimes I forget that not everybody is trapped in my nightmare with me. Please forgive me. I am glad to have you here. I shall say so to Monsieur Poirot when I see him at dinner.'

'Thank you. And there is nothing at all to forgive.'

'You are very kind. Cynthia has told me so much about her wonderful, handsome, clever son.'

I tried not to wince at this. Mother never said anything complimentary to me for my own sake. She never had, though I had heard her praise-boast about me as a way of elevating her own social capital in the eyes of others.

'Now that I have met you, I am not at all surprised that you are such a source of pride to her,' said Vivienne. 'She adores you, you know. I am so pleased for her sake that you are able to spend the coming Christmas with her. Family is so important. The young do not always know it. I am sure you do, Edward, as an only child. It must be hard without . . .'

Whatever she had been about to say, she thought better

of it. Instead, she produced a rather artificial smile and said, 'In any case, Cynthia is overjoyed, and it does me good to see her happy. It is like being cold in your bones and knowing there is a roaring fire nearby, even if its warmth cannot reach you. One is still grateful it is there.'

The cloud of pain surrounding Vivienne Laurier was heavy enough without me adding to it. Now was not the time to explain that I had not agreed to spend Christmas with Mother, nor did it seem an opportune moment to point out that a roaring fire, or preferably twenty of them, was exactly what Frellingsloe House needed—that and some more Christmas tree decorations.

I assured myself that I did not need to say it out loud in order to make it true: I would not be spending Christmas in this house. My resolve grew stronger each time someone told me otherwise.

'Cynthia is a treasure,' Vivienne went on. Had Mother given her a script to commit to memory? 'No one listens to me properly apart from her. The rest of them all get angry or impatient, or try to correct me, or else they tell me I have lost my mind. Before Cynthia arrived, I heard nothing all day long apart from how wrong I am about everything. Your mother is a godsend, Edward.'

It was incredible to me that a rational being could hold this opinion.

'She is the only one willing to do anything that might actually help. It was her brilliant idea to involve Hercule Poirot.'

Of course it was.

'When did she arrive?' I asked.

'Three days ago.'

Goodness, but Mother worked quickly. I had assumed she had been here for at least two weeks. Did she not make a remark, in Poirot's drawing room, about endlessly staring out of her window at the sea? That must have been her impatience talking.

'She was due to arrive the day after tomorrow, but then . . . well, the truth is, three days ago I woke up and found that, despite feeling perfectly well physically, I could not get out of bed. My misery had glued me to the sheets, or it might as well have done. I don't suppose you have ever felt as bad as that. Probably most people have not. The only thing that got me out of bed was Cynthia's voice in my head saying, "Vivienne, stop being so feeble. You must get up at once and take action." I realized that I needed her to be here, rather urgently: Cynthia is mainly *mine*, you see, though she is a friend of Arnold's as well, and is on friendly terms with Douglas and Jonathan. They are my two sons.'

I nodded.

'The thing about Cynthia is that she always knows what to do in a crisis. And no one else was sorting it out. Stanley Niven's murder was—is—still unsolved, and . . . well, you've seen how determined my husband is to take himself off to that wretched hospital where people are bludgeoned in their beds. I couldn't bear it any longer, not without help or support. I telephoned Cynthia, and she agreed to drop everything and come straight away.'

She must have been beside herself with glee. Mother loved nothing more than a drama, and one involving a murder would have suited her perfectly. Did she spot, instantly, the opportunity to tamper with Poirot's and my Christmas plans? Three days after arriving at the Lauriers', she had set off to London to rope us both into her scheme.

'Tell me, does Monsieur Poirot believe that he can solve Stanley Niven's murder?' Vivienne asked. 'Cynthia says that he will do so quickly, before Arnold takes up residence at St Walstan's. Do you agree with her? Does he always succeed, once he applies himself to a . . . problem of this kind?'

'So you have not given up, then,' I said.

'Pardon?'

'In the study, earlier, you told your husband that you had given up.'

'Trying to talk him round—yes, that I have sworn off. I don't want Arnold to expend what little energy he has left trying to persuade me why he is right and I am wrong. Since Stanley Niven was killed, I have tried and failed hundreds of times to change his mind about going to St Walstan's. By far the best thing would be for him to stay at Frelly.' A tear had escaped from the corner of her eye. She did not wipe it away. 'I could keep trying, but it wouldn't work, not unless all four children agreed, and they never will.'

'You have four children?' I had heard only about the two sons.

'I think of them all as my children,' she said. 'Douglas

and Jonathan, and Maddie and Janet, my two daughters-in-law. Enid and Terence have become family too—how could they not, when both of their girls are married to my two boys? That is not merely an in-law relationship, is it, when we are all tied together as closely as we are?'

I made a non-committal gesture. Not everyone in Vivienne Laurier's position would invite their Enid and Terence Surtees equivalents to live in their home. Had the two lodgers, Dr Osgood and Felix Rawcliffe, also been designated as honorary Lauriers? How many nights could one safely spend at Frellingsloe House without being reclassified as a member of the family?

'Your sons and their wives agree with your husband, then, that he should go to St Walstan's?'

'Everyone agrees with him, apart from Cynthia and me,' Vivienne said sadly. 'Dr Osgood says Arnold should be in a hospital where he can receive the proper medical attention he needs. He has persuaded Felix—Felix Rawcliffe, the curate—to take the same view, though Felix was initially sympathetic to my concerns. Douglas says, "Why not let Pa try and solve a murder if it would make him happy?" and of course Maddie thinks it's a marvellous idea. She seems to believe that Arnold might succeed in his quest. There is no hope of that, I am afraid. If you could only hear his ludicrous theory about the disgruntled woman from the post office . . . Really, I cannot bear it.'

Had I not been ordered from the study by Poirot, I might have known all about the much-advertised 'two leads' by now. Was the woman from the post office one of them?

Poirot was probably having a high old time in that comfortable leather armchair, listening to a variety of delectably implausible hypotheses.

'Maddie and Douglas are determined, always, to say the opposite of what any sensible person would say.' Vivienne's voice ached with despair. 'And Maddie is adamant that it would be better for *me* if I were to be relieved of the burden of Arnold's day-to-day care, which is quite untrue. Does she ask me what I think is best for me? Of course not. And Enid and Terence are no help. I don't know what they think about it all; they will not be drawn on the subject. Jonathan and Janet are adamant—as is Arnold— that a decline followed by a death cannot be permitted to happen here at Frelly. They have even persuaded our parish priest, Father Peter, to take their side. Felix was hardly going to go against Father Peter, was he? Everybody except Cynthia seems to agree that on no account must this wonderful, perfect house be sullied by the mortality of its inhabitants!'

This last outburst seemed to shock her, as if she had not known herself to be capable of such biting sarcasm. When she next spoke, her tone was more doubtful. 'Frelly is a happy place, of course. It has been in Arnold's family for three generations. We have enjoyed many wonderful times here, but the way everyone talks about it now, what they all believe . . . it is nothing more than superstition! What rule, invented by whom, dictates that if something sad happens in a house, that sadness takes over the whole building, never leaves it and changes the entire character of the place? Yes, it will be devastating for us all if Arnold dies here at home, but it will be equally unbearable if he dies at the hospital. The tragedy is that he won't be with us any more, and it has absolutely nothing to do with Frelly, which . . .'

She stopped and looked over her shoulder. Turning to face me again, she lowered her voice and said, 'Jonathan would have my guts for garters if he heard me say this: no house is anything more, really, than a collection of bricks held together by . . . lime putty, or whatever it is. The rest is people: their feelings and their memories. And the possibility of Arnold dying here is hardly the only problem that Frelly faces. They all carry on as if they are ignorant of the truth! You know about the house, I assume. Cynthia has told you?'

'The coastal problem?' I said, hoping I had phrased it with sufficient tact.

'The sea laying waste to our village, yes. In a few years, Frelly will no longer be here. There is no way to save it. But we are all determined not to acknowledge that. It's funny: you accommodate a delusion for a short while, then a little longer, to spare the feelings of others . . . then suddenly you wake up a year later to find that you are as complicit as everybody else in the denial of reality. We all pretend that Frelly can be saved somehow, that it will last forever. It is madness!'

'Then why not speak the truth?' I said.

'I love my husband more than I care about truth,' said Vivienne. 'If Arnold finds it consoling to believe that Frelly can survive, then I must pretend I believe it, for his sake. Besides, Jonathan and Janet are as convinced as Arnold is that the house can be saved. And if I spoke up, Douglas and Maddie would add their voices to my campaign for the truth, I have no doubt. It is for my sake and for no other reason that they silently collude in the fantasy that Frelly can be rescued. They know how I suffer when they are at odds with Jonathan and Janet. It causes me the most agonizing pain.'

She grimaced. 'Family is everything, Edward. When Arnold and I met, I had nobody left. I was twenty-nine years old and completely alone in the world. Arnold became my family—my whole world. I will be utterly lost without him. He is the life force in me.' Pain blazed from her eyes. 'Once Arnold and I are both gone, Douglas and Jonathan will need one another like never before. The girls too—Maddie and Janet. One does not realize until one loses a loved one how precious they are, how precious every moment is. Oh, I know what you are thinking.'

I was thinking that not all blood relatives could accurately be described as loved ones.

'You are about to tell me, as so many others have, that Arnold will soon die of his illness whether he is murdered or not,' said Vivienne. 'That it hardly matters if he dies or is killed, and so why not let him have his bit of sleuthing fun? I will tell you why: because every second that he is alive, each moment I can spend with him, means more to me than you could possibly imagine. I will not lose him any sooner than I have to.'

'Quite right too,' I said. 'And also, quite wrong: I was not going to say that it would not matter if your husband were murdered.

'That is what most people seem to think,' said Vivienne. 'And I am cast as the killjoy wife, set on thwarting her dying husband's last wish to have fun solving a crime. I don't care! I refuse to allow Arnold to become a second victory for a murderer. It matters how a person dies, Edward. If anything violent were done to Arnold, anything evil, I should not be able to grieve in the only way that I can imagine grieving. I could not go on. Not even for my children's sake.'

'I understand,' I told her.

'Dr Osgood says Arnold has no more than six months left, but he cannot know for certain. No one can. What if he has another eight months, or a year? What if he has two years left? Instances of this sort are rare, but Dr Osgood admits it can happen—though he also tells me I should not expect such a miracle. Why not, I want to know, when Arnold is exceptional in so many other ways? You have seen how he is: fizzing with *joie de vivre*, even now. Which is why I do not wish to argue with him any more. He will not be persuaded; I must accept that. Tell me truthfully, Edward: do you believe that Hercule Poirot can solve Stanley Niven's murder before Arnold moves to St Walstan's?'

'I hope so,' I said. 'That is why we are here.'

'You have plenty of time,' said Vivienne. 'Arnold will remain at Frelly until the beginning of January. That will be long enough, surely, if Monsieur Poirot is as talented a detective as everyone says he is.'

'I have watched him untangle the most baffling mysteries with astonishing speed,' I told her. 'If anyone can do it, he can.'

This did not seem to mollify her. 'If the police have failed, why should Monsieur Poirot succeed? What will he be able to discover that they could not? No one had a reason to kill Stanley Niven. By all accounts, he was a good, kind man. It seems likely to me that his death will never make sense to anybody but his killer. Then there is no chance that even Monsieur Poirot will solve it.'

It would have been futile to tell her to try not to worry.

'And Inspector Mackle is determined to pin the blame on one of the Nivens, for which he should hang his head in shame,' Vivienne went on. 'They are a lovely, happy *family*.' She said the last word as if she truly believed it to be sacred. 'None of them would dream of committing a murder.'

'Do you know the Nivens personally?' I asked her.

'No. I know only what Robert—Dr Osgood—has told me. I trust his judgement far more than I trust that of Inspector Gerald Mackle.'

'Well, you can trust Hercule Poirot,' I told her. 'I have never known him to fail. May I ask you a question?'

She nodded warily.

'Why are you afraid that Stanley Niven's killer will try to kill your husband?'

'Is it not obvious? If Arnold is determined to find out who did it, and if you were the murderer—a person who has already killed once—what on earth would stop you trying it again?'

82

I took a risk. 'Forgive me,' I said, 'but were you not frightened for Arnold even before he announced his intention to investigate Stanley Niven's murder?'

Vivienne's eyes widened. 'Ah. You have been speaking to Robert, I see. Very well, then: yes. Yes, I was afraid for Arnold from the moment I was told that Mr Niven had been murdered. And now you will ask me why, and I shall get my hopes up that perhaps at last someone will listen to me and take the threat to Arnold seriously—only to have you tell me, no doubt, that I imagined it all and there is nothing to worry about.'

'Whatever you say, I shall not dismiss it out of hand,' I assured her.

'Thank you. It was the other patient—what he said to me, and the way he looked when he said it. There was no mistaking it: he meant to warn me. He was trying to tell me that Arnold would be next. No one will believe me, because he did not use those words, but—'

'Wait,' I said. 'I am a little lost. Start at the beginning. Which other patient are you talking about?'

'Mr Hurt-His-Head,' said Vivienne.

'Dinner is ready!' a voice called up from the hall below. I looked down and saw a small woman: an elderly, be-spectacled, bird-like creature. Her hair was grey and sparse; patches of pink scalp were visible between the meagre strands. She wore a dirty blue kitchen apron that was several sizes too large for her. Her bare hands were a livid red that indicated recent scrubbing. Had Maddie not said that her mother, Enid Surtees, was presently occupying the role of cook at Frellingsloe House? I suspected this was Enid.

'We had better join the others,' Vivienne said quickly. She lowered her eyes as she turned away from me, as if we had been jointly involved in a shameful activity. Soon she was at the bottom of the stairs and hurrying away, leaving me alone with many questions, unasked and unanswered, about the man she had referred to as 'Mr Hurt-His-Head'. Who was he, and what did he have to do with the murder of Stanley Niven? And what had he said or done to make Vivienne believe that her husband would be the hospital killer's next victim?

CHAPTER 8

At Dinner

I found Frellingsloe House's empty drawing room by accident while looking for its dining room. Once I had succeeded in finding that, I reached the conclusion that someone had deliberately arranged things the wrong way round. The room that plainly ought to have been the drawing room had been designated as the dining room, and vice versa. I wondered which contrarian member of the Laurier family, belonging to which generation, had decided he wanted a long, rectangular drawing room with only a few small windows, and this large, square dining room with wide French doors at one end.

Both rooms boasted tall, undecorated Christmas trees of the sort that seemed to be *de rigueur* at Frellingsloe House. The dining room's tree stood wretched and forlorn against a backdrop of red velvet: one half of a pair of curtains that had not yet been drawn against the night. The many windows revealed only blackness and the blurred reflection of the scene at the centre of the room: a long, narrow table of dark wood (it would have been perfectly suited to the shape of the rectangular drawing room, alas!) with people positioned around it and three empty chairs. Poirot was at the far end of the table, next to my mother. I took a seat between Dr Osgood and the curate, Felix Rawcliffe

This left only two chairs unoccupied. Arnold Laurier had not yet arrived, and I worked out that the other empty chair would soon be taken by Enid Surtees, who had appeared in the doorway with a large serving bowl that looked twice as heavy as her. I considered standing up and offering to take it from her. What stopped me was the expression on the face of the man I assumed was her husband, Terence Surtees. He was watching Enid with what looked like paralysed anxiety—as if he were afraid she might not be able to get the bowl all the way to the table, but even more reluctant to help in any way.

Had Maddie not said that Terence Surtees was Frellingsloe House's gardener? If so, then this had to be him. He had the dirtiest fingernails I had ever seen on hands that were otherwise clean, and fingers that brought to mind swollen sausages. His hair was white, and as thick as his wife's was thin. It had something of the shape of a lion's mane about it.

I saw that Poirot, in spite of being engaged in conversation with Mother, had also noticed Terence Surtees' look of frozen consternation. No one else in the room seemed to be aware of it.

Enid placed the heavy bowl on the table next to the tower of clean plates. Relief washed over me that our dinner had not ended up splattered all over the floor. Then, a few seconds later, I wished that it had. Enid had pulled the plates towards her and was serving up a species of stew which was quite the most unappetizing thing I had ever seen slopped onto a plate. It had a shiny surface and a lumpy texture. Even the smell of it was vile.

'Shall we wait for Arnold?' Vivienne said.

'It will go cold,' was Enid's curt reply. The ladling out of the lumps continued. It might even have picked up pace, though I could not swear to it.

'I am sure he will be here any second now,' said Vivienne in a strained voice. I guessed that she was not happy to have her wishes ignored. This was the problem with turning your sons' mother-in-law into your cook, I supposed. To an employee who played no other role in one's life, one could give clear orders. It was much harder when dealing with a close friend in such a role. Though, come to think of it, the stilted atmosphere between Vivienne Laurier and Enid Surtees did not suggest to me that friendly feelings flowed freely between them. Presumably Enid and Terence were not being paid a wage for their cook and gardener services. Mother had definitely said that the paid servants had been dismissed in order to save money.

'Could something have delayed Monsieur Laurier?' Poirot asked Vivienne. 'Catchpool, perhaps you could go and find out.'

'No,' said Vivienne. 'Nobody needs to do anything. Arnold will be down shortly. I am not worried about him. I simply thought it would be nice to . . . But Enid is right. We should eat the food while it is hot.'

Once each plate had a pile of the grey lumpy matter at its centre, Enid dripped globules of other unidentifiable substances around the edges from the other serving dishes. There was something dark green and wet, and a sludge-like substance the colour of rust. I restrained a shudder when the same serving spoon was used for all the different pots of slurry.

Soon everyone present had an individual portion of this collage of culinary offence in front of them. Enid sat down opposite me and between the two youngest men at the table. These were obviously Douglas and Jonathan Laurier, sons of Arnold and Vivienne. Douglas, I guessed, was the one who had Maddie on his right-hand side. He was handsome in a rakish way, with slightly unkempt dark hair that was almost black and eyes the same colour. Despite his smart attire—he was impeccably turned out—his slouched posture and lopsided, mischievous smile created a dissolute impression. His brother, Jonathan, had lighter brown hair and was rounder and not quite so handsome. A teddy bear, I thought, and a remarkably cross one. He had not smiled once, at anybody, since I had entered the room—not even when he had nodded at me in greeting.

His wife, Janet, was small and delicate like her mother, and beautiful. It was as if a china doll had been placed among humans. She had an oval-shaped face, blue eyes, golden hair and a mouth like a small pink bow which produced very brief smiles now and then. She was engaged in conversation with Dr Osgood and her father, Terence Surtees, though her role in the proceedings seemed confined to listening and nodding occasionally as she ate.

There was no sibling resemblance between her and her sister; the two women could not have looked any less alike. Maddie was handsome, buxom and not at all doll-like. I was pleased to note that she was no longer draped in all kinds of ill-matched clothes. Apart from my mother, who was still busy boring Poirot and enjoying her own performance as much as she always did, Maddie and Douglas were the only people at the table who seemed to be having fun. They were teasing each other and laughing. I wondered if Poirot had noticed that Maddie, Janet and their parents were the only ones eating. No one who was not a Surtees—now or by birth—had touched their food yet.

Arnold's plate awaited him on the table in front of the one remaining empty chair, its contents slowly solidifying. Enid must have wanted to do all the serving at once, or she would surely have left Arnold's food in the large lidded bowls where it could have stayed warm. Vivienne was pushing food around her plate with her fork, her eyes fixed on Arnold's untouched meal. Without warning, she stood up and started to pour wine and water from the jugs on the table. She had not got very far when Enid sprang up out of her chair and said brusquely, 'Leave that. Let me do it.'

'No, I will do it,' was Vivienne's quiet but firm reply. Enid sat down again.

I had not been wrong: there was a hostility between these two women. Something about Vivienne's manner silently implied that the drinks ought to have been taken care of already, and not by her. We waited and watched in silence as she filled all twenty-six glasses: thirteen with wine and thirteen with water.

'Well, this is jolly!' said Maddie. She raised her wine glass. 'Chin-chin, everyone!' Douglas snorted and raised an eyebrow. Jolly, then, was not the word he would have used. I had to concur. The atmosphere was so strained that I was sure Maddie's remark had been deliberately sarcastic.

'Madame,' Poirot addressed Vivienne Laurier. 'Are you sure you would not like Catchpool to ascertain the where-abouts of your husband?'

'I am sure. Thank you,' she replied. 'If Arnold is not here by now, then he is likely to have fallen asleep. I would rather not disturb him.'

'Catchpool could open the door quietly,' Poirot pressed her.

I tried to catch his eye so that I could send him a questioning look. He sounded concerned that something unto-ward might have happened to Arnold Laurier, and I could not work out why. Was his anxiety related to Laurier's illness, or driven by something else?

'I could also open my father's door quietly,' said Jonathan Laurier. 'Would that suit you just as well, Monsieur Poirot? I am only the son and heir, mind. You might prefer it if the check were carried out by your Scotland Yard lackey who only met my father today.'

'Jonnells!' Douglas laughed. 'I have never heard you say something so rude that was not addressed to me.'

'Do not call me that,' said Jonathan.

'Oh, boys, do stop,' said Mother. 'Douglas, do not goad

him. Jonathan, resist the temptation to rise to the bait. As for you, Monsieur Poirot: do not entertain the notion that you might be offended by what has just occurred—that will do you no good whatsoever.'

I waited for her to add that I should also not take offence, but no such direction came. I decided to make the most of this opportunity to do whatever I wanted, uncoerced by Mother, and aimed the most condemnatory look I could muster at Jonathan Laurier.

'It was my brother's childhood nickname.' Douglas turned to me with a grin. 'You should call him Jonnells every time he calls you a lackey. I would.'

Jonathan, whose face was beetroot red, said to me, 'I'm sorry, Inspector Catchpool. I did not mean . . . You did not deserve that. Please accept my heartfelt apology.'

'Edward has a very forgiving nature,' Mother told him. 'You needn't fret.'

I made a non-committal noise and busied myself by sampling the congealing greyness on my plate. It had no flavour at all, which was a welcome surprise. I had expected it to taste hideous.

'Would this be a good time for me to explain the rules of the Morality Game to Monsieur Poirot and Inspector Catchpool?' said Maddie.

'Not without Arnold,' Vivienne said. 'He won't want to miss any conversation about Christmas games.'

'It is a pity that Catchpool and I will miss this Morality Game, which sounds intriguing,' said Poirot. 'We shall be in London for Christmas.'

Douglas frowned. 'I was told you would both be with us until the beginning of January.'

'You were given incorrect information, I am afraid.'

'Vivienne, I do think someone should check on Arnold,' said Maddie.

'So do I,' said Poirot forcefully, and again I wondered what lay behind his unease.

'The son and heir could nip up, perhaps,' Maddie said pointedly to Jonathan. 'Though come to think of it, there are two sons and heirs, are there not?'

'I certainly thought so,' said Douglas.

'So, really, it is not the definite but the indefinite article we should be using when we speak of such things, Jonnells,' said Maddie.

Janet threw her fork down on the table. 'Will you ever stop causing trouble for no good reason?' she said to her sister.

'Will you?' Maddie fired back. In a high-pitched voice that I assumed was intended as a mockery of Janet's, she said, '"Oh, how terrible, I can see a courtyard, with windows on the other side of it. I'm not upset by life-destroying illness or death but a courtyard—well, that is the limit! Who could possibly endure having a courtyard outside their window?"'

'Girls, please desist from this nastiness immediately,' said my mother. 'Enid, if you won't tell them then I am afraid I will have to.'

'Sorry, Cynthia. Sorry, everyone,' said Maddie. 'I apologize for having mentioned something as hellish and disgustingly intolerable as a . . . *courtyard.*' She lowered her voice to a whisper for the last word. She and Douglas started to laugh.

Poirot looked as if he would have liked to know what this courtyard business was about. I was curious, too; one could hardly ask, however. No doubt it was some decades-old family argument.

Jonathan was looking at Douglas in apparent confusion. 'I never said that I was our father's only son.'

'"The son and heir" were your exact words,' said his brother. 'Not "*a* son and heir". It was a tiny detail, and you hoped Maddie and I wouldn't notice. Well, we did.'

Jonathan shook his head. 'I said "the" because, in that moment, I was thinking only about myself and Inspector Catchpool. He is a policeman. I am the son and heir. Do you see?'

'I don't see how the "heir" part is relevant at all,' said Maddie. 'I find it fascinating that you did not simply say "son".'

Vivienne stood up suddenly. 'I will go!' she cried out: a howl of anguish. Everyone observed her in silence for a moment or two. Then she gathered herself and said in a matter-of-fact voice, 'I will go and see what has become of Arnold,' as if that had been all she meant. Clearly she had found the bickering between her sons and their wives unbearable—in which case, why not say so? She would have had the silent support of most of the table. She was not a straightforward person, I thought; far from it.

'No, please, I will go, Vivienne.' Dr Osgood rose to his

feet. 'Sit yourself down. Eat, for heaven's sake. You are the person at this table most in need of sustenance. You've lost half your bodyweight since all this started.'

'Oh, nonsense, Robert,' Vivienne waved away his concern. 'I shall be back in a minute or two—please do not wait for me. Excuse me, everybody.'

She left the room slowly. It was only once she had disappeared from sight that we all heard the speeding up of her footsteps, accompanied by the sound of stifled sobbing.

CHAPTER 9

The Courtyard View

Dr Osgood drummed his fingers on the table. 'Well done, Douglas and Jonathan.' He glowered at the two younger men.

'Thank you,' said Douglas smoothly. 'For what am I being congratulated?'

'You are responsible for what just happened. You, Jonathan, Madeline and Janet.'

'I did warn them to stop,' my mother said with a sigh.

Douglas aimed a cold smile at her. 'I am afraid your unblemished perfection of thought and deed is unattainable for some of us mere mortals, Cynthia. Yours too, Dr Osgood. Speaking of which, how is your delightful fiancée? When is the special day again? Not too far off now, I dare say.'

Osgood's mouth moved, but he said nothing. He might have been chewing a tough piece of gristle; it was hard to tell.

'Monsieur Poirot, may I ask you a question?' said Maddie before Osgood could respond. 'If you were in a private room in a hospital, receiving the best possible care, would you mind if your room overlooked a small courtyard full of lovely trees and plants, if other patients' rooms were on the other side of that courtyard? Would you think it was worth the risk of one of those other patients glimpsing you in your hospital room now and then—and bear in mind, these rooms all have curtains, so you could close them whenever you wanted to—and risk catching sight of other patients yourself—at a safe distance, of course—if in exchange you had the beautiful courtyard as your view?'

'Why are you asking Monsieur Poirot?' Jonathan snapped at her. 'He is not the patient in question, therefore his opinion is irrelevant.'

'The opinion of Poirot is never irrelevant, monsieur. But . . .' My friend shrugged. 'To answer this question, I would need to see the precise distances involved. If there were a reasonable amount of space between my room and any other, and if the beauty of the courtyard pleased me greatly . . . why, then it might suit me. To be able to watch people from a distance, but not have to listen to them; to try to understand them when all they are to me is a silent, moving image—this I would find fascinating. And as Madame Maddie says: there are the curtains that one can always close if one does not wish to see or be seen.'

I waited for Maddie to crow, but she did not. She said to Jonathan, 'As you say, Monsieur Poirot is not the patient in question. Arnold is. Why, then, did neither you nor Janet think to ask for *his* opinions about courtyards and privacy?'

'Because they were not thinking of him at all,' said Douglas. 'They were thinking of themselves. *They* did not want to be seen by the patients in the rooms across the courtyard when they visited Pa in hospital, so they sought to deprive him of the best view St Walstan's has to offer.'

'Oh, I think they are far too selfish to visit Arnold in hospital,' said Maddie, as if the people she was denigrating were not present in the room. 'You watch, once he gets there: Vivienne will be there all day every day, and you and I will visit often. Janet and Jonathan, meanwhile, will make excuses and avoid the place.'

'Such hatred,' Janet murmured. 'When did you become so wicked, Madeline?'

'I simply want our father to have the best . . . situation that I can create for him,' Jonathan said quietly. 'That includes a reasonable amount of privacy.'

Douglas leaned forward, resting both his elbows on the table. 'You know perfectly well that Pa cares not a jot about privacy and would love to spy on his fellow patients. If you deny it, you are a liar.'

'Will you all please stop provoking each other?' said my mother. 'You have already driven Vivienne from the room, and goodness knows how Enid and Terence must feel. What is to be gained by carrying on in this way? And might I remind you that we have guests?'

'"We?"' said Douglas. 'Are you not also a guest, Cynthia?'

'Why, of course. I simply meant—'

'I am going to bed,' said Enid Surtees, standing up. She had eaten every last bit of food on her plate. So had her husband, who mumbled something indecipherable and followed her out of the dining room.

Janet watched them go, looking stricken. Jonathan shook his head slowly. I feared the stultifying silence might stretch on endlessly, but Dr Osgood broke it. 'What is that noise?' he said. 'Can you hear it?'

'All I can hear is a barrage of needlessly unpleasant—' Mother began.

'Listen!' Osgood cut her off. 'There: crying. Almost howling. You must be able to hear it.' He stood up and walked over to the window. 'It's Vivienne,' he said. 'She is out there alone in the dark and the rain, weeping.'

'Brave, strong doctor to the rescue . . .' Douglas Laurier made a gesture with his arms that suggested running—moving his arms back and forth vigorously—though he remained in his seat. Whatever his remark had meant, it had made him smirk.

'I hear nothing,' said Felix Rawcliffe with a trace of impatience in his voice. 'There is, perhaps, no need for a rescue on this occasion.'

'You cannot possibly see her out there in the darkness,' Jonathan told Osgood.

'I can hear her, I tell you,' the doctor snarled at him.

'Well, where is Arnold?' Mother asked impatiently.

'How should I know?' said Osgood. 'I am going to bring Vivienne in from the garden.' He marched out of the room.

Poirot, too, had stood up and was on his way to the door. 'I shall go and find Arnold Laurier myself,' he said.

Mother had sat down again. 'You had better go and

rescue Vivienne, Felix,' she told the curate. 'Dr Osgood, in his present state of heightened emotion, is the very last thing she needs—and I shudder to think what he might do to me if I try to intervene. Well, go on! You are the only one of us who has divine protection. Yes, I know He protects us all, but you have the credentials.'

Rawcliffe looked surprised, but he did as he was told.

I had no desire to stay at the table with only Mother and the Fractious Four for company, so I made my excuses, citing my urgent need for an early night, and left the room.

I was at the bottom of the house's main staircase when Jonathan Laurier caught up with me. 'Inspector Catchpool?'

'Hello!'

'I want to say again how sorry I am for my rudeness before. I do not know what possessed me, only that . . . well, sometimes with my brother and his wife around it is hard to keep one's cool.'

'Please, think no more of it,' I told him. 'I quite understand. And . . . you have had my mother as a guest in your home for some days now, so you might understand why I understand, if you catch my drift.'

Jonathan smiled, but the disquietude in his eyes did not shift. He was all snarled up about something. Whatever it was, instinct told me that it was the true reason for his having followed me; the desire to repeat his apology was secondary. 'Well, goodnight, then,' I said and turned to go upstairs, suspecting I would not get far before he called me back.

Sure enough . . . 'Inspector Catchpool, may I ask you—do

you know if my father has spoken to Monsieur Poirot yet about this house?'

'Frellingsloe House?'

Jonathan nodded.

'I left them talking earlier, before dinner,' I told him. 'I suppose the house might have been mentioned. I have not had a chance to speak to Poirot properly since then, I'm afraid. Was there something in particular—?'

'Yes, there is,' said Jonathan. 'It was my idea that Father should ask for your Belgian friend's help. The man is his hero, after all, so please remind Monsieur Poirot of how very sick he is—how little time he has left. Kindness, sparing his feelings—these things are more important than anything else. Please make sure your friend understands that.'

'What exactly does Arnold . . . ?' I stopped, since there was little point in continuing. Jonathan had turned his back on me and was walking away, uninterested in any comment I may have wished to make.

How extraordinary, I thought—and did not get much further than that. A heavy blanket of exhaustion had descended upon me, making it difficult to reason clearly.

I was about to take off up the stairs when I heard a door close or open, followed by voices. Even for a tired man such as I, these were easily recognizable as belonging to Felix Rawcliffe and Vivienne Laurier.

'Then I do not understand why you allow it to continue,' Rawcliffe was saying.

'It is none of my business.' Vivienne sounded desperate.

'I did not ask for any of this. I have done nothing! Why do you care so much about a stranger you have never met?'

'For as long as you allow him to live under this roof—' Rawcliffe began.

'If you want him to leave, get rid of him yourself,' said Vivienne. 'Do not worry about what I might want or need. Evidently you care nothing for my feelings.'

'You love him, then,' Rawcliffe said. 'If you did not, then you too would want him gone. Admit that you love him and I shall not raise the matter again. Or if you will not, then at least explain to me why you care so little for a stranger. Do we not have a moral duty to others, whether or not they are known to us personally?'

I had no time to reflect upon what all of this might mean; their footsteps were coming closer. I hastened up the stairs to the second floor and was planning to knock on Poirot's door when I heard shuddering snores. So he was asleep already. Excellent; I decided this meant that he had found Arnold Laurier safe and well—as well as a man could be in his condition, that is.

I was pleased to find that my room—the one opposite Poirot's—contained my suitcase. I made sure the door was securely closed and then lay down on the bed. My last conscious thought before falling into a deep sleep was, 'I must on no account fall asleep while fully dressed.'

20 DECEMBER 1931

CHAPTER 10

Poirot's Bad Dream

I was roused by a loud *rat-a-tat-tat*. I lurched upwards into a seated position, still half asleep and aware of the words 'Someone is firing a gun', though I could not discern if this was another person's voice or my own thoughts.

It felt important to move quickly, but I could not. Then I was flat on my back again. When I opened my eyes a few seconds later, I wondered if I had imagined the whole episode. Then I heard it again: a hard rapping on my door. Relief that it was someone knocking and not 'the stuttering rifles' rapid rattle' was short-lived as I noticed it was still fully dark outside. There had to be some sort of crisis if I was needed at this hour.

As quickly as I could, I staggered to the door of my bedroom and opened it. Poirot walked in, wearing a red dressing gown over his pyjamas, with a red and gold brocade belt and matching slippers. He looked tired but full of purpose. In his right hand, he held an envelope. There was writing on the front of it, but I could not read it.

'Did you wake me, Catchpool?'

'No. *You* woke *me*, by banging on the door. Don't you remember?'

'I knocked on your door because you knocked on mine first. You were shouting.'

I told him I had been fast asleep until a few seconds ago.

He eyed me suspiciously. 'You were perhaps sleepwalking?'

'I have never sleep-walked,' I said. 'Nor, to my knowledge, have I ever sleep-shouted.'

'I see.' He stood perfectly still in the middle of the room.

'It must have been someone else,' I said, feeling a pinch of alarm. A commotion in the middle of the night did not bode well.

'No. I know the voice of my friend Catchpool.' Poirot frowned. 'It was you.'

'I tell you, it was not.'

'You are certain? You did not knock at my door? You did not call out in alarm that the sea was inside the house and had reached the floor below ours?'

I smiled. 'It sounds to me as if you had a very vivid nightmare.' I pointed to the gap between the curtains and said, 'The sea, for the time being, still knows its place. I shall prove it to you when the sun starts to rise. What time is it?'

'Twenty minutes after four o'clock.' Poirot shook his head. 'It is most strange to think that I could have been dreaming. I was certain that I had been awake the whole night.'

'Well, that's not true. I heard you snoring.'

'*Non*. That was not me. When was this?'

'When I came up to bed. I was going to knock on your door—'

'What time was it?'

'A little after a quarter to ten.'

'I was not asleep then,' said Poirot. 'And I too heard the snoring. It came from Arnold Laurier's bedroom, which is below mine. I found it most reassuring, once I had satisfied myself that it was Monsieur Laurier who was the source of the terrible rumbling sound—though it kept me awake for some time. There is too much noise in this house, Catchpool. Snoring, the ceaseless agitation of the ocean—I do not care for it.'

'Shall I try to find us rooms somewhere else?' I asked.

Poirot looked tempted for a second, but was soon shaking his head. 'Not yet.'

'You said you were not worried about the erosion of the cliff when I asked you before. If you are having nightmares about it, isn't that a good enough reason to—?'

'Hercule Poirot does not worry about forces of nature. They cannot be changed or reasoned with. It is people who cause me to feel alarmed, Catchpool. If I am having peculiar dreams, if I am unsettled, then that is because of the behaviour of human beings. Here at Frellingsloe House, there is the strong flavour of danger. Do you not smell it?'

'You're mixing up your senses,' I told him. 'If it were a flavour, I would taste it, not . . .'

Seeing the impatience in his eyes, I stopped myself and

said, 'The main danger, as I see it, is that you and I will be trapped here for the whole of the Christmas holiday. If we cannot set off back to London in the next day or so, I might be banging on your door in the middle of the night shouting about that.'

I nodded at the envelope he was holding. 'What's that letter?'

He looked down at it as if noticing it for the first time. 'Someone pushed it under my door. I thought it was you, but . . . It is addressed to "Monsieur Poirot and Inspector Catchpool".'

'Are you going to open it?'

He proceeded to do so, then sat down at the desk to read it. I could see that it was not short. There were at least two pages, covered with untidy handwriting.

'Well?' I said, when I thought I had waited patiently for long enough.

'It is from Arnold Laurier. In it, he describes the two leads he spoke of—the ones the police are not taking seriously.'

'Why has he put them in a letter? I assumed he would have told you about them after I left the two of you alone earlier.'

'He did not have the chance. Seconds after you went in pursuit of Vivienne Laurier, I became dizzy and excused myself. Our long journey and my hunger got the better of me. I needed to lie down.'

'Dizzy?' I did not like the sound of that. 'Poirot, are you all right? You do not look entirely well, you know.'

'Do not fuss, Catchpool. I am merely tired. In a moment I shall return to my room and sleep for one or two more hours. That will suffice. And then tomorrow I must find somewhere that can provide me with edible food, or I am in danger of starving to death. It would be a grave error to rely upon Enid Surtees for sustenance.'

'So Arnold wrote us a letter about his two leads, did he?' I mused. 'I wonder when he did that. Vivienne thought he had fallen asleep before dinner. She said that was the only reason he would have missed the meal.'

'In his letter, he explains what happened,' said Poirot.

'May I read it, please?'

He made no move to pass it to me. 'All in good time, *mon ami*. Tell me: do you have anything to report? What did Vivienne Laurier say when you spoke to her?'

I knew from extensive experience that he was not asking for a mere summary; he expected me to omit nothing. I spent nearly half an hour telling him in detail everything that Vivienne Laurier and I had said to one another, and then I reconstructed for his benefit the conversation I had overheard on my way up to bed.

'And the man speaking to Vivienne Laurier was Monsieur Rawcliffe? You are certain?'

'I would hardly mistake him for anyone else,' I said. 'You can hear his teeth in his voice.'

Poirot nodded. 'This conversation you overheard . . . it seems to make no sense,' he said. 'Who is this stranger living under the roof of Frellingsloe House that Vivienne Laurier either does or does not love? We have met everyone who lives here. Not one of them is a stranger to Madame Laurier.'

'The stranger and the "him" referred to must be two different people,' I concluded. 'Oh, and I must say, I do not agree with Dr Osgood. He led us to believe that Vivienne Laurier's predominant emotion is fear, but that was not how she struck me at all, neither when I was speaking to her nor when I was eavesdropping on her and the curate. The overwhelming impression I got was of a deep sadness and despair.'

Suddenly, I knew what it was that I meant to say. 'She strikes me as devoid of all hope. Fear, by necessity, contains an element of hope—only no one would think so, because we conceive of the two as opposites: frightened people are miserable, whereas the hopeful are jolly and contended. Yet it is undeniable that fear has a sort of frenzied hope as one of its ingredients.'

'That is an interesting idea, certainly,' said Poirot.

'It is odd. Now that you are here, why is she not confident that you will catch the killer? She asked if I believed you would and I told her I did, but that did nothing to lift her spirits. Oh—she mentioned somebody called Mr Hurt-His-Head.'

'You will read all about him in this letter.' Poirot held it aloft but still did not pass it to me.

'Speaking of jolly and contented people, what was it about Stanley Niven being a happy man that aroused your interest?' I asked him.

He looked surprised. 'I have at no point said that I am interested in the happiness of Monsieur Niven.'

'No, you have not. But you are, aren't you? Very much so. Why?'

'Such happiness is unusual. That is all.'

'It is quite plainly not all. I suppose, as always, you will tell me when you are ready. Is there anything in Arnold Laurier's letter about Frellingsloe House?' I asked.

'No.'

'Did he talk about the house, once I had left the study?'

'*Non.* Why do you ask?'

'His son, Jonathan, said that Arnold plans to ask for your help with something. He implied it was a house-related matter.'

'*Non.* Monsieur Laurier said nothing about it. We spoke for hardly any time after you left.'

'May I see the letter?' I asked in a tone that I hoped sounded fresh and inspired, as if the idea of my reading it had only just occurred to me.

'You may. Though first you will do me a favour, please. It will require going downstairs.'

I sighed. 'You want me to check that Arnold Laurier is still breathing.'

Poirot nodded. 'The snoring we both heard—it has stopped. Also, it occurs to me only now that it was suspiciously loud.'

'It must be contagious, this belief that Arnold Laurier will be Stanley Niven's murderer's next victim,' I said.

'Very amusing,' said Poirot. 'I shall give you this letter to read as soon as you return, *mon ami*. I am sure you will find it as fascinating as I did.'

'Do you really believe that whoever killed Niven is here at Frellingsloe House tonight?' I asked him. 'Why, for goodness' sake?'

At that moment, we both heard a woman's voice: 'Arnold? Is that you up there?' It was coming from the floor below ours. It sounded like Vivienne.

I heard a door open or shut; it was hard to tell which. I stepped out on to the landing. Poirot followed me.

'There you are! What are you . . . ? Is that thing clean?' Yes, that was definitely Vivienne Laurier's voice. She was not speaking to us.

Next, I heard Arnold: 'Hello, dear. Did I wake you? I'm sorry. I was cold.'

'That thing looks moth-eaten,' said Vivienne.

'It's as clean as I need it to be,' her husband replied. 'Do not fuss.'

'Go, Catchpool,' Poirot whispered, inclining his head. I knew what he meant, though I could scarcely believe it. He wanted me to see Arnold Laurier with my own eyes; both of us hearing him speak was apparently not evidence enough of his continued presence in our mortal realm.

I crept as quietly as I could towards the top of the stairs. From this vantage point I saw Arnold clearly. Wrapped around his shoulders was a blanket: rust-coloured stripes alternating with yellow ones. I agreed with his wife's assessment: it looked fuzzy, matted, and suitable only for a dog's basket.

'It was him?' Poirot asked when I returned to his side.

'Of course it was him. You plainly believe him to be at

great risk, and not only from his illness. Will you please tell me why?'

Poirot regarded me calmly. Maintaining his infuriating silence, he passed me Arnold Laurier's letter without any further prevarication.

CHAPTER 11

The Two Leads

Once Poirot and I were back in my room with the door closed, I unfolded the sheets of paper and began to read. The first thing that leapt out at me was that I had been put into parentheses for no reason that I could fathom. The letter was addressed to 'Dear M. Poirot (and Inspector Catchpool)'. This irked me, but I set it aside as a petty distraction and tried to concentrate on what Arnold Laurier had written:

As my illness has progressed, my sleep patterns have become unpredictable. M. Poirot—when you left my study to ready yourself for dinner this evening (yesterday evening, I suppose I should say, since it is now three o'clock in the morning), I intended to do the same, after taking a short and efficient nap in my chair. Usually I close my eyes and open them again between three and five minutes later, feeling substantially refreshed. On this occasion, alas, I awoke to find that two hours had passed and I had missed dinner entirely. Never mind: dear old Enid is not the world's finest cook, and my appetite is not what it used to be in any case.

I stood up, hoping to seek you both out, apologize for my inadequacy as a host, and recommence our discussion of the murder of Stanley Niven. Once I was up on my feet, unfortunately, it became evident that I was still comprehensively exhausted. I did not in any way feel like one of the brightest and best of the sons of the morning. You will not understand this if you have never been gravely ill (and I hope you are feeling much better after your peculiar turn), but there was only one course of action I could contemplate . . .

'I do not like the sound of your "peculiar turn",' I told Poirot. 'After such an event, you need to take good care of yourself.'

'Do not agitate yourself, Catchpool.'

'The food we are expected to eat here can hardly be considered proper nourishment. Please allow me to find us rooms elsewhere.'

'*Non*. Close observation of the inhabitants of Frellingsloe House will be required. Here is where we must stay, though our stomachs will not thank us for it.'

'Why must we be here? Nobody in this house killed Stanley Niven. How will observing them help us?'

'You take too much for granted, Catchpool. Five members of the Laurier family were in the room next to Monsieur Niven's at the very moment that he was being murdered.'

'In the room next door, yes. With the door closed. Not in the room where Stanley—'

'Do you know that the door was closed for the whole time they were in there?'

'Well . . .'

'Ah, you have heard that they all said so, *n'est-ce pas*? And a nurse who was with them said so too.' Poirot shook his head. 'So far we have spoken to nobody about the events of 8 September apart from Dr Robert Osgood. *Eh bien*, he was also at the hospital that day, also on Ward 6. And where were the other residents of Frellingsloe House? The curate, Monsieur Rawcliffe? Enid and Terence Surtees? Arnold Laurier himself? Where were they, Catchpool?'

'They were all *not* at the hospital that day.'

'*Bien sûr*, this is what we have been told.' Poirot smiled. 'Also, we are encouraged to believe that Stanley Niven was not personally known to anyone at Frellingsloe House—he was a complete stranger to them all—so there can have been no possible reason for anybody living here to murder him. This was contradicted by Arnold Laurier, was it not? Monsieur Laurier informed us that he and Monsieur Niven had met at St Walstan's in August. I was surprised to hear that, and I believe you were too. Why? Why were we both so secure in our assumption that Stanley Niven and Arnold Laurier had never met? *Because we had been briefed in a manner both precise and thorough*.'

'Then . . . are you saying you believe Niven wasn't a stranger to the Lauriers, and that someone in this house killed him?'

A weary look had appeared on my friend's face. 'No, Catchpool. I intended to say only that you assume too much. I try to correct you and what happens? You rush to assume too much in the opposite direction. Please, *mon ami*,' he nodded at the letter, 'continue to read, if you can decipher Monsieur Laurier's handwriting.'

I did as I was told. The letter continued as follows:

. . . but there was only one course of action I could contemplate: getting myself into bed and back to sleep as soon as possible. I would have been no use to you at all, M. Poirot, or to poor, late Stanley Niven, if I had attempted any other enterprise. Please forgive what must have seemed to be unpardonable rudeness on my part. Believe me, the very last thing I wanted to do was miss the first evening of you being here at Frelly. I am delighted to know that I will have many other opportunities to spend time with you and learn from you, since you are to be with us for the whole of the Christmas holiday.

The fact of someone having written something down did not make it true, I reminded myself. Neither did my having read it. I took a deep breath and read on:

And now, to the business of detection. I did not have the chance to tell you about my two leads in the matter of Stanley Niven's death. I cannot understand why Inspector Mackle patted me on the head and sent me on my way when I told him these two stories, both of which might be of great significance. I am eager to share them with you and see if you agree. Since I find myself wide awake, feeling well rested and full of the joys of spring at three o'clock in the morning, I shall do so now, in written form. I should add that I feel inordinately guilty for trying initially to withhold this information from you earlier, as a form of leverage. As you correctly pointed out, it was a dishonourable way to proceed and I feel thoroughly ashamed. I share the following information without asking for any favour or concession in return (though neither my wishes nor my intentions have changed. I cannot be deterred from my investigative mission!).

Lead 1

When I met Stanley Niven at the hospital in August, we conversed on several subjects. One of these was our former professions: his work at the post office and mine as a teacher of mathematics. He told me various things I did not know about the life of a postmaster, including that customers were occasionally rather brusque and even sometimes rude. This surprised me. Naturally, I had encountered the occasional obnoxious attitude among my pupils over the years, but it was rare, and I was dealing with eleven-to-sixteen-year-olds. At that age, one has not yet learned that it pays, always, to be courteous and cooperative. As an adult customer of a post office, however, one is reliant upon those who work in that establishment to convey one's letters and parcels to their intended destinations. Why on earth would you insult the very chap whose job it is to ensure the safe arrival of your every correspondence?

The above might seem to be a digression, M. Poirot, but it provides context. Mr Niven, after relaying several tales of customer rudeness that I could scarcely credit, laughed and said, 'The encounters that really stick with you are not the ones where some fellow lashes out impatiently. Those are very common, I am afraid. No, the episodes that lodge themselves most powerfully in the memory are the truly extraordinary ones—those so peculiar as to be unbelievable even once one has lived through them.'

After that introduction, I was beside myself with curiosity. Mr Niven then held me in thrall with a story involving a lady whose name he did not tell me—which, regrettably, makes this lead rather difficult to follow up. (Though not impossible, M. Poirot. Nothing is impossible, is it? I am certain you agree with me about that.) In any case, this woman arrived at the post office one day and demanded to speak to the person in charge. That was Stanley Niven, and this happened a few years before he retired. I cannot tell you when he retired, though I dare say you could find out easily enough. The woman insisted on speaking to him in private. He took her to his office, whereupon she burst into floods of tears and accused him of ruining her life.

He was startled, naturally, having never met her before. She was beside herself, weeping and wailing, and at first would not be pacified. This made calm clarification impossible for at least twenty minutes. Eventually Mr Niven quietened her down and asked what he was supposed to have done to her that was so heinous. It turned out that a man called Henry had been sending her letters that she would have preferred not to receive. There had been four so far, and she believed more would follow. The point was that Henry lived close to Mr Niven's post office, and all his letters had been posted from there, the woman said. She held Mr Niven responsible for the distress she had suffered so far, and told him she found his conduct in the matter both disgusting and shocking. By this, she meant that he had failed to prevent those letters from reaching her. Worse than that: he had positively allowed them to be posted to her.

Is it not extraordinary, M. Poirot, that people can be so illogical and blinkered? This woman had come to tell Mr Niven that he must on no account allow this Henry chap to send her any more letters; he must refuse to cooperate, refuse to sell him the stamps, and banish him from the post office the moment he appeared.

I looked up. 'You have read this?' I asked Poirot.

He had. 'Like Monsieur Laurier and Monsieur Niven before him, you are surprised by the irrational expectations and beliefs of the woman in the post office. I am not. Good

sense is not the driving force in the lives of most people.'
Nodding at the paper in my hand, he said, 'Continue.'
I read on:

Stanley Niven did what most men in his shoes would
have done. He told the lady that he and his employees
had no idea what words were contained within the many
sealed envelopes they handled every day. Tactfully he
explained that, even if he were able, somehow, to know
the content of each missive, he could not, in his profes-
sional capacity as postmaster, decide which letters were
acceptable and which should be refused safe passage.
Everyone was entitled to express themselves freely, within
the confines of the law—surely the lady could see that?
Gentlemen, she could not. She screamed many
unpleasant insults, told poor Stanley Niven to rot in hell,
and left. As I have said, I cannot understand why
Inspector Mackle is so profoundly uninterested in this
story. When a murder occurs, one surely looks for anyone
who might have had a grudge against the victim, and
here we have a grudge of rot-in-hell strength and a
personage of, I would argue, obviously unsound mind.

Lead 2

My hand is a little sore and stiff from all this writing, so
I shall be succinct. The second lead is Mr Hurt-His-Head.
That is not his real name, which I believe is Burnett.
Professor Burnett, Inspector Mackle called him, though I

would not take that young man's word for anything without a thorough checking of the facts. He means well, but is no bright spark.

Mr Hurt-His-Head is what Vivienne called this Burnett chap when she first told me about him. As a nickname, it is apt. You will soon see why. He is a patient at St Walstan's, and made an appearance on Ward 6 on the day Stanley Niven was killed. I do not know if he is still in the hospital.

When Vivienne and the children went to have a look at Ward 6 on 8 September, they argued about whether or not it would be suitable for me to have a room with a window that looked over a courtyard.

'That explains the strange courtyard argument at dinner,' I muttered.

Courtyard or no courtyard, I told Vivienne, I do not mind in the slightest. Put me in a cupboard, so long as I can pursue my murder investigation. While inspecting this courtyard, Vivienne noticed a distinctive-looking man standing at the window of his hospital room on the other side. Ask her to describe him to you: his physical appearance sounds remarkable. The man was staring, though not directly at Vivienne. Instead, he seemed to be looking off somewhere to her right— through his window and across the small yard. Jonathan, Janet, Douglas and Maddie all say they didn't notice him. Gentlemen, if Vivienne says he was there, that is good enough for me. Ask her about it. She will tell you, now she knows Stanley Niven's room was next to the one reserved for me, that she is entirely convinced Mr Hurt-His-Head was watching what was happening in that room. She believes he must have witnessed Mr Niven's murder.

Unfortunately, Mr Hurt-His-Head suffers from a severe cognitive impairment which affects his linguistic skills. Vivienne reports that, after seeing him staring into Stanley Niven's room, she returned her attention to the silly courtyard contretemps on which the children were still wasting their time and energy. A little later, though by no means soon enough, the Lord had mercy upon my wife: that argument ended. Vivienne says she opened the door of my room (permit me to call it that, though it is not yet mine) and there, standing in front of her, was Mr Hurt-His-Head. She said he looked poised to knock or barge in.

This next part is corroborated not only by Janet, Jonathan, Maddie and Douglas but also by the nurse who was showing them my room—Nurse Zillah Hunt—and by our very own Dr Osgood. This patient, Mr Hurt-His-Head, said in an agitated tone of voice, 'Son of man has no place to hurt his head.' He kept looking at the bed, Vivienne said: the hospital bed in my room. He stared at it pointedly, as if he wanted to say something about it but could not. And he kept declaiming those same words, though after a while he abandoned the first part and simply repeated, 'To hurt his head! To hurt his

123

head!' over and over again, quickly and breathlessly. Nurse Olga Woodruff eventually had to intervene, for he was becoming increasingly hysterical. Luckily, Olga is a person of strong and steely character. Vivienne said it was a ghastly scene. The poor man was begging her with his eyes, she told me—begging her not to let Nurse Olga take him away. He reached out to Vivienne as if inviting her to grab his hands and commence a tug of war. She did not, of course. Then, once Nurse Olga and Mr Hurt-His-Head had gone, Dr Osgood broke the terrible news: that there had been a murder on the ward, in the room next to mine.

'Is it not a quote from the Bible?' I asked Poirot.

'With one significant difference,' he said. 'The correct quote is "The son of man has no place to *lay* his head." Professor Burnett—Monsieur Hurt-His-Head—did not say that. It was not the word "lay" that he repeated in a frantic manner. No, it was the word "hurt". And he said it a very short time after he had, in all probability, watched someone bring down violently a large vase upon the head of Monsieur Niven.'

'This Nurse Olga,' I said. 'How does Arnold, or Vivienne, know about her strong and steely character? He writes as if he knows her well—even refers to her as "Olga" without the "Nurse".'

'He is a dying man, Catchpool. Is it so strange that he should be well acquainted with a nurse at the hospital nearest to his home?'

This, I had to concede, was a fair point. I read the last paragraph of Arnold Laurier's letter:

Inspector Mackle has been kind enough to check on Mr Hurt-His-Head at regular intervals, and has assured me as recently as yesterday morning that the poor fellow has come to no harm, which is a relief. Yet Mackle refuses to see sense and treat this episode as undoubtedly the best available lead in the investigation of Stanley Niven's murder. Perhaps you will be able to persuade him to take it more seriously, M. Poirot. I have every faith in you, and very much look forward to working with you in the service of clarity and justice. It will be the great honour of my life to do so.

Yours with immense admiration,

Arnold Laurier.

'I am inclined to agree with Inspector Mackle that Miss Post Office can be ruled out,' I said. 'Even the most irrational neurotic would not murder a post office manager, many years later, because he allowed someone she disliked to send her some unwelcome correspondence.'

'Indeed, she is unlikely to be the killer,' said Poirot. 'However, we can learn something valuable from her example: an unreasonable person might see a strong motive for hatred, perhaps even murder, where a reasonable one perceives nothing untoward, or nothing at all. This is worth keeping in mind. A truly deranged motive might be invisible to sane men such as ourselves, *mon ami*.'

'Mr Hurt-His-Head, on the other hand . . .' I said. 'Now there's a valuable lead if ever there was one. I don't know about you, but I plan to tell Inspector Mackle tomorrow— this morning, in fact—that he would do well to—'

'*Non.*' Poirot cut me off. 'You will say nothing to Inspector Mackle. I shall go alone to the police station and to the hospital.'

'But—'

'I have other plans for you, here at Frellingsloe House: among other things, the decorating of many Christmas trees.'

'What?' I spat out the word in disgust.

'What better way to contrive to be spoken to, perhaps confided in, by several members of this household, eh? You are sure to pick up all sorts of interesting morsels. Already you have overheard something fascinating and inexplicable, *n'est-ce pas?*'

'Poirot, for pity's sake, do not—'

'Catchpool,' said my friend in a tone of stern finality.

I fell silent. It was the lack of choice that was hard to stomach, so I determined, in that moment, to make it a choice. I chose, as wholeheartedly as I was able to, complete obedience to Poirot; I had made the same decision many times before.

'It makes no sense for both of us to be in the same place, *mon ami.* We must deploy our resources in the most effective fashion. To leave Frellingsloe House unsupervised by at least one of us would be reckless indeed. Here you will be ideally placed to find out about the Lauriers and the

Surteeses, Dr Osgood and Felix Rawcliffe: their relationships, their secrets.'

Next out of my friend's mouth came five words that
turned my guts to ice: 'Your mother agrees with me,' he
said.

CHAPTER 12

A Sea Swim, a Bath and a List

I spent the first two hours of the next day (it was, strictly speaking, a continuation of the same day, but in my book a day begins only at six in the morning) feeling bitter and suspicious. Those words—'Your mother agrees with me'— had affected my mind as rotting meat affects the body. My first thought, upon hearing them, was: 'Poirot must not see that I am upset.' No doubt I am an aberration in this respect as in so many, but for me distress has always brought with it a fear that someone will detect my true psychological state. The dread of being 'found out' is always the worst aspect of the ordeal.

I had therefore made sure to seem as chipper as I could at breakfast, even when Mother sat down beside me and told me, chirpily, that she would show me where to find all the bags and boxes full of Christmas tree decorations. 'Tell me sincerely, Mother,' I said, employing what charm I could muster in the hope of getting to the truth. 'Poirot says this Christmas trees plan was his idea and that you merely endorsed it . . . but do I detect the genius of Cynthia Catchpool behind the scenes, too modest to take the credit?'

Only once or twice in my life had I flattered Mother so outrageously—always when I had wanted something from her—yet I knew she would not suspect a thing. In her assessment, I ought to have been lavishing praise upon her every day from dawn until dusk. Besides, she was a person who chose to believe in the world as she thought it should be, in preference to the world as it truly was—so when I aimed a compliment at her, she never questioned it. 'Don't be silly, Edward,' she said. 'If Monsieur Poirot told you it was his idea, why would you doubt it?'

'I think you probably told him that I would take it better if it came from him.'

She denied it all, and I told her it was no skin off my nose either way, as I was looking forward to the Christmas trees project.

After breakfast, as I walked along the path that ran from Frellingsloe House's door to the steps that led down to the sea, I heard Mother's voice call out my name. I turned and saw her hurrying to catch up with me.

'Are you a lunatic?' she demanded, eyeing the rolled-up towel in my hands. 'You surely to do not intend to swim in the ocean in Norfolk—in winter? You will die.'

'No, I won't. I shall only stay in for a short while. Two minutes at most. I've done it before. You know that perfectly well. As I recall, you mentioned sea-swimming in your initial attempt to lure me here for Christmas.'

'I did not!' Mother lied.

'Yes, you did. A brief immersion in very icy water is invigorating. You should try it.' I was looking forward to the divine shock of cold sea making the blood in my veins zing. Perhaps it would drive away my lingering resentment at the knowledge that Poirot and Mother had conspired to arrange my day's activities.

Before breakfast, I had watched from the dining-room window as Poirot had been driven off in a car sent by Inspector Mackle. First he would go to the police station and then on from there to the hospital. Lucky old him.

'Well, it is no business of mine if you wish to freeze to death.' Mother turned and strode away.

I proceeded in the opposite direction, and was stopped once more by her calling my name. This time she made it clear that she expected me to walk over to her. I did so, cursing under my breath. When I reached her, she lowered her eyes and said quietly, 'There is no need to be horrid to me, Edward. One day you will have children and you will understand that no parent has a child hoping that he will grow up to be horrid. Or maybe you won't ever have children, and I shall end up like poor Enid Surtees, who is quite desperate to be a grandmother, but it seems that both her daughters . . . Well, there is either something wrong with them or with the two Laurier boys, perhaps something that runs in the family—'

Mother stopped suddenly. Then she said, 'I cannot even talk to you about perfectly ordinary things, without you being determined to turn it into something it is not.'

I pointed out that I had said and done nothing.

'Oh, I saw the look on your face. What possible connection could there be between Enid's desire for grandchildren and the murder of Stanley Niven? Enid was not at the hospital that day—she was here. She did not know Mr Niven. None of us did.'

'Mother, would you do me a favour?' I said. 'Do you remember, when you were trying to persuade me to come here for Christmas, you told me all kinds of things about everybody at Frellingsloe House? Could you tell me those things again, in as much detail as you are able to provide? I did not give it my full attention first time round.'

'I have no intention of indulging in gossip,' Mother said primly.

It took some effort for me not to laugh at this. She was as keen on gossip as I was on swimming in cold water.

'I am not a fool, Edward. You are trying to trick me into telling you things. It won't work. Anything I tell you, you will twist in order to justify your belief that the answer to the mystery of Stanley Niven's death is to be found here at Frelly. It is not. It is to be found at St Walstan's hospital.'

'Mr Hurt-His-Head might know the answer,' I said casually, testing her.

She looked relieved. 'Yes, he might. He very well might, but you try making the Norfolk police pay attention. Goodness knows how Inspector Gerald Mackle has ended up in a supervisory role. I would not leave him in charge of a jar of jam, let alone a murder investigation.' With that, she took off, and I made my way down to the sea.

I both survived and enjoyed my swim, then returned to the house and undertook the climb to the top floor, where I ran myself a bath. There is nothing better than a hot bath after the kind of swim that seems to embed the essence of cold deep inside you; you believe you will never be warm again and then, hey presto, you are.

The bath water was too hot for me to stay in for long, so I climbed out and returned to my bedroom, thinking about Mother's refusal to help me. To the devil with her. I had not paid full attention to her witterings about the people I would meet if I accompanied her to Munby, but I was sure that, if I tried, I would be able to remember most of what she had said.

Some minutes later I was dressed and sitting at the desk in my room, which was perfectly positioned beneath a large sash window that offered a splendid view of the sea. I opened the window to let in some fresh air—my preference even in winter, and one that Poirot claims he will never understand—and then wrote down every snippet of information I could recall from Mother's original description of the residents of Frellingsloe House. Each time I thought I had finished, I stared at the rolling waves and said to myself, 'What else? There is more. There must be more.' This approach proved so fruitful that I would earnestly recommend it to anyone who wishes to improve the function of their mental faculties.

By the time I had finished, my list was substantial. The only thing I could not judge with any accuracy was how much of what I had written down was hard fact and how much was mere opinion, gossip or mistaken speculation. The list read as follows:

What Mother said about the people at Frellingsloe House

1. The illness killing Arnold Laurier is a rare kind of cancer. Hardly anybody suffers from it or dies of it.

2. The doctor lodger, Robert Osgood, is engaged to be married to somebody. (Who? Mother probably knows, and so, I am sure, do most people at Frellingsloe House.) Dr Osgood is not in love with this person and does not really want to marry her. Rather, he is in love with Vivienne Laurier.

   NB: might the Osgood and Rawcliffe 'Romeo and Rosaline' discussion be related to the above? My best recollection of that conversation is as follows: Osgood seemed a little irritated with Rawcliffe, and his manner grew increasingly heated as they talked. Poirot is right: Osgood ended the discussion abruptly. Everything Rawcliffe said seemed to enrage him, and he did not want to have a row in front of Poirot and me. From what I could gather, his argument was that *Romeo and Juliet*, the play, is only as beloved as it is because the characters Romeo and Juliet adore each other. That is what makes

133

it a great love story. If Romeo had lost interest in Juliet as he did in Rosaline, no one would have cared about them as a pair at all. There would have been no great love to ruin. Anyone sensible would think that Rosaline was far better off without Romeo, because his love for her had proved to be so transitory and fickle.

Could this have been Osgood trying to persuade Rawcliffe that the woman he is expected to marry would be better off without him? That, since he is not especially keen on her, there is no great love to be destroyed? Is Vivienne Laurier the 'Juliet' in this picture? Did Osgood stop loving his fiancée when he fell in love with Vivienne?

3. Vivienne Laurier and Felix Rawcliffe are involved in some kind of secret business together, which is not of a romantic nature. But they are certainly hiding something, or conspiring together in some way. (This is likely to be what lies behind the conversation I overheard between Vivienne and Rawcliffe last night.)

4. Maddie and Janet Laurier hate each other. Before meeting the Laurier family, the sisters were close. Maddie, the elder of the two, met and married Douglas first. Later, Janet married Jonathan, the younger Laurier brother. Maddie and Douglas had not been happy about this development and the two couples had remained at loggerheads ever since.

5. Enid and Terence Surtees are angry (both of them, or only one of them?) with Arnold Laurier, and their anger is somehow linked to the marriage of Jonathan and Janet. Because they believe Arnold encouraged it? Cannot remember. Maybe Mother did not tell me.

6. Enid Surtees and Vivienne Laurier have something in common. Enid views it as a tragedy that her girls no longer love one another as much as she loves both of them. She cannot believe, having brought them up in the way she did, that they have allowed two men to come between them. Vivienne, for her part, lost all of her family at a relatively young age. She came from a large clan and had always hoped she and Arnold might have at least five children. She has always fretted about the lack of a strong bond between Douglas and Jonathan. They do not seem to love each other unconditionally in the way that she loves them, and she wishes they did.

7. Enid Surtees is disappointed that neither of her daughters has yet given her a grandchild. She believes there is something wrong with the Laurier brothers—that the lack of progeny can be laid at their door and has nothing to do with either of her daughters. (Mother disagrees, and blames Enid's appalling cooking. Maddie and Janet must have been malnourished as children,

she believes, and are infertile as a result. She has no evidence whatever for this claim.)

8.   Happy Men—a recurring theme. Mother said that Arnold Laurier was irrepressibly happy despite being terminally ill. An optimistic and cheery nature is something he has in common with the late Stanley Niven. Does Vivienne think Arnold might be the next victim of a killer targeting happy men? Surely not; that would be ridiculous. Yet both Vivienne and Poirot seem to think Arnold might be the killer's next victim. *Why?*

9.   Arnold Laurier inherited much family wealth. He and his wife Vivienne agreed that they would spend as little of it as possible in order to leave their sons with as much as they could after their deaths. This was a joint decision made long ago. A much later, more recent decision was then made to let all the domestic servants go and to replace them with Terence and Enid Surtees. This (I am almost certain Mother implied) was Arnold's doing, and Vivienne had not been happy about it initially, though she had accepted it.

Twice I read through what I had written. Satisfied that I had made all the progress I could for the time being, I stood up and readied myself to go downstairs and decorate the various Christmas trees of Frellingsloe House.

CHAPTER 13

Inspector Mackle's Own Two Hands

I had assumed the car that came to collect Poirot that morning was sent by Gerald Mackle of the Norfolk police. In fact, Poirot told me later, Mackle had not sent the vehicle; rather, he had driven it himself. 'There is one sure way to know that a task will get done, and that is to do it with your own two hands,' he had said to Poirot. Having made his point, Mackle elaborated upon it unnecessarily with an extended soliloquy about seeing with one's own two eyes what one's own two hands were doing, and walking on one's own two feet in order to sniff out a puzzle with one's own nose.

'I am sure you feel as I do, Mr Prarrow,' the inspector concluded, after the crime-solving responsibilities of all relevant parts of his anatomy had been inventoried.

'Not at all, inspector. Myself, I favour the opposite approach. If dashing from place to place is required, I am happy to rely on those who are kind enough to help me. I prefer not to travel back and forth like the ping-pong ball. Once everything I have requested has been told or brought to me, that is when I rely entirely upon my little grey cells. They have not yet let me down.'

'Is that so, Mr Prarrow? Well, fancy that.' Mackle was a tall young man—thirty at most, Poirot estimated—with a long, rectangular face and the sort of fair hair that was as close to the primary colour of yellow as it is possible for hair to be. Even for someone of his height, the inspector's hands and feet looked excessively large. It was no wonder, Poirot thought wryly, that he had decided to make trusted colleagues of them, since they took up so much space in his immediate vicinity.

The motorcar was following a twisting road through a small hamlet, with a few thatched cottages clustered around a crossroads at its centre. Poirot looked out for a sign that said 'Police Station', assuming that was where Mackle was taking him; it was certainly where he had asked to be taken when he had telephoned to arrange the car first thing that morning.

'I suppose you have only the finest men working for you,' said Mackle with a baleful sigh. 'That's the difference, you see. I like my men well enough, but they don't have my persistence. Not a one of them is as stubborn as I am when I know I'm right. Take this Stanley Niven murder case. Sure as I am born, it's one of the man's own relations that did it—his wife, his son, his daughter or his brother. They all claim to have alibis but one of them is a lie, and I think I know which. Proving it, though: that's the tricky part.'

'Please, inspector, look at the road, not at me. It is not a straight road.'

'I know every curve and crimp of this coast road as well as I know my own two hands, Mr Prarrow. As I was saying: I am almost positive I know whose alibi—'

'Please, hold the steering wheel with both of your hands, inspector.' Poirot pulled a handkerchief out of his coat pocket and used it to mop his brow.

'I expect they all drive as proper as anything in London, do they?' said Mackle cheerily. 'They won't know the roads as well I know the roads here, mind. Tell me, as a London chap—why do you need so many?'

'So many of what?' said Poirot.

'Roads,' said Mackle.

'I only live in London,' Poirot told him. 'I am Belgian.'

'Is that so? Fancy that. Well, I don't mind where you're from, as long as you're not a quitter. Quitters fairly turn my stomach. I know you're not one, mind you, from everything I've been told. It will be a welcome relief, working with you, after what I have had to endure from my own men. All day long it's "There's no point, Inspector Mackle" and "It won't work, Inspector Mackle." Well, of course it won't if you give up, lads. Eh? Tell me, Mr Prarrow, are you a lover of poetry?'

'*Bien sûr.*'

'I am too. I always say: when there's a murderer to be caught, the only person I want to listen to is my friend Mr Guest.'

'Who is he?'

'Edgar Albert Guest. American writer. He had the right attitude to quitting:

> *'So he buckled right in with the trace of a grin*
>   *On his face. If he worried he hid it.*
> *He started to sing as he tackled the thing*
>   *That couldn't be done, and he did it!*

'And I, Gerald Mackle, will do it too—with your help, Mr Prarrow. Do I presently know beyond doubt which of my four suspects is the guilty party? No, I do not. Am I determined to find out? Yes, I am. It is exactly as Mr Guest wrote. He expressed it perfectly:

> *'There are thousands to tell you it cannot be done,*
>   *There are thousands to prophesy failure,*
> *There are thousands to point out to you one by one,*
>   *The dangers that wait to assail you.*
> *But just buckle in with a bit of a grin,*
>   *Just take off your coat and go to it;*
> *Just start in to sing as you tackle the thing*
>   *That "cannot be done", and you'll do it.'*

Mackle seemed to be driving ever deeper into the countryside.

'Pardon me, but how far is the police station?' asked Poirot. Almost all of the daylight had disappeared a few moments ago as the car had entered a wood, and now they were in a thin, shadowy, green tunnel with a ceiling of thick leaves and bowed branches.

'Ah, we are not going there,' said Mackle. 'I am taking you to meet somebody instead. Two somebodies, actually— from St Walstan's. Nurse Beatrice Haskins and Nurse Zillah Hunt. I promise you, you will want to hear what they both have to say.'

'Then we are going to the hospital?' This was acceptable, thought Poirot; it was on his list of places he planned to visit today.

'No, we are not going there either,' said Mackle. 'We are going to Nurse Haskins' home, where Nurse Hunt also lives. She is Nurse Haskins' second cousin, you see. That's how she got her job at St Walstan's. Lovely girls they are, both of them. Well, Bee Haskins is hardly a girl. She's my mother's age if she's a day, but she has a girlish quality. Laughs a lot. Nurse Hunt is young, and very attractive indeed. Big lips that seem to be begging a fellow to kiss them, if you catch my drift, Mr Prarrow. If I were not a happily married man . . .' Inspector Mackle turned to wink at his passenger, who gripped the sides of his seat with both hands as the car narrowly missed a tree.

'I would like to visit Ward 6 of St Walstan's Hospital,' said Poirot, once the immediate danger was past.

'And you will,' Mackle promised. 'All in good time. I shall drive you there myself. But first I want you to hear what Nurses Haskins and Hunt have to say. They agree with me, you see, that the killer must be one of the Niven relatives.'

At last, the motorcar emerged from the tunnel of trees and into the light again. It was unusually bright for a day in December.

'Inspector, I must ask you to cease, immediately, all attempts to influence my opinion,' said Poirot. 'I intend to ask my own questions and form my own conclusions.'

'Understood, Mr Prarrow. Understood. Though do keep in mind, please, that one of the four Nivens must have done it. The deceased's wife, Audrey, is my least favourite for the role of murderer. She seems far too sad about her husband's death to have killed him—though I suppose she might be pretending. The son and daughter, Daniel and Rebecca, are both more likely culprits than their mother, I think. They are the beneficiaries of the will—not that Mr Niven left anything to speak of. His parents are both still alive, you see—both nearly a hundred years old, if you can credit it—and all his money went towards looking after them. His brother, Clarence, is most likely the one who killed him. He is also the one whose alibi is the hardest to put a dent in.'

'Do any of these people have a motive for the murder?' Poirot asked.

'Yes, one of them does,' said Mackle. 'Whichever of them did it, they must have had a motive. Stands to reason.'

Poirot took a deep breath. 'Why do you believe that Monsieur Niven's brother Clarence is the most likely to be guilty?'

'Ah! A very good question.' Mackle chuckled to himself. 'I think you will appreciate my reasoning here, Mr Prarrow.

You of all people will understand the logical path I followed, and I expect you will say that you'd have come to the same conclusion yourself. Quite simply: thirty-two people say they were at Clarence Niven's London club, in the same room as him during the hour in which his brother Stanley was killed. *Thirty-two people.*'

'He appears to be eliminated from suspicion most conclusively, then.'

'By my reckoning, his supposedly solid alibi is the main point against him,' said Mackle. 'I think he fancies himself as an intellectual, and he has gone to elaborate extremes on the false alibi front, hoping it will cause us to make certain assumptions.'

'Such as?' said Poirot.

'Why, the assumption that he must be innocent—for surely no man could persuade thirty-two people to lie for him,' Mackle declared triumphantly. 'Think about it: persuading one acquaintance to lie for you is easier than persuading thirty-two, is it not? Eh? A solver of crimes might calculate that a guilty man would surely offer an alibi that requires the cooperation of *only one person*, since one is all he needs. Once he has that one safely in the bag, he's in the clear, so why the blazes would he go to the trouble of lining up a further thirty-one? No murderer would. Do you see what I mean, Mr Prarrow? That is what Clarence Niven believes I will think. It is why he arranged for such a large number of people to give him an alibi—but he did not reckon with the ingenious brain of Inspector Gerald Mackle! I apologize for blowing my own horn, but some things cannot be denied. Now, if you and I can convince just one of those thirty-two dishonest alibi-suppliers to break the pact and tell the truth—'

'Are the thirty-two a group of some sort?' Poirot asked. 'Do they know each other? Do they all know Clarence Niven personally?'

'Aha! You are asking all the right questions, Mr Prarrow. They say not. Only two of them will admit that they know him at all. The rest are all members of the same club, but claim never to have spoken to Clarence Niven. If only one of them would tell me the truth, I could—'

'Do not call it "the truth", inspector.' Poirot was unable to contain his impatience any longer. 'You offer nothing to substantiate your belief that one of the four Nivens must be the killer. *None* of them has a motive, *n'est-ce pas*? And they all have alibis.'

'But . . . one of the alibis must be a lie.' Mackle sounded confused, as if he distinctly remembered having explained this clearly already but was now wondering if he had merely imagined doing so. 'It is the lack of motive that tells me I am on the right track,' he told Poirot.

'How so?'

'There is nobody in the world, as far as I can see, who has an actual motive for murdering Mr Niven. Therefore it must be one of the four favourites, as I like to call them: Audrey, Daniel, Rebecca or Clarence Niven. One of his family.'

'*Sacré tonnerre*. Why must it be so, inspector?'

'Why, it hardly needs to be said, Mr Prarrow. This case

has got "nearest and dearest" written all over it. Who but the very closest of kin would hit a person over the head with an enormous vase—more than once—for no reason at all?'

CHAPTER 14

Decorating Two Christmas Trees

I shall always remember 20 December 1931 as the day I made a valuable discovery: if you want to find out more about a person connected with a murder case, the traditional method of asking them questions about all the usual things—their relationship to the victim, for instance, or their whereabouts when the crime was committed—is significantly less effective than this lesser-known method: begin to decorate a Christmas tree in their vicinity.

This is what will happen. First, your quarry will approach and make casual conversation along the lines of 'Good to see someone tackling the tree at last!' Then they will start to suggest what you might do differently—'Oh, you're putting that there? I would place it higher up, myself.' Next, once you have implemented at least two of their recommendations (this part will require you to ignore your own aesthetic wisdom), they will start to talk freely about other matters, especially if you are mostly on your hands and knees, surrounded by paper garlands and tinsel and not looking in their direction.

I feel duty-bound to add a caveat, since I have just referred to a person 'connected with a murder case': it was not at all clear to me at this stage whether the Lauriers, their house-guests and their lodgers were or were not connected to the murder of Stanley Niven. I had no reason to believe they were, and would have thought it unlikely were it not for the fact that Poirot, for reasons I could not fathom, seemed to be operating on the assumption that there was a definite link.

One further explanatory note: the conversations that follow have been abridged only in a very specific way—I have trimmed to the bare minimum all references to the tree decoration side of things. If anyone is eager to hear about how Janet Laurier would hang gewgaws on a Christmas tree differently from how I, left to my own devices, would have arranged them, I am afraid you will be disappointed. I will, however, offer this summary: I was right in every particular and she was wrong.

'How about that, then?' I said to her once most of the work had been done. I stood back so that she could see the results of our joint labour. The drawing room, though it looked a thousand times better than it had yesterday, was still too long and thin, and its windows were still too few and small.

'It's beautiful,' Janet said. 'Have you done this before? You must have. I can imagine Cynthia giving very thorough lessons in how to dress a Christmas tree.'

'I can imagine it too, but it did not happen. My childhood memory of Christmas trees is that they were simply there: like Christmas lunch, and my presents, and snow so deep it went up to my waist.'

'It's sweet how excited Cynthia is that you'll be with her for Christmas,' said Janet. 'But . . . you said at dinner last night that you do not plan to stay.'

'No. Poirot and I will have left by then.'

'I am not sure that is Cynthia's understanding of the situation.'

'Families,' I sighed, forcing a smile. 'They are a blessing and a curse.' I bent down and moved things around inside the boxes that contained the remaining decorations, deliberately not looking at Janet.

After a few seconds, she said, 'I was not going to mention it, but . . . well, now that the subject of families has come up, I should like to apologize to you for the behaviour of several members of mine. I have never felt more ashamed. My mother's cooking . . . I am used to it, but it must have been rather an ordeal for you and Monsieur Poirot. I am sure he is accustomed to the finest French cuisine. And Jonathan was unpardonably rude to you at dinner.'

'Your husband has apologized very graciously,' I told her. 'It is forgotten.'

'Do you find it easy to forgive people?' she said quietly. 'I wish I did. Sometimes it is altogether too difficult. My brother-in-law, Douglas, is so venal and vile, as is my sister Madeline. He has corrupted her. The Madeline I knew as a child was never cruel to me in the way that Douglas's Madeline is now.'

I remembered that Maddie Laurier had told Poirot and me soon after meeting us that only her enemies called her Madeline.

'It is unusual to come across two sisters married to two brothers,' I said.

'Not really,' Janet said quickly. 'It must happen all the time. How else do people meet? The people we already know introduce us to new people.'

'I suppose so,' I conceded. 'Still, it must have—'

'I am sure you noticed Douglas's obsession with his inheritance—all that talk last night of him being son and heir. He cannot leave the subject alone. It was unconscionable of him to bring it up at dinner, in front of you and Monsieur Poirot, whom he had only just met.'

'Was it not Jonathan who first said it?'

Janet recoiled. 'Jonathan might have said something incidental, but it was Douglas—it is always him or my sister—who turned it into an embarrassing scene by accusing Jonathan of trying to steal his share of Arnold's estate.'

'Did he do that?' I tried to give the impression of struggling to recall the finer details, though I vividly remembered what both brothers had said. 'I don't think I heard an accusation of attempted theft.'

'It was not made overtly,' said Janet. 'Douglas would give anything to be able to claim the whole of his father's estate for himself. The only person standing in the way of that is Jonathan, for whom he cares not a jot. And I sometimes wonder how much he loves Arnold. Jonathan *adores* his father. It is hardly right, really, that Jonathan and Douglas are each to get half of everything once Arnold is gone, if the love felt for him by the two of them is anything but equal. Would you not agree?'

I made a face that indicated I was giving her opinion thorough consideration.

'It is Vivienne's fault,' said Janet impatiently. 'Her stupid belief that fair and equal mean the same thing. Reprehensible woman! Both Douglas and Madeline are inordinately fond of her. They will make sure she wants for nothing as a widow. Madeline treats her as if she is her own mother. It must upset our real mother, Enid—though my sister doesn't seem to care about that. I could tell you many tales of her and Douglas's selfishness, but I do not like to speak ill of family. Even though Madeline is quite the most . . .' Janet stopped. 'But I do not like to be disloyal. One should not publicly denounce one's own relations. Do you not agree, Inspector Catchpool?'

Either this question was a trap or Janet lacked the ability to assess her own behaviour in a realistic fashion.

'I imagine it is easy to slip up, even if one has such a policy,' I said.

'The correct standards must be upheld or else we are no better than beasts,' she said. 'I have always tried to be a good person and to consider the feelings of others. But if I were like Madeline, if I cared only about myself?' She let out a bitter laugh. 'Why, then I would *beg* Arnold to die here at Frelly instead of taking himself off to St Walstan's to do it. But I care about *his* wishes, and Jonathan's, so I say nothing of my true sentiments. I tell no one, no one at all, that I would secretly like Frelly to be forever ruined. Then I would be free.'

'I am not sure I follow,' I told her.

She made a small noise: a stifled groan. 'If Arnold were to die here, the house would become a place of sadness, sullied by tragedy. That is what Arnold himself thinks, and so Jonathan accepts it unquestioningly. As soon as Arnold knew his illness was terminal, he said, "I must not die here at Frelly. This is a place of joy and life. I will not allow it to be destroyed by death." That became the truth for Jonathan—do you see? He worships Arnold as if the man were a god. Only if this house were ruined could Jonathan be free of it.'

'Ruined by Arnold dying here?' I said.

Janet nodded. 'My conscience will plague me for having told you that.' Her voice shook. 'How easy life must be for those without a conscience, like my sister. She and Douglas will be free of this house as soon as Arnold dies. Douglas would have bought a house for the two of them years ago if he could have afforded anything he deemed grand enough. Well, soon he will be able to—his father's death will make him a wealthy man.' A sneering expression passed across her face. 'I'm sure Vivienne will move in with them immediately. The three of them will all be as thick as thieves together. Besides, Vivienne knows she cannot stay here indefinitely.'

Janet eyed me doubtfully. 'I assume you know that Frelly will not be here for very much longer?'

151

'The erosion problem? Yes.'

'Arnold refuses to accept the fact. It was your mother who started him thinking that way. On one of her visits, soon after we received the sad news, she said, "Surely something can be done?" I am afraid Arnold seized upon her words, and Jonathan always ends up believing whatever story his father tells. Now they are as resolute as each other and constantly affirming to one another this belief that Frelly can be saved. It is torture for me, inspector. I love my husband. I *love* him, and I cannot bear to watch him squander his next three years trying to honour his late father by saving this house. It simply cannot be done. Sometimes one must admit defeat, whatever Arnold believes. And then, to have to watch the house crumble into the sea, and endure Jonathan's misery and listen to him endlessly blaming himself for having failed Arnold. I don't think he would ever forgive himself. It will blight his life forever, and mine too.'

'You want Arnold to die here at home because then Jonathan would view the house as tarnished and not devote the next few years to trying to save it,' I summarized the situation as I understood it.

Janet nodded. 'I hope he would, yes. Surely if a terrible tragedy were to happen here at Frelly—the death of his beloved father—Jonathan would feel differently about wanting to save the place.'

I had barely made a start on the tree in the dining room when I heard a man's voice: 'Well, blow me down!' It was Douglas Laurier, looking and sounding like an overgrown schoolboy keen to enliven his day with some high-jinks. 'Hi, Maddie,' he called over his shoulder. 'Come and have a look at this. Ma wasn't joking—not that she ever does any more.'

'Joking about what?' I heard Maddie's footsteps as she hurried to see the cause of her husband's astonishment.

'Inspector Catchpool is in here playing Cinderella—quite willingly, by the look of it.'

'I am starting to enjoy it,' I told him. It was true. The Christmas trees project was making my mind work in new and unpredictable ways. This tree was going to end up looking far better than the one in the drawing room.

'Golly, you're a brick, Edward,' said Maddie with a giggle. She leaned to the left, scrutinizing my work so far. 'A brick with lashings of artistic talent, by the look of it. I would never have thought to put that paper lantern over there. Not Cinderella, Douglas—that is quite wrong. No one has swanned off to have fun at the ball and left Edward here alone to suffer. It seems to me *he* is the one having a ball, beautifying this gorgeous, neglected tree while the rest of us mope around in dreary spirits, accomplishing nothing.'

Douglas put his arm round her waist, pulled her towards him and kissed her. 'Let us help you, Edward,' he said. 'Or better, let us take over and you can help us if you would like to. It's not right that you are doing this alone.'

'Oh, do let us help!' said Maddie. 'That sounds jolly!'

The two of them seemed positively gleeful. I wondered if they were always so effervescent when Jonathan and Janet were not around. 'Do not imagine I need to be rescued,'

I told them. 'Truly, I am having more fun doing this than I would have thought possible.'

'What he is too polite to say, Madds, is that he doesn't want us messing up his creation. Very well, then, you can be in charge, inspector—but do assign us the odd menial task. Untangling, for instance.' Douglas pointed at the decorations box. 'I have never done anything menial in this house. In the good old days we had proper servants, and now Pa and Ma have turned Enid and Terence into servants, which is amusing and appalling in equal measure. I remember watching Terence do one of the trees a couple of years ago and there seemed to be an inordinate amount of untangling involved.'

I laughed. 'The secret is to resist the temptation to resent it.' I pretended I had not noticed Douglas's remark about the servitude of Enid and Terence Surtees. 'I use the time I spend untangling to develop my vision of the end result.'

'A true artist speaks,' said Maddie.

'Will you be cross if I make one small alteration?' Douglas removed a paper reindeer ornament from a low branch of the tree and placed it higher up. 'Don't you think that looks better? Surely we want the longer what-nots closer to the top and the shorter ones around the bottom?'

'Don't be silly, darling,' said Maddie. 'Balance is what's needed: a mixture of both long and short decorations at every level. Don't you think so, Edward?'

Douglas shrugged. 'Maybe you are right, my love. I shall put it back.'

'No, leave it,' I said. 'You have given me a useful

opportunity to apply my newly invented "Now that it's there" principle.'

'What's that?' Maddie asked.

'I don't want to bore you,' I said, embarrassed. 'I'm sure neither of you is particularly interested in—'

'I am *agog*,' said Maddie. 'I cannot live without hearing more about the "Now that it's there" principle. Please explain it.'

'My wife is fascinated by almost everything.' Douglas eyed her affectionately. 'I advise you never to travel with her. You find yourself on a train, seated beside the most tedious person imaginable, who wants nothing more than to tell you all about their dullest recent irritations. You are just about to make your excuses and escape when you hear Maddie say, "Do tell me more about your aunt's aching hip joint. In what month of which year did it begin to plague her?" In that terrible moment, you know you might as well kiss goodbye to the next three hours of your life.'

Maddie was laughing heartily. 'Whereas Douglas is interested in almost nothing,' she said.

'That is true,' he agreed. 'Almost nothing. Though I shall make an exception for your "Now that it's there" principle, inspector. I think I can guess what it is: the policy of leaving something in place because it's easier than moving it, even if it looks worse in its present position? Avoiding effort rather than pursuing perfection?'

'No, not that,' I said.

'Well, now I am curious,' said Douglas.

Both of them were watching me and waiting. After such

a build up, this was going to be excruciating. 'It is far from exciting,' I said hastily. 'All right, I will tell you: though be warned, it might sound potty. Imagine you have a decoration—a paper reindeer, say. You hang it on a branch and then decide it doesn't look quite right. Most people would move it immediately to somewhere where it looked better. But there is an alternative: one can say to oneself, "How can I improve the look of things *without moving the reindeer*?" The surprising thing is that, usually—based solely on my experience of decorating the tree in the drawing room earlier, which I admit is not all that much experience—there will be a way to do it. Your visual imagination is compelled, because of the constraint, to travel in directions it would not ordinarily consider. You think to yourself, "What if I put this here, and that there, and balance it out like this?" Before you know it, you discover that starting from the "Now that it's there" principle can very often lead to something more ambitious, and more visually impressive, than you would have ended up with if you had succumbed to your first impulse and moved the reindeer.'

'Ah, yes, but . . .' Douglas wagged a finger at me. He had started to rock gently back and forth as I spoke, impatient to explain to me why I was wrong. 'There would be no temptation to try this method in the first place if one placed no value on the avoidance of effort. That must be the main advantage of your method, or else why not move the reindeer straight away and take that more obvious route to the tree looking good?'

'He has already explained why, darling,' said Maddie.

'Ruling out the obvious means you end up with a superior result.'

'It ends up being more of a challenge, not less,' I said. 'Contrary to what you might imagine, no energy is conserved if you take the "Now that it's there" approach. There is little that taxes the brain more than forcing it to deviate from its customary ways of thinking and imagining.'

'Yes, I see. I see.' Douglas was taking my theory more seriously than I had thought he would.

I made a small concession: 'It is true, though, that I would not have hit upon the "Now that it's there" method if I had not initially entertained lazy thoughts like, "That looks terrible but it can damn well stay there, or else this will take me until next Christmas"—so you are not entirely wrong.'

Douglas laughed. 'I am never entirely wrong. My wrongness rarely reaches the halfway mark. Isn't that right, my love?'

Maddie's face had taken on a more serious expression. 'Edward, I feel terribly guilty,' she said. 'Dinner last night must have been unutterably awful for you and Monsieur Poirot. The fuss about the courtyard . . . You must have been desperate to understand what it was all about.'

'My wife always wants to know what everything is all about,' said Douglas. 'She assumes others do too. Please speak up if you do not, otherwise I fear you are about to hear a tale or two.'

'You will have noticed that my sister and I are not exactly fond of each other,' Maddie said sadly. 'We were once. We were the best of friends until she fell in love with Jonathan. They met at our wedding. And then some months after we returned from our honeymoon, Janet approached me with a grave expression on her face. She told me Jonathan had been courting her, but things had not progressed very far. She asked me . . . I shall never forget it! She said, "Maddie, please tell me if you would rather I discouraged him. It might be peculiar for me to be romantically involved with your husband's brother. Everything might get rather complicated. If you hate the idea of it, you must say so. I am not sure *I* would like it, if our situations were reversed," she said. And I knew precisely why she would dislike it, too,' Maddie said with feeling. 'She described my own unease to me very vividly: "As an adult, one creates an independent life, away from one's original family," she said. "Surely the last thing one would want is for one's sister to barge into the new life one has created. And I am not yet in love with Jonathan, so I can extricate myself without too much trouble. Besides, there are plenty of other men in the world, quite a few of whom are just as sweet on me as he is, so if you would rather I put an end to it, I will. All you need do is ask."'

'And did you?' I said.

'I told her my preference would indeed be for her to choose a beau who was not my husband's brother, but that she should almost certainly disregard my preference and think only about her own. I believe people should be entirely free to make their own choices, don't you, Edward?'

'Well—'

'Now, if Janet had set her sights on Douglas, that would have been a different matter. I had, and have, a legitimate claim to him, but there was no possible justification for my asking Janet to give up Jonathan for my sake. If she had met and married him first, and I had met Douglas at *their* wedding, why, I would not have cared a jot if anyone had disapproved. If somebody is unmarried and available, and somebody else falls in love with them, then that is that. No one else's opinion ought to count for anything.'

'A very reasonable way to look at it,' I said.

'Indeed,' said Douglas. 'You might think, mightn't you, Edward, that Janet would have been happy with that answer, but it was not good enough for her.'

'She turned instantly cold,' said Maddie. '"So you would prefer it if I gave Jonathan up," she said. "We do not, then, have your blessing?" I thought she must have misunderstood. I said, "You have my blessing to do as you please and that is what you must do. I would disapprove if you did anything else." But it was too late. I had committed what was, in Janet's eyes, a terrible offence. I had not realized there was only one answer she would not deem unforgivable: "Oh, how spiffingly splendid, Janet! I am thrilled! Nothing could give me more joy!" By admitting to a preference for her falling in love with a man who was not my brother-in-law, I had betrayed her in the most appalling way and could never be forgiven.'

Maddie sounded deflated, suddenly, as if she had only just realized the story she was telling was actually rather a sad one. 'I tried to explain that I had only wanted to be as honest as possible, but it was too late. Janet pretended she had never said she would have hated it if Douglas and I had got together after she and Jonathan were already married. She lied calmly and brazenly, as if we did not both know perfectly well that those very words had been said by her and heard by me.'

Maddie sighed. 'That was what I thought at first, anyway: that she was purposefully lying. I was wrong. I have come to realize that Janet simply does not remember anything that no longer suits her view of the world.'

'I call that lying.' Douglas scowled.

'But that is not how it feels to Janet,' said Maddie. 'If she wants something to be true, she convinces herself that it is. Your father's will is the perfect example.'

'Don't mention Pa's will in front of the inspector, my love. He might start to think Ma's ridiculous notion is worth investigating after all.'

'What notion?' I asked.

'Ma is convinced that someone at St Walstan's wants to kill Pa,' said Douglas, as casually as if he were describing the weather.

CHAPTER 15

At Duluth Cottage

Nurse Beatrice Haskins and Nurse Zillah Hunt lived together in the coastal village of Trimingham, in a long, stone house that took up nearly a quarter of the side of the road on which it stood. Its name, painted on a sign at the front, was Duluth Cottage.

This sturdy little domicile, less than a quarter of the size of Frellingsloe House, struck Poirot as a friendly and welcoming prospect. Its thick, stone walls were the colour of butter—'the exact creamy shade of butter melting in the sun, Catchpool'—and its window frames and door were painted pale green.

There was no front garden to speak of. Duluth Cottage sat sociably at the edge of the road, looking as eager to meet passers-by as a house could, in an arrangement that raised the question of whether an inexpertly-steered motorcar—one driven by Inspector Mackle, perhaps—might one day make an accidental appearance in its sitting room.

Until he arrived at the door of Duluth Cottage and found

himself instantly cheered by its outward appearance, Poirot had not realized how low his spirits had sunk after thirty minutes confined to a small car with only Inspector Gerald Mackle for company. 'Attempting to converse with that man is as futile as trying to make raindrops fall backward into the sky,' he told me later. 'He refused to listen to reason. Stanley Niven's brother must have killed him because he had no motive for doing so! Thirty-two unconnected strangers must be lying because Inspector Mackle wants it to be so! We must spend as little time with him as we can, Catchpool. Proximity to a dull mind removes the lustre from even the brightest intellect. The little grey cells of Hercule Poirot must be protected.'

Nurse Beatrice Haskins had opened the door of Duluth Cottage in response to Inspector Mackle's knocking. Fifty years old or thereabouts, Poirot guessed, she had a round, pink face, fair hair and a broad, generous smile. Her intelligent green eyes sparkled. Like her house, she was wide but not tall.

Poirot liked her straight away. She told him he must call her 'Bee'. Then she introduced Nurse Zillah Hunt, a blonde of about thirty who was wispy and ethereal, with a too-large mouth that made Poirot think of a duck and not at all of kissing, as Inspector Mackle had suggested. He found it hard to imagine Zillah Hunt doing the heavy lifting work that nursing required, and noticed that Gerald Mackle could hardly take his eyes off the young woman, who was manifestly aware of his interest; it seemed to make her uncomfortable.

Eventually, the four of them—Mackle, Poirot, Bee Haskins and Zillah Hunt—were settled in the house's cosy and tastefully decorated sitting room. Nurse Bee had prepared a selection of sandwiches and cakes that made Poirot want to sing with joy. He could see at once that everything was of the finest quality: the bread was thick and soft and there were pieces of real fruit in the jam. 'You have a delightful home,' Poirot told the two women. 'There is more of interest on the walls here than in most art galleries.'

He found himself especially drawn to a print of two boys holding spades and crouching beside a small pond, both wearing Wellington boots. From the water, three smiling frogs looked up at them, and there was a fourth in mid-air, as if it had jumped out to greet the human visitors.

'This house and all the pictures belong to Verity, my cousin and Zillah's mother,' said Bee. 'Zillah is my second cousin, though she has always called me Aunt Bee. Verity is out this morning, which is a shame. She would have loved to meet you, Monsieur Poirot. She could tell you the history of every picture and every piece of furniture in this room. I'm afraid I cannot take credit for anything apart from the food.'

'This sandwich is absolutely divine, madame . . . or is it mademoiselle?'

'I am not sure,' said Bee. 'I'm afraid French is not my strong suit. Does it depend on whether I am old or whether I am married? I'm not married—never have been—and I *feel* old sometimes, but Verity still calls me a silly girl.

Maybe she is right. Maybe I am still young, relatively speaking.' She laughed.

'Mademoiselle, then.' Poirot smiled at her. 'I do not believe I have ever before used the word "divine" about a sandwich. This one is extraordinary. I shall have another. It has been too long since I last ate well.'

This led to a confused mock-altercation between Nurse Bee and Gerald Mackle, caused by the nurse's mistaken assumption that the inspector was responsible for keeping Poirot fed and watered. Naturally, Mackle failed to provide effective clarification, and Poirot was too busy appreciating the victuals to offer any assistance.

Eventually, Mackle remembered that his purpose in coming here was not merely to stare at Zillah Hunt. 'I was saying to Mr Prarrow on the way here, ladies, that you and I are of one mind in the matter of Stanley Niven's murder. I should like you both to tell our esteemed guest the same thing, if you don't mind. He still needs some convincing that it must have been a member of the Niven family who did it.'

'Well—' Bee Haskins began, but had managed no more than one word before Mackle started to speak over her.

'Both of these ladies have told me right from the start, Mr Prarrow, that it cannot have been anyone on Ward 6 that day who killed Stanley Niven.'

'It must have been,' Poirot contradicted him, stifling a sigh.

'I beg your pardon?' said Mackle.

'Death was caused by blows to the head—a murder method that requires the killer to be physically present.'

'Aha! Yes, of course. Quite right. There's no putting one over on you, is there? What I meant is that the murderer cannot have been anyone who was *supposed* to be on the ward or at the hospital that day. Tell him, ladies.'

Bee Haskins impressed Poirot with her first statement: 'I will not say what must or must not have happened, because I simply do not know. I do, however, know all the doctors and nurses at St Walstan's. The porters, too, and the kitchen staff. Everybody. There is not a person working there who is capable of committing a deliberate, cold-blooded murder. And I know most of the patients and their families too—not all, but most. Ward 6 is for long-term patients, and I get to know them all very well indeed.'

'They all love Aunt Bee,' said Zillah. 'They confide in her.'

'I knew Mr Niven, and was extremely fond of him. We all were.' Bee's eyes filled with tears. She blinked them away. 'I cannot believe anyone would want to . . . to do that to him. He was one of the loveliest people I have ever met. So kind and thoughtful and funny. The stories he told! He used to have the ward in fits.'

'Aunt Bee and I cannot imagine why anyone would want to kill him,' said Nurse Zillah. 'There must have been a mistake of some kind. They must have meant to kill someone else.'

Poirot thought immediately of Vivienne Laurier's fear, reported to us by Dr Osgood, that Arnold Laurier would be the next victim. Was it possible, he wondered, that the killer had believed it was Laurier he was killing at the hospital on 8 September and not Stanley Niven?

Inspector Mackle laughed. 'You think our killer got the wrong victim, Miss Hunt? There is a problem with that theory: whoever he or she is—and personally I think it's a he; I think it's Clarence Niven—he has managed to evade capture for more than three months. He must be clever if he has done that, must he not? No clever man would get his chosen victim mixed up with a stranger he cares nothing about, now, would he?'

'You should not speak so publicly of your suspicion of Clarence Niven, who might be innocent,' Poirot told him.

'I must admit, inspector, that Zillah and I have been wondering . . .' Bee Haskins began tentatively. 'You seem so very sure that the murderer must be one of Mr Niven's close relatives, and most probably his brother, Clarence. Is there a particular reason why you think so?'

'There is indeed,' said Mackle amiably. 'His excessively elaborate alibi. Thirty-two people, might I remind you. Besides, it is always a close family member who turns out to be responsible.' He nodded, confident that he had covered all relevant points.

'I met Clarence Niven several times,' said Zillah Hunt, with an edge of defiance in her voice. 'He seemed a gentle soul. He and his brother seemed to like each other a lot.'

'There was real love between those two men,' Nurse Bee agreed. She pressed her eyes shut, but not before some tears had escaped.

'An evil nature and a talent for acting—for deceiving—often go hand in hand,' said Mackle.

'I know the difference between a loving sibling and an unloving one,' Bee Haskins said sharply. 'Monsieur Poirot, Inspector Mackle and I are *not* of one mind about this murder. Not at all. I am sorry, inspector, but I completely disagree with you.'

'So do I,' said Nurse Zillah.

'Well, well.' Mackle scratched the side of his face. 'Fancy that.'

Having eaten enough to keep him going for the time being, Poirot put down his plate and said, 'Inspector, I should like to hear a thorough account of what happened on Ward 6 of St Walstan's hospital on 8 September. May I ask you, please, to omit your own theories. I wish to hear only the bald facts.'

'Of course,' said Mackle. 'Well, if I might start with the basics, and at the risk of stating the obvious: Stanley Niven was murdered. Death was caused by two blows to his head with a vase that had been in his room, on his nightstand. Flowers and water had been inside it, but those were on the floor. The killer must have emptied the vase before using it to strike Mr Niven—probably didn't want to end up covered in water. Someone drenched to the skin might attract attention if they were sneaking out of a hospital ward.'

'So water and flowers were found on the floor,' said Poirot. 'Were there fingerprints on the vase?'

'There were,' said the inspector. 'Unfortunately, one of my men mislaid them before we had a chance to do anything useful with them. We realized our mistake soon enough but it was too late. The vase had been thoroughly scrubbed by then.'

'I see,' Poirot said in a voice devoid of expression.

'Yes, it was a crying shame. Still, these things happen, don't they?'

'How was it established that the vase was the murder weapon?' Poirot asked.

'It had . . .' Mackle eyed the two women, then cleared his throat. 'It was apparent from the condition of the vase afterwards. There was blood on it.'

'Time of death?' said Poirot briskly.

'Between two o'clock and ten minutes before three. We were not able to narrow it down any further.'

'And why could Monsieur Niven not have been killed before two or after ten minutes to three?'

'Well, because Dr Osgood . . . I believe you have met him, Mr Prarrow? He lodges at Frellingsloe House.'

Poirot nodded.

'Dr Osgood entered Stanley Niven's room at ten minutes to three to give him his medicine,' said Mackle. 'Found him dead.'

'And I saw him myself at two,' said Bee Haskins. 'Alive and well, or as well as a hospital patient can be, at any rate. I was accompanying Dr Wall on his rounds. Two o'clock was when he knocked on Stanley Niven's door and was invited to enter. We both went in and found Mr Niven in good spirits. But there is something that has never made sense, Monsieur Poirot.'

'What is that, mademoiselle?'

'The door,' Nurse Bee said with a sigh. 'It cannot have been open and closed at the same time.'

'I hardly think we need to bother Mr Prarrow with—' Mackle started to say.

'Silence, please, inspector. I should very much like to hear about this door. Do you mean the door to the hospital room of Monsieur Niven, mademoiselle?'

'No,' said Bee Haskins. 'The one next to it—the door to Arnold Laurier's room . . .'

CHAPTER 16

Decorating More Christmas Trees

'Why is Vivienne so convinced that whoever killed Stanley Niven also wants to kill Arnold?' I asked Maddie and Douglas.

They exchanged a look. Then Maddie said, 'It makes no sense, Edward. She has not been herself since Arnold received his terminal diagnosis. And then after the murder . . . why, she stopped eating. She is disappearing right in front of our eyes.'

'Whereas Pa seems more sprightly than ever,' said Douglas. 'The prospect of catching a murderer at St Walstan's has enlivened him no end. Which has enabled my appalling brother to say, "I only want for Pa what he wants for himself. Who among us would not gladly grant the final wish of a dying man?" *Et cetera ad nauseam*.'

'Jonathan and Janet do not care what Arnold wants,' said Maddie. 'It is *they* who do not want to live in a house in which a protracted death is taking place. How unpleasant for *them* it would be. Just wait until Arnold gets properly sick—we won't catch sight of them at the hospital. Douglas and I will be the ones taking over from Vivienne, insisting she goes home and gets some rest now and then.' She sighed. 'I sincerely hope Arnold dies as quickly as possible once his illness progresses to its next stage. Until he is gone, Vivienne cannot begin to recover.'

Douglas, far from looking shocked, was nodding. 'All this dying he's doing is torture for Ma. She, of course, wants him to live forever. At least once a day she says something like, "He really might last as long as a year, or two if we're lucky. Even the cleverest doctors cannot predict the future."'

'And meanwhile, she is loathing every second of the present.' Maddie's tone was defiant. 'The worst part of any terrible thing, always, is the dread one feels in advance. Anything that has already happened, however ghastly, can be recovered from, or at least incorporated somehow. It is a wonderful thing to be able to say "The worst is over".'

I said to Douglas, 'You implied before that Janet and Jonathan lied about your father's will. What did you mean?'

'I did not imply it. I stated it proudly. It's a fact: they are liars.'

'Douglas and I disagree about this,' said Maddie. 'I prefer to think that Janet is not aware of her distortions. You must think I hate my sister after hearing the way I spoke to her at dinner last night, Edward, but I don't. I love her deeply. Lord knows I wish every day that I could stop loving her, but I cannot. It is wounded love that pours out of me in her presence, not hate.'

'Whereas I merely dislike Jonnells,' said Douglas. 'I never

took to him, truth be told, though for my parents' sake I tried to be pleasant—but from the moment he was old enough to display any sort of personality, I found it to be conventional, self-aggrandizing and duplicitous. It is a relief not to have to feign fond brotherly feelings any more. I only feel sorry for the parents: Ma, Pa, Enid and Terence. They are the ones who suffer as a result of this feud that Jonathan and Janet have instigated.'

'Not your father,' Maddie corrected him. 'He has always insisted that the four of us are on the verge of making friends. Any day now, he believes that this grand reconciliation will happen—and from that point on it will be sunshine and roses all the way.'

'What is the lie about Arnold's will?' I asked again. I was comfortable asking directly, since both Douglas and Maddie seemed eager to confide.

'Janet and Jonathan tell anyone who will listen that Douglas and I are counting the days until Arnold dies, so that we can claim Douglas's share of the inheritance,' said Maddie. 'Apparently we are wildly impatient to leave Frelly and buy a house of our own.'

Douglas said, 'It was entirely my brother's idea that we use the money bequeathed to us by Pa to buy a house as far away from here as possible. Oh, and they also want Ma out, once Pa is gone.' Douglas's face contorted in disgust. 'Our clear instructions were to take her with us—and of course that is now presented as us trying to kidnap and make off with her in order to have her all to ourselves.'

'Janet's view of Vivienne is deranged.' Maddie shook her

head. 'She will not let go of the ridiculous notion that Vivienne prefers Douglas and me because we are both eldest siblings and so was Vivienne. It is nonsense! Vivienne has never in her life uttered a single word that could be construed as taking a side between the four of us. No matter what the disagreement is, she maintains an agonized silence—never caring about how the matter is settled, wishing only for peace. If she does prefer Douglas and me, it is probably because we are nice to her. She cannot have failed to notice that her younger son and daughter-in-law are thoroughly vile people.'

There was a light knock at the dining-room door, though it was standing ajar. Terence Surtees appeared, looking rather shellshocked. 'Oh,' he said when he saw the three of us together.

'Hello, Dad,' said Maddie. 'What you looking so glum about?'

To me it seemed likely that her father had just overheard his youngest daughter being described as vile by his eldest, which would surely be enough to wipe the smile off any chap's face.

'I was hoping to have a word with Inspector Catchpool, but . . .'

'Daddy, wait.'

It was too late for Maddie to hand me over, graciously, to her father; Terence Surtees had already left the room.

Three people looked in on me as I decorated the Christmas tree in Arnold Laurier's study; this struck me as noteworthy. The drawing room and dining room were both rooms that members of the household might pass as they went about their day—walking between the front door and the back door, for instance, or from the main stairs to the kitchen—but Arnold's study was at the end of a small, out-of-the-way corridor that led nowhere else; one would not pass its open door unless one took a deliberate diversion in order to do so.

The first person to appear was the curate, Felix Rawcliffe, who asked when I had last seen Vivienne Laurier. At breakfast that morning, I told him. He frowned and searched the room with his eyes, as if dissatisfied, then left abruptly.

A few seconds later, Dr Osgood walked in. 'Oh, it's you,' he said. 'Did I hear you talking to Rawcliffe a moment ago?'

'He asked me if I knew where Vivienne was.'

'Do you?'

'No.'

'She is perhaps with Arnold,' said Osgood. 'She was looking for him a moment ago.' He hesitated, then said, 'Did Felix tell you what he wanted her for?'

I shook my head. The doctor looked as if he would have liked to object to my answer, but could find no grounds that would seem reasonable. 'I don't like the way you have arranged the ornaments according to their colour,' he said, nodding at the Christmas tree. 'Nobody wants a mass of red on one side and a clump of silver on the other. The colours should be evenly distributed. Let me show you.'

Piece by piece, he destroyed my design and created something more predictable and mundane. I made noises that were suggestive of admiration.

'I believe you are unmarried, inspector,' he said as he re-hung two shiny bell ornaments. 'Much to your mother's consternation, I gather. I too am unmarried. It makes life very easy in some ways, does it not?'

'Life is never easy,' I told him. 'There are different kinds of difficult, and one must choose between them.'

'Some lives are considerably easier than others, inspector.'

'Perhaps. Such things are never discernible from the outside, however. Only the one living the life can judge. I say, those bells look superb in that spot. I had not thought to put them there. You have made the tree look positively regal.'

'Yes, it does look rather good,' Osgood agreed. 'Better, anyway.'

'I shall make sure everyone knows you saved the day,' I said, trying not to mind that my handiwork had been vandalized.

'The question is: should one marry only for the motive of love?' Osgood said this as if it followed logically from my remark about the tree. 'Or should one decide that to marry is a worthy goal, and then select the best available . . . candidate?'

'The former, in my opinion. Though my mother would prefer me to favour the latter strategy. Are you not engaged to be married?'

'I am, yes,' the doctor said quickly and without interest.

'I don't suppose . . . Have you had a chance to speak to Vivienne properly since you arrived yesterday?'

'I spoke to her at some length before dinner last night.'

'Did she . . . ? Did the name of Felix Rawcliffe come up at all in your conversation?'

'No.'

'I was afraid that he might be making things rather awkward for Vivienne. But . . . she did not complain of any such thing to you? Good, good. He must be your age, or even younger. And Vivienne is completely devoted to Arnold. Who knows if she would even consider marrying again.' With that, Robert Osgood turned and walked away.

I was still puzzling over his remarks when, ten minutes later, my third visitor appeared—Jonathan Laurier, unsmiling and exuding an air of dissatisfaction. 'Inspector Catchpool. I was hoping to find you. Have you spoken to your friend Poirot yet?'

A mischievous impulse came over me. 'Many times in my life,' I said.

'Do not play the fool, please. I am referring to—'

'I have not had the chance,' I cut him off.

He sighed heavily. 'I would greatly appreciate it if you could attend to the matter as soon as possible. Poirot must promise to deliver my father's desired result.'

I cast my mind back to the previous night. This was something about Frellingsloe House, as I recalled. Jonathan Laurier had given me no further details.

'Just the promise will be sufficient,' he said now, 'followed by the pretence that something is then underway—something likely to do the trick. I would not normally ask anybody to enter into a deception, but in this case I have no doubt that it is the right thing to do.'

'Poirot does not take orders from me,' I told him. I was tempted to add, *And I do not take orders from you.*

'He will surely listen to you,' said Jonathan impatiently. 'He is a foreigner. You are an Englishman, and a Scotland Yard inspector. Come to think of it . . . perhaps you could exert your influence with our infuriatingly stupid Inspector Mackle while you're here.'

'In what direction?'

'There is a lunatic man at the hospital who has been shouting about hurting people's heads.'

'Ah. Mr Hurt-His-Head,' I said.

'He was standing in the corridor outside my father's room, mere footsteps from Stanley Niven's room, immediately after Niven was killed. Is it not obvious that he must be the murderer? He was the only raving mad person present, and he repeated his confession several times: "To hurt his head, to hurt his head." There could hardly be a more blatant admission of guilt. What I want to know is: why wasn't he arrested days ago?'

'Have you said this to Inspector Mackle?' I asked.

'Mackle heard a very different interpretation of events from my mother first and, unfortunately, believed it,' said Laurier. 'Mother is wrong. She claims this lunatic was scared, and was trying to warn her that my father would be killed next. What rot! He was trying to admit what he had done, but, hampered by his limited powers of speech, was unable to do so effectively. I can tell you precisely what the wretched creature was doing: holding out his hands so that handcuffs could be put on them, not appealing to my mother to rescue him.'

'How can you be sure?' I asked.

'I heard it from the lunatic's own mouth: "To hurt his head. To hurt his head." That was what he had wanted to do to Stanley Niven, and it was his way of announcing to all of us there that he had, in fact, done it.'

CHAPTER 17

The Doors and Mr Hurt-His-Head

'Very well, then, I shall tell you about the doors,' Nurse Bee Haskins said to Poirot. 'It's a mystery Zillah and I cannot solve between us.'

'Do not worry, mademoiselle. Poirot, he will solve the puzzle.'

Zillah Hunt looked up in surprise at this bold statement.

'Well . . . good,' said Nurse Bee. She settled herself in her chair and started to tell her story. 'Once Dr Wall and I had checked on Stanley Niven at two o'clock, we looked in on the remaining Ward 6 patients, the ones we had not yet been in to see. Then we set off for Ward 7, which was next on Dr Wall's list. That is the one across the courtyard from Ward 6. One of the patients there is Professor Burnett.'

Monsieur Mal-de-Tête, Poirot thought to himself, but did not say.

'It is a terrible shame that such a brain as his should turn to mush,' Inspector Mackle said with a sigh. 'Age and infirmity come to us all, more's the pity—but Professor Burnett was an eminent scientist in his heyday. One of the cleverest men in England, I was told.'

'Of all the brains that could be described as mush . . .' Bee Haskins began emphatically. Whatever she had been about to say, though, she thought better of it. 'Professor Burnett's mind still works perfectly well, Monsieur Poirot, though admittedly it is impossible to know what thoughts it produces. His emotional state is easier to read. Feelings always make themselves known, even when verbal expression fails. Language is the problem, you see. Professor Burnett has lost most of his, and it frustrates him terribly. He has retained only a handful of words, which he repeats over and over.'

'His predicament sounds most unfortunate,' Poirot agreed.

'When Dr Wall and I visited Professor Burnett's room on 8 September, he was not in bed where he usually is. He was standing by his window. I tried to get him back into bed, but he was intent on staying where he was and staring out at the courtyard, or so I thought at the time.

'As I stood beside him, I spotted Zillah across the courtyard, in the room on Ward 6 that is soon to be Arnold Laurier's. She was also standing by the window, with a young couple beside her: a small, golden-haired woman who looked like an angel ornament that you'd hang from a Christmas tree, and a taller man. Now, of course, I know from Zillah that they were Jonathan and Janet Laurier, though I didn't know it at the time. Behind them, I could see vague shapes of other people—'

'Vivienne, Madeline and Douglas Laurier,' Zillah Hunt told Poirot.

'Yes, but I didn't see them clearly,' said Nurse Bee. 'I only registered them as people in the background. The main thing, the thing I noticed immediately, was that Zillah looked ill at ease. And Jonathan and Janet Laurier looked angry and appeared to be speaking to Zillah in a harsh and unfriendly manner. And the poor love was looking more and more desperate and trapped.'

'That was exactly how I felt,' Nurse Zillah told Poirot. 'I spotted Aunt Bee, too, standing by the window with Professor Burnett, and I thought, "If only she were here. She would know what to do." That Jonathan Laurier is a horrible man. He kept shouting at me, and his wife was echoing everything he said, but sounding more scared than angry. I've met that type of wife before: scared the husband will turn his fury on her if she doesn't make a show of being just as angry as him. And then the other couple, Douglas Laurier and his wife . . . well, it was the strangest thing. They started to list all the character flaws of Jonathan and Janet in such minute detail. It was horrible. They didn't once raise their voices, but what they said came across as all the more vicious for being spoken in that quiet, dry way, as if these were all obvious facts that everyone sensible already knew.'

Inspector Mackle leaned over and patted Nurse Zillah's hand. 'Captivating though this is, my dear, it has no connection with the crime we are trying to solve: the murder of Stanley Niven. He and the Lauriers did not know each other. There is no connection—'

181

'How can you be sure of that?' Poirot asked him.

'Why, they all say so—all the Lauriers and all the Nivens. And I didn't take their word for it, I will have you know. I looked into it myself and found no connection between the two families.'

'Nurse Hunt, please continue,' said Poirot.

'Well, Aunt Bee could tell from across the courtyard that I was stuck in a room with some horrid people—not Arnold's wife, mind. She seemed kind and gentle, and as upset by it all as I was.'

'I wanted to hurry back to Ward 6 and help Zillah, but I was accompanying Dr Wall on his rounds,' Bee Haskins added. 'I thought, "I'll just stand here at the window with Professor Burnett and keep an eye on things for a while." The shouting seemed to subside a little, and I saw Zillah recover some of her composure—'

'They ran out of steam in the end, once they had said every wounding thing they could think of,' said Zillah. 'The argument limped on for a bit longer, then stopped, then started again—but only because no one wanted to admit defeat. You could tell that all the vim had gone out of it. I knew the worst was over when Vivienne Laurier stopped crying. I put on my best cheery, practical face and started to tell her all about St Walstan's. Didn't look at any of the others—only at her, for the rest of the time we were in the room together.'

'When I saw Zillah perk up, I decided it was safe to move away from Professor Burnett's window,' said Nurse Bee. 'But he stayed where he was and would not be talked back into his bed. And now, having set the scene for you, Monsieur Poirot, I will come to the point: I am certain— could not be more so—that the door of that room on Ward 6, Arnold Laurier's room, was *open* while the worst of the row was taking place.'

'Whereas I am positive that it was shut,' said the younger nurse. 'Aunt Bee and I have discussed it endlessly, as you can imagine. Neither of us can be persuaded out of our opinion.'

'Did you see anybody or anything in Stanley Niven's room?' Poirot asked Bee Haskins.

She shook her head. 'I'm afraid my attention was entirely focused on Zillah and the Lauriers. But I believe Professor Burnett saw something. I think that's why he wouldn't abandon his vigil at the window. Before Stanley Niven was killed, Professor Burnett had a particular phrase that he used to repeat endlessly. It was the only thing any of us at St Walstan's ever heard him say. His family warned us when he was first admitted that he would say nothing else. Well, that has turned out to be untrue! But I mustn't get ahead of myself. The phrase is a quotation from the Bible: "Son of man has no place to lay his head." The professor would normally say it at least once or twice if you looked in on him, and he *always* said it when he first saw you, as a sort of greeting. On the afternoon of 8 September, however, he did not. He said nothing when Dr Wall and I entered his room—made no sound at all. He was staring out of the window, fixated on the courtyard or on something on the other side. I assumed it was the Laurier family drama that had so transfixed him; it was not audible to us on Ward 7, but it was certainly dramatic to watch it unfold even without sound. Now, though, I don't think that was what the professor was watching. I think he witnessed the murder of Stanley Niven. For somebody to lift a heavy vase in the air, more than once . . . why, he could easily have seen it.'

'*Oui*,' Poirot agreed. 'It is not a subtle way to kill a person. In your opinion, could a woman of average strength have lifted and . . . wielded this vase easily?'

'Oh yes,' said Nurse Bee. 'We nurses do it all the time.'

'And the professor's room is directly opposite the one in which Monsieur Niven was killed?'

'Not quite but almost. Monsieur Poirot, I believe with all my heart and soul that Professor Burnett knows who the killer is. The tragedy is, he cannot tell us.'

'Mr Prarrow, you are welcome to speak to the professor yourself,' said Inspector Mackle. 'You try getting the name of a murderer out of a man capable only of repeating the same five words all day every day. Besides, he does not know the names of Stanley Niven's relatives, does he? So he can hardly say, "It was the brother, Clarence, who did it."'

'Ten words,' said Zillah Hunt.

'Pardon, my dear?' Mackle turned to face her.

'"Son of man has no place to lay his head." It's ten words,' said the young nurse. 'And those words have changed, Monsieur Poirot, since Stanley Niven was killed. Quite often now, Professor Burnett says "hurt" instead of "lay": "Son of man has no place to *hurt* his head." We never heard that variation before Stanley Niven's murder. Never.'

'And he started to say it that same day,' said Nurse Bee. 'He said it for the first time to the Laurier family, when they and Zillah came out of Arnold's room. I had left Ward 6 by then, so I didn't see it myself, but Zillah was there. She heard it.'

'He became almost hysterical,' said Zillah. 'And now he says it all the time: "To hurt his head! To hurt his head!"'

'He says it to me at least twice a day,' Bee Haskins said. 'Sometimes he yells it while pointing at me. It's horrible.'

'Most interesting,' said Poirot. 'Tell me, would the killer have been covered in Monsieur Niven's blood after committing the crime?'

Inspector Mackle shook his head. 'There was some on the vase and on Mr Niven himself, obviously, but—'

The sound of a telephone ringing made everyone jump, so immersed were they in the conversation.

Zillah Hunt excused herself and left the drawing room. A few moments later, she returned, wearing an anxious expression. 'Oh, dear,' she said. 'I do hope . . .'

'What is it, mademoiselle? Tell me at once.'

'It was Dr Osgood. He says you must return to Frellingsloe House at once, Monsieur Poirot. Arnold Laurier is missing. Dr Osgood and Vivienne Laurier have looked everywhere and cannot find him.'

CHAPTER 18

The Tree in the Library

I was making good progress with the Christmas tree in the library when Terence Surtees appeared. 'No Maddie or Douglas to help you?' he enquired.

'No.'

'What about your friend Poirot?'

'No. He will be with Inspector Mackle for most of the day, I expect.'

'I see.' Surtees was staring at the tree. 'Is that the right position for those paper snowflakes?'

'I think so, yes. But that will not become apparent for some time.'

'They do not look like individual flakes. The impression, rather, is one of a flower with snowflakes for petals.'

'That is deliberate,' I told him. 'It will look impressive, once I have finished.' Rather than asking what he wanted, I described what I was hoping to achieve with my snowflake-flower idea.

It took him less than ten seconds to interrupt me. 'I have

sought you out only to apologize,' he said. 'It must have appeared rude when I left the dining room so quickly, without so much as a goodbye. I overheard something that was not intended for my ears, and quickly realized I had been misled.'

'By whom?'

'Our dear host and master,' Surtees said in a hard voice. 'Arnold. I ran into him earlier, and he told me . . . Dash it all, he has done it to me again! I was a fool to believe him then, and today I am a fool once more. Well, this is the last time.'

I moved a bauble on the tree. 'Do you think this looks better over here?'

'He told me the children were all helping you to decorate Christmas trees together—hurried over to tell me, as if it was cause for great celebration. When I came to witness the joyous spectacle with my own eyes, what did I find? Only one of my daughters describing the other as "vile" to a police inspector she met just yesterday.'

'I am sorry you had to hear it,' I said.

'The animosity between Maddie and Janet has robbed Enid and me of every last shred of our happiness,' Surtees said. 'Enid has all but given up. Her hair is falling out from the misery. It is more painful than words can describe to compare what she is now to the woman she used to be.' He ran his hands through his own hair, rearranging the lion's mane. Lowering his voice, and with a quick glance over his shoulder in the direction of the door, he said, 'I don't even mind about grandchildren. I could be perfectly happy without them, if only Maddie and Janet would resolve their differences. Enid thought that if we came to live here, in the middle of the girls' battleground, they would feel compelled to do something to improve matters. Well, it has not happened yet, and we have been here seven months—keeping ourselves wretchedly busy in the kitchen and the garden, and not getting paid a penny.'

'It is an unusual arrangement,' I said.

'Of course, we get our food and lodging, and we are able to see our daughters every day. Arnold would call it ideal. That is how he presented it to Enid, when she spoke to him and Vivienne without saying a word to me first. It was Enid who went to the Lauriers and asked if they would consider having the two of us to stay for a short while in the hope that we might be able to sort out our girls, who were both already living here. Arnold could not have been more delighted. The timing of Enid's request was perfect: Vivienne had just let their cook and gardener go in order to save money.' Surtees snorted. 'Which is ludicrous when one considers that Arnold is sitting on a small fortune. Refuses to spend any from that pot, though. He sees his "family money", as he calls it, as being for Douglas and Jonathan.'

'Many fathers would not be so generous,' I said, thinking of my own, who had reminded me regularly throughout my childhood that his financial contribution to my life would end on the day I became an adult.

'Even leaving his heaps of family money out of the equation, Arnold could afford a proper cook and gardener if he wanted one,' said Surtees. 'He *did* afford it, for many years. I don't know what changed. I don't want his money, anyway. Wouldn't take it if it were offered. Enid and I are making more than enough by letting our house in London while we live here. Of course, it has not occurred to Arnold for one second that Enid and I might grow resentful in our positions of servitude. He is altogether too nice, that is Arnold's problem: too happy about everything. He would not mind being a servant, I am sure—he would find a way to turn it into an adventure. He always thinks everything will be the most enormous fun. That is why he cannot be trusted. Hearing from him that everything will be fine does not mean that it will be; it merely means he is not willing, ever, to adopt a more pessimistic cast of mind.'

'I doubt he deliberately misled you about the decorating of the trees,' I told him. 'Maddie and Douglas helped me with one and Janet helped me with another, earlier this morning. Arnold could have heard mention of both and got the wrong end of the stick.'

'You are right,' Surtees said. 'Arnold would never do any harm on purpose. That almost makes it worse.'

'I think this silver bauble would look better on the other side of the tree,' I said. 'So that it can be seen from the garden, if one were to look up. What do you think?'

Surtees ignored the question. He walked over to the window and looked out. After a silence of some seconds, he said, 'There is no way to return to the past, but if I could . . . if only I could . . . I would not allow Arnold to persuade me.'

'Of what?' I said while repositioning the bauble, trying to sound as if I were only half listening.

'Enid knew, you see. She has always known what the girls were up to, long before they told us anything. She knew Janet and Jonathan were sweet on each other. One day she sat me down and said, "Now, listen, Terence. You will not believe me, and you will be indignant, I expect, but I am going to tell you what is about to happen and what you must do about it. Jonathan Laurier will very soon come to you and ask for Janet's hand in marriage. And you must say no. On no account! You will tell him that he does not have your permission. Promise me you will do it." I laughed, naturally. How could Enid know what Jonathan would do? And whyever should we wish to keep apart two young people who were besotted with one another? I had gladly given Douglas permission to propose marriage to Maddie, after all.

'I reminded Enid of this and she said, "That is why you must do all you can to deter Jonathan. I have heard about this sort of thing happening: two brothers and two sisters. Believe me, it can cause all manner of trouble." I told her I did not see how, and she said something complicated about the rearrangement of loyalties.' Surtees sighed. 'My wife uttered many wise words that day, inspector. How I wish I had listened to her.'

'Rearrangement of loyalties, eh?'

'Yes, and not only that. Invasion of territory too. Oh, she saw it all, did Enid, long before it happened. She said, "If Janet marries Jonathan Laurier, she will immediately think of everything about his family as entirely hers by right. She will be all the more furious with Maddie for having got there first, and she'll blame her for all of it as if Maddie were the encroacher, quite forgetting that the order of events proves her wrong."'

Surtees lowered himself into the nearest armchair. 'There is something about a severe danger warning that goads a person into disregarding it,' he said. '"Surely not," one thinks to oneself, feeling oh-so-reasonable and measured. "Surely it is an exaggeration, and things will not be as bad as all that." And if the warning is delivered with great certainty, well, we are naturally suspicious of those who are too certain of anything—often with good reason. I took Arnold's advice and gave Jonathan my permission to ask for Janet's hand in marriage.'

'Arnold advised you?' I said.

'Oh, he was full of the joys of spring, as he always is. He thought it would be wonderful for all four of our children to be married to each other. Vivienne was delighted too. She said we would soon all be able to be one big, happily family, all eight of us. In fact . . .' Surtees frowned. 'Yes, she did, if I recall correctly—and I think I do. Vivienne immediately invited Enid and me to move in with them, here at Frelly. For once Arnold was the more cautious of the two of them. He said, "Do not be too hasty, dear. Jonathan has not yet proposed and Janet has not yet said yes." We all laughed, then. I was touched by Vivienne's kindness. She comes from a large family herself—one of five siblings, like me. It was understandable, I thought, that she wished to create a new, big, happy family. I had no idea how soon afterwards she would seek to turn some of her newly acquired relatives into servants.'

Surtees grimaced. 'Maybe Janet gets her unreasonable streak from me.'

'I don't follow,' I told him.

'Enid and I agreed to Arnold and Vivienne's offer of residence here in exchange for our work. And here we still are, when we could easily have left, and even though we hate our subservience more and more with each passing day. Anyway, all of that is beside the point,' he said brusquely. 'You asked if Arnold advised me. He did. And five minutes into my discussion with him, I was convinced that Enid's doom-laden predictions were wildly unrealistic. I told her I would give Jonathan permission to marry Janet if he asked for it. When my wife wept and begged me to reconsider, I quoted Arnold's words: "Why would I wish to take the side of fear against love?" And now, every day, I pay the price for my foolishness. I inhabit—Enid and I both do—the nightmare scenario that she was so desperate to avoid. My greatest fear . . .' He faltered and his voice shook. 'My fear is that I shall go to my grave, and Enid to hers, knowing that Maddie and Janet are still not reconciled. If they could only love each another as they did before, I would happily die today. So would Enid.'

'I'm sorry,' I told him. 'It must be very hard for you and for your wife.'

'I know I had a hand in creating the problem, yet I blame Arnold for all of it. Is that not wicked of me? Sometimes

I think I hate him. "Why would you wish to take the side of fear against love?"' Surtees muttered. 'For a very good reason, as it turned out. If Arnold had not asked me that question . . . May he suffer the torments of the damned for uttering those words in my presence!'

CHAPTER 19

Unanswered Questions

This was how Poirot described to me, later, his journey back from Duluth Cottage: 'It was unbearable, Catchpool. I suffered the agonies of the damned—and it was not helped by the ceaseless chatter of *l'imbécile* Mackle, in whose presence no restful silence can flourish. He wished to speak only of the murder of Stanley Niven, because he knew of no other murder, no *second* murder, connected to that case. I, meanwhile, was certain that Arnold Laurier, missing from Frellingsloe House, had been murdered too—and I was to blame! I should not have left him unattended, fearing as I did that Vivienne Laurier was right about him being the killer's next victim. I was a blind fool who had not listened when my intuition spoke to me more clearly than it ever had before! Catchpool, I had no doubt that Monsieur Laurier's body would have been found by the time I returned.'

As I say, it was much later that Poirot allowed all of his pent-up anguish to pour out. I do not wish to get ahead of myself, so I will return to an earlier point in the story: the moment of his arrival back at Frellingsloe House. I was on my knees, putting the final decorative touches to the Christmas tree in the entrance hall, when I heard a car pull up on the gravel outside. Then came the sound of fast, impatient footsteps. 'This cannot be Poirot,' I thought. My Belgian friend was neither habitually nor by preference a fast mover.

There was a frantic pounding on the front door. 'Catchpool! Let me in, *immédiatement*!'

I had no idea why he was so agitated, and assumed the cause was something that had occurred while he was at the police station or the hospital; I did not know, at this point, that he had visited neither. Nor did I know that anybody had telephoned first to the local police station and then, after hearing from one of his men where Inspector Mackle had taken the famous Hercule Poirot, to Duluth Cottage to ask Poirot to return as a matter of urgency. Certainly no one had mentioned to me anything about Arnold Laurier having gone missing.

I tried to stand up quickly, stumbled and ended up back on the floor.

'Catchpool! It is I, Poirot! Let me in.' He banged on the door again.

As I moved in the direction of the front door, I heard footsteps above me, on the staircase. 'Do not fret! I shall be there in jiffy!' a merry voice called out. I calculated that the voice's owner would reach the door before I did, so I turned back to my tree, which—though I say it myself—was by now looking positively regal. It was a king among trees, festooned with an abundance of shiny, beautiful objects, each of which had been placed in its optimal position with great delicacy and skill.

The front door was opened for Poirot seconds later—by none other than Arnold Laurier. Yes, it was he who had skipped down the stairs, calling out reassurances as he went.

Poirot's face was a picture. It made me think of a goldfish that had fallen out of its bowl and could not understand why there was suddenly no water for it to breathe. Behind him, through the open door, I saw the same car parked in front of the house that had come to collect him this morning. Once he had recovered himself, Poirot turned and gestured at the vehicle, indicating that it was free to leave.

'I owe you an apology, Monsieur Poirot,' said Arnold Laurier. 'You have been inconvenienced and no doubt greatly alarmed, and all for no reason. As you can see, I have not disappeared.' He performed a full turn where he stood, allowing Poirot—and me, though only in parentheses, no doubt—to view him in the round. 'I am not missing. I never was missing. I simply went out without informing anyone—something I have done all my life, I might add— but I should have taken into account my wife's baseless fear that I am about to be murdered by the beast of St Walstan's, whoever he might be. Haha! No doubt she believes he has grown tired of waiting for me to turn up at the hospital and is now set on seeking me out here at Frelly to administer a grisly punishment.' Laurier laughed, apparently finding it all immensely entertaining. Then he remembered Poirot's recent experience and adopted a more sober expression. 'I am very sorry if we gave you a shock, old boy.'

'I am delighted to find you alive and in such good spirits, *mon ami*.'

'Why don't you ask him where he has been, Monsieur Poirot?' came Vivienne Laurier's voice from the back of the hall. 'He refuses to tell me.' She sounded sad and resigned as usual.

'All will be revealed, dearest,' said Arnold. 'When I am ready, I shall tell you every last delectable morsel. I would far rather present you with a problem nicely solved, not one that is still proving to be rather a headache. And I know just the man who can help me solve it. Monsieur Poirot, may I speak to you for a moment in private?'

'Of course.'

'Thank you. Let us go to my study. Vivienne, I am confident that, after a brief confabulation with our good friend Poirot, I shall have some happy news for you . . . for all of us; the children too.'

Vivienne and I watched the two of them leave. 'What do you think of my decorative efforts?' I asked her.

She made no response and did not even look at the tree. I watched as she moved slowly and aimlessly around the hall as if she were sleep-walking, first in the direction of the front door and then back towards the foot of the stairs, where she came to a standstill. 'It is not fair,' she said. She was talking not to me but to herself—that much was apparent.

'What is not fair?' I asked.

'We imagine it is the injustice that stings, but the worst pain is caused, always, by the idea that things should be fair, when they never have been and never will be. If only I could see things differently . . . but how?' She looked at me suddenly. 'Does it not strike you as horribly, awfully unfair, Edward, that something as morally irrelevant as biological accident—the hereditary physical traits one is born with, that one has done nothing to earn—should be of such consequence? If spirit, courage or faith counted for anything, if creativity or determination had any bearing upon what becomes of a person, Arnold would live forever and I would waste away into nothingness.'

'I think you are being unnecessarily cruel to yourself,' I told her.

'Instead, whether we live or die is decided by genetics, which are entirely random,' she went on. 'Arnold is a uniquely inspiring, talented man. Yet he is the one who is dying. I knew he would go first. I always knew, from the moment I first met and fell in love with him. He was recovering from an illness then. Since he was twenty years old, he has suffered from every constitutional weakness it is possible to suffer from. He was an ailing child, born weeks before he should have been. You find all of this hard to believe, I see. Oh, I understand why. When one meets Arnold, one notices only his vitality—the power of his mind and his character. He has no interest in the many disasters that might befall him. He wastes no time thinking about his own death, because he is so full of life.'

A sob burst from her. 'And here am I, feeling hollowed out and barely alive, not even sure I want to be here any more. I shall live for another thirty years, I have no doubt, and every one of those years will be empty and miserable.'

I hovered ineffectually, not knowing what to do or say as Vivienne Laurier stood next to me, howling like a wounded animal.

'And that is only the suffering that awaits me after Arnold dies,' she erupted again. 'Before he dies will be the worst part. He will move to St Walstan's—he is determined to do so—and . . . and . . . oh, he knows nothing of the danger he courts.'

'Unless Poirot catches the killer first,' I said.

'I do not believe he will,' said Vivienne.

'May I ask why not?'

'Believing that good things might happen has become impossible,' she said.

'Well, I have known Poirot for years. During that time, I have watched with astonishment as he solved case after case. I am certain he will catch Stanley Niven's killer.'

'Cynthia thinks so too. Whyever would I doubt someone who has never failed, she wanted to know. But hope cannot take root in a heart that knows only despair, and my despair is like a poison spreading inside me. There is not much of anything else left. The tragedy is that emotional poisons have an insufficient effect upon the physical robustness of a person, which is entirely down to genetic inheritance. Dr Osgood is always telling me and everybody else in this house—he has told you, I dare say—that I have lost too much weight and am wasting away. If I could only believe him, that I will soon shrivel to nothing . . . But no, it is the likes of Arnold who are susceptible to that fate, not the likes of me. Do you not think it terribly cruel of Mother Nature to arrange things this way? Why not put a temperament and mind like Arnold's into this inde-structible body?' She pointed at herself. 'I would not be surprised if my shattered heart has at least two decades left to beat.'

I could not think of a single thing to say. The thing about dealing with excessively melancholy people, I have noticed— those who carry clouds of gloom with them everywhere they go—is that one loses the will to cheer them up. In their orbit, one is robbed of the notion that one can do anything to improve one's own situation or theirs.

'Your mother is much less tolerant of my despondency than you are,' Vivienne told me. 'It is odd, perhaps, but I will forever be grateful to her for her refusal to submit to it or indulge it in any way. If she were not here at Frelly, I would spend all my time walking around like a ghost, through the corridors and halls of this house, which is itself a ghost. That is the sort of thing I would not get away with saying to Cynthia. She would shout at me.'

I hoped she was not suggesting that I ought to do the same.

'Only she is able to pull me away from the abyss for short stretches of time. It is her absolute intolerance of anything she dislikes that does it, and the sheer force of her personality. The best I am capable of feeling, I feel in her presence.'

My eyebrows must have shot up at this. Then paranoia took hold of me. Had Mother inveigled her grateful friend into praising her fulsomely in my presence each time an opportunity arose? Had a bargain been struck? *You do your best to persuade my unappreciative son that I am the best thing since bread was wrapped, and I shall bring Hercule Poirot here to make St Walstan's safe for Arnold?*

The object of my suspicion was marching briskly towards me. 'Edward!'

'Hello, Mother.'

'Have you finished all the Christmas trees yet? Is that one finished? It doesn't look finished.'

'Almost. I just need to add the last few bits.'

'I don't know why you're chinwagging, then, with the job unfinished.'

'It is my fault,' Vivienne told her. 'I'm afraid I have been—'

'Oh, Vivienne.' Mother looked cross. 'You haven't been spouting all your favourite tommyrot, have you? What has she been telling you, Edward? That she is doomed to live to be a hundred and ten, growing more desolate by the day? As I keep telling her: having some misery to contend with does not preclude joy. We must simply wrap up our unhappiness as we would a treasured possession—if we have lost a loved one, or suffered a betrayal—and carry it around with us carefully, taking it out and tending to it every now and then, and then putting it carefully back in its special place, once we have admired it sufficiently for the present moment.'

'What the devil are you talking about, Mother?'

'And never *ever* telling it to go away, or that it has outlived its usefulness,' she went on. Vivienne was transfixed. No wonder Mother liked her. 'And at the same time, one looks around for any little bits of joy that one can find. No, it is more than that,' she corrected herself. 'One makes sure to create joy. The biggest misunderstanding of all is the assumption that we will stumble across joy by accident if we are lucky. No, no. It is something we must manufacture ourselves. As soon as you are ready to attempt it, Vivienne, I shall show you how. Now, Edward, hurry up and finish that tree. Vivienne, go to the kitchen. Have Enid take some tea and cakes to the library—that will be Edward's reward, once he has completed his task.'

Vivienne moved swiftly, eager to obey her mistress's instruction.

'Does Enid Surtees ever leave the kitchen?' I asked Mother once she and I were alone.

'Do not be facetious, Edward. You saw her in the dining room at dinner last night and at breakfast this morning.'

'Every time I have walked past the kitchen today, she has been in there.'

'Well, what do you expect? She is Frelly's cook.'

'Why is she? She has no talent for cooking.'

Mother smiled. 'You used to do this as a young boy—do you remember?'

'What?'

'If ever you wished to put something off or delay your bedtime, you would ask a series of ever more convoluted questions. I fell for it sometimes, but not often.'

I had no memory of what she was describing.

'And I shall not fall for it now. No more questions! Go and finish that tree.' She strutted away.

I considered leaving the tree in the hall unfinished, then decided against it. There was no point ruining something I was pleased with only to spite Mother.

I disobeyed her other instruction, however, and continued to ask questions, if only to myself: about something Vivienne had said that, as far as I could see, had only one possible meaning, and also about a remark Arnold Laurier had made before taking Poirot off for a private conference. I had only half noticed it at the time. Now that I came to think about it properly, it puzzled me. I resolved to ask Poirot for his view later, because to me it made no sense at all.

CHAPTER 20

Rules of the Morality Game

Once I had finished with the tree in the hall, I made my way to the library, trying not to look forward to the 'tea and cakes' that Mother had forecast. Doubtless Enid Surtees' definition of both was very different from mine.

When I arrived there, I saw that no refreshments had appeared yet, but there was a large notebook lying open on the long table that ran almost the full length of the room. The pages I could see were covered in small, neat handwriting. Moving closer, I saw the word 'Morality' with a capital M. I sat down and started to read.

It soon became apparent that these notes must have been written in preparation for the playing of the Morality Game on Christmas Day. Somebody had jotted down a list of the game's rules, then, beneath it, a list of six names. My eyes widened when I got to the last one. Beneath each of them, someone—almost definitely Maddie Laurier, I decided—had written a brief description of that person's misdeeds, for example: '*H. H. Holmes (real name Herman Webster*

Mudgett): owner of the "Murder Castle" hotel, murdered employees and guests.' I smiled to myself. Had Poirot been with me, I might have quipped that, personally, I would have made sure to avoid any hotel that went by that name.

Having read the rules, I knew that each player had to come to the game with their chosen 'worst person in the world' contender. The winner was the player who ended up, after several eliminatory rounds, with the most votes for their nominated evil-doer.

The list of names in front of me seemed to be Maddie Laurier's shortlist of potential Most Evil Persons. Judging by the large tick beside the name, she had chosen Elizabeth Báthory, 'The Blood Countess', as her winner, who would now go forward to compete with everybody else's worst people. Aside from the Blood Countess and the Murder Castle chap, the four other names on Maddie's shortlist, all with crosses beside them, were Emperor Caligula of Rome, Maximilien Robespierre, Gilles de Rais and, finally, Janet Laurier. I was relieved to see that Maddie had retained at least some sense of proportion and ranked her sister lower on the evil scale than at least one of history's most depraved and bloodthirsty killers.

The library door opened and Enid Surtees appeared with a tea tray, which she placed carefully on the table. Her eyes moved to the pages that lay in front of me. 'Is that . . . ?' she started to say, but did not finish the sentence. Leaning over, she pulled the notebook towards her and lifted it so that she could see its cover, which was white and had printed on it the words SUPPLIED FOR THE PUBLIC

SERVICE. Beneath these were the capital letters G. and R., for George Rex, the King, with the insignia of a large crown between them.

'The crown notebook,' she said, eyeing me with undisguised disapproval. 'Where did you get this?'

'It was lying open on the table when I got here.'

'I'd put it somewhere out of sight if I were you. If Vivienne comes in and sees it . . . I'm surprised she didn't burn it.'

Before I could ask her to explain these puzzling remarks, Enid Surtees had left the room and closed the door behind her.

I went through the notebook to see if there was anything in there apart from Maddie's detailed scribblings about the Morality Game. There were only two more pages that had been written on, one in the middle and one near the back. The first was a list of Christmas preparations that needed to be done, including what presents should be bought for members of the household and one or two other people. This was in a different handwriting. Vivienne Laurier must have written this, I concluded, since she was the only person who lived at Frellingsloe House whose name did not appear on the list with a Christmas present idea next to it. I was pleased to see that my name and Poirot's were not on the list, and chose to take this as a sign from Fate that we would be long gone by Christmas Day.

Two names on the Christmas presents list belonged to people who did not live at Frellingsloe House: Father Peter and Olga Woodruff. I wondered if both were expected for Christmas luncheon, and why Nurse Olga Woodruff had been invited. Perhaps she was going to be the main nurse responsible for Arnold Laurier's care at St Walstan's.

On a page towards the back of the notebook, someone had scribbled in pencil—big loops and messy zigzags—over a large and quite detailed drawing of a gravestone that had been done in pen and ink. The pencil scrawl looked as if it had been added by a careless child, and in no way obscured what was beneath it: a picture of a headstone— mainly square, but with curved flourishes at its top corners. At the very top of the stone, in handwriting I recognized from his letter to Poirot and me as Arnold Laurier's, were the words: '*In loving memory of beloved husband and father, Arnold Laurier, called to rest ?? 1932*'.

The library door opened again and Mother appeared, carrying a small drink. 'Don't let your tea go cold, Edward, after Enid went to the trouble of making it for you. Here, I have brought *un sirop* for Monsieur Poirot. I thought he would be here by now.'

'Never mind that.' I told her what Enid had said about Vivienne burning the crown notebook, and asked if she knew what it might have meant.

'Oh, that,' she said. 'Enid is terribly melodramatic. A month or so ago, Arnold presented Vivienne with a sketch of the sort of headstone he wants. He thought it would make sense to order it as soon as possible and offered to do so himself, to save Vivienne the trouble. I'm afraid she reacted rather badly when she saw he had written "1932" as the year of his death. She picked up a pencil and . . . well, she scrawled all over his drawing. She felt terribly ashamed afterwards, knowing Arnold had only been trying to help, but she also insisted it was a terrible thing for him to assume he would die in 1932 when he might last several more years. He won't, of course,' Mother concluded. 'But I would not advise that any of us say so to Vivienne. Now, you drink your tea,' Mother clapped her hands in front of my face, 'and I shall go and find Poirot for you.'

'There is no need to . . .' I stopped and sighed. She was already gone and would have paid no attention anyway.

I looked down at the list Maddie Laurier had made (it could be no one but her, surely) of miscreants, historical and contemporary: Emperor Caligula, The Blood Countess, H. H. Holmes of the 'Murder Castle' hotel . . . If Maddie could put her sister on the list for the crime of 'unreasonable and vindictive hatred and vilification of the innocent', then surely it would be acceptable for me to add 'Cynthia Catchpool: determination to consider no one's wishes or opinions but her own'.

If only I had been equipped with a pen or pencil in that moment . . .

CHAPTER 21

The True Pattern

'Ah, Catchpool? Here you are. Your mother said I would find you here in the library. Ah—and there is my *sirop*!'

'I wondered when Arnold would set you free,' I said. It is hard to describe how I feel whenever Poirot walks into a room I am in. It is the mental equivalent of light being transformed into colour by a diamond's fluorescence.

'What is that notebook?' he asked.

I told him about Maddie Laurier's Morality Game notes, Arnold's gravestone drawing and Vivienne defacing it. Then I asked him how close he was to solving the murder of Stanley Niven.

'Not at all close,' he said. 'But this thought, it encourages me.' He walked to the farthest end of the room and lowered himself into the green leather chair in the corner by the window. 'I have told you before, though you might not remember: it is when the mystifying details of a case start to proliferate, when the contradictions begin to amass and each new fact that comes to light explodes the emerging

209

picture instead of helping to make it whole . . . that is when I know I am moving inexorably towards the moment of full understanding.'

'Yes. You have said that before.'

Poirot smiled. 'And you believe me no more now than you did then, but it is true. Nothing is truer. Most people believe that making progress entails feeling as if one is moving forward. They think they will be able to say to themselves all along the way, "Ah, yes, now I see. How perfectly it all comes together!" *Non, non, non!* One perceives only chaos and the absence of progress until the one or two final elements make themselves visible. Only then does the apparent mess resolve itself into a story that makes sense, in which everything fits together.'

'What did Arnold Laurier wish to say to you that he could not say in front of his wife?' I asked him. 'And what happened today at the hospital and the police station? What did you find out?'

'I went to neither St Walstan's nor the police station. I went to Duluth Cottage.'

'What is that?'

'A most delightful little house. Its owner is a Mademoiselle Verity Hunt. She lives in the cottage with two other women: Nurse Bee Haskins and Nurse Zillah Hunt. I will tell you all about it, but first, tell me about your day. What has happened at Frellingsloe House since I left it this morning? Omit no incident or conversation, please.'

'I have decorated five Christmas trees, including the one

in this room,' I told him. 'They all look splendid, I must say. Each one has a distinctive style.'

Poirot regarded me with evident impatience.

Once I had described in detail the various events and interactions of my day, I told him about the two things that were bothering me. 'One of them was said by Arnold Laurier and another by his wife. Arnold's came first. You heard it too. It was just after he let you in, when you came back to the house. He was poking fun at Vivienne's theory that the St Walstan's killer might kill him next. He said, "No doubt she believes he has grown tired of waiting for me to turn up at the hospital and is now set on seeking me out here at Frelly." Do you remember?'

'I do,' said Poirot. 'What of it?'

'Well, it made me think. For as long as Stanley Niven's murderer is out there and at large, Vivienne wants Arnold to avoid the hospital, yes? She thinks he will be killed if he is admitted there, and she wants him to stay here at home where he will be safe. She has also, according to Dr Osgood, expressed the opinion that it was Arnold the killer intended to murder, not Stanley Niven. In which case . . . why does she think that this person will only kill Arnold once he has arrived at St Walstan's? Why would this chap— or lady, if the killer is a female—not travel to Frellingsloe House, which is a relatively short distance from the hospital, and murder him here? How many homicidal criminals have you known whose attitude has been "I am going to kill my enemy, or the person who threatens me, but only if he presents himself at this particular location. Otherwise, I

211

will not make the effort to go and kill him elsewhere"? It makes no sense. Does this miscreant wish to finish off Arnold Laurier or not? Surely the answer cannot be "Only if no travelling is involved"?'

'Yes. I see.' Poirot stroked his moustaches with his index finger. 'If the murderer works at the hospital, it would be hard for them to enter this house and kill Arnold Laurier without getting caught. Far easier to do it at St Walstan's. Though you raise an interesting possibility: what if the killer would feel threatened by Monsieur Laurier *only* if he were to take up residence at St Walstan's?'

'Poirot, I am about to make a bold claim. I would not be at all surprised to learn that Vivienne Laurier knows exactly who the killer is and the precise nature of his or her grudge against Arnold. When she and I spoke earlier, she said, "Arnold knows nothing of the danger he courts." I would not have been suspicious if she had said, "He cares not a jot about the risk," or something of that sort. But she did not say that. It very much sounded to me as if she knew more specific details about the danger—details of which her husband is unaware.'

Poirot nodded slowly. 'If that is so, and she fears for his life, why does she not tell him? She must be too afraid of something or somebody.'

'Or she is protecting somebody,' I said. 'One of her sons, maybe.' Poirot's smile of admiration told me that he was considering the very same theory.

I asked him again about the recent private conversation in Arnold Laurier's study to which only he had been invited.

Immediately, his eyes clouded with sadness. 'Monsieur Laurier wanted to talk to me about Frelly.'

'Must you call it that?'

'It is what he calls it, with a voice that is full of emotion.' Poirot sighed. 'It is concerning to me. To love a building as if it were a person with emotions and a soul when it is no such thing . . . When Monsieur Laurier went out this morning without telling anyone, it was to attend a meeting. Over a period of months, he has conducted a series of secret meetings. Today's was the last one—with a geologist from Norway. Gudbrand Klemesrud is his name. He is a world expert in a discipline I had not, I confess, heard of before: geomorphology. It is the study of landforms and how they change in response to the activity of air, ice and water.'

'The land being worn away by the sea,' I said.

Poirot nodded. 'For several months now, Arnold Laurier has, at great expense and without the knowledge of any member of his family, been bringing to Norfolk one world expert after another. One by one, they have dashed his hopes by telling him the unalterable truth: that nothing can be done to save his beloved family home. Determined to believe that what he wants is possible, he has sought out opinion after opinion. Today, Gudbrand Klemesrud told him the same thing: there is no hope of saving the house.'

'One has to admire his persistence,' I said.

'*Non*. He has wasted time and money on this foolhardiness. This is why the paid servants were let go, so that the money could instead be spent on this fantasy. Vivienne Laurier has no idea how much has been squandered.

Monsieur Laurier believes she will be overjoyed, one day, when he tells her how he spent it, and this he intends to do only once the problem has been solved and a happy outcome secured. Do you know what he said to me, Catchpool? "The great victories come only if one is willing to risk losing everything."' Poirot cursed under his breath. 'Between them, he and the dim-witted Inspector Mackle are enough to put a person off optimism altogether. And now you tell me that Jonathan Laurier has requested that I lie to his father and promise to save the house when I have no expertise at all in the field of geomorphology.'

'Do you mean . . . Did Arnold Laurier ask *you* to save Frellingsloe House from the forces of coastal erosion?'

Poirot nodded. 'I am his last hope.'

This seemed absurd beyond belief.

'In Monsieur Laurier's estimation, it is ideal that I have never before solved a problem of this sort. It has for him the appeal of the unconventional. Besides, he says, I am the only person he can think of who never fails. The sum of money he offered to me . . .' Poirot blinked several times. 'I cannot and will not take it, naturally.'

'You must tell him at once that even you, the great Hercule Poirot, cannot suspend the forces of nature.'

'You are sure, then, that honesty is the correct course of action, *mon ami*? All I need do in order to ensure Monsieur Laurier dies a happy man is tell him I will put my little grey cells to work—'

'No, Poirot. That would be quite wrong.'

'I agree,' he said with a sigh. 'It is only that I do not

wish to make a happy man unhappy.' He stood up, walked over to the table and took a sip of his sirop, then another. 'The happiness of Arnold Laurier . . .' he murmured, staring out the window. I was about to ask him what his special interest was in Laurier's happiness and also in Stanley Niven's, but I was not quick enough. He had drained his glass and was now in action mode—which for Poirot means assigning actions to me. 'Do you have your notebook and pencil to hand, Catchpool?'

'I can get them.'

'Do so, please. I wish to transfer from my head to paper everything I have learned about what occurred on the day Stanley Niven was killed.'

CHAPTER 22

I Take Notes

I was hurrying back to the library when someone stepped in front of me without warning, apparently not minding if I barrelled into him. It was Jonathan Laurier. His face was red, his mouth set in a hard line. 'I have just spoken to my father,' he said. 'He tells me that he has now asked for Poirot's help, but as yet he has received no assurance that your Belgian friend will do whatever it takes to save Frelly.'

'What your father wants is impossible,' I said. 'It cannot be achieved, not even by Hercule Poirot.'

'What is wrong with you people?' Jonathan demanded. 'Have you no compassion? My father will soon be dead. After that, he will be completely ignorant of the fate of this house. Poirot must tell him what he wants and needs to hear, so that he can go to his grave with a peaceful heart.'

'Poirot will do no such thing. He has made up his mind.' There was something about this man's unshakeable conviction that everyone ought to put aside their own principles and do his bidding without question that made me happy

216

to challenge him directly, though normally I preferred to enact a much quieter sort of rebellion. 'Misleading people about the things that matter most to them is not the best solution to any problem. I am surprised you cannot see that.' I walked away at a brisk pace, leaving Jonathan Laurier floundering in the fug of his unjustified anger.

When I entered the library armed with my notebook and pencil, I caught Poirot with a grimace on his face that he tried to hide when he saw me. 'Is something the matter?' I asked him.

'Nothing important,' he said. 'The air in this house does not agree with me.'

'Sea air is meant to be extremely invigorating. Good for a variety of ailments.'

'Maybe so. It is, I think, the atmosphere here and not the air that is the problem. Someone in this house intends harm to another, Catchpool. Murderous harm. If only we could leave immediately . . . But we cannot. Not until we have ensured that whoever killed Stanley Niven does not also kill Arnold Laurier.'

I laughed. 'Poirot, Stanley Niven's killer might never even have heard of Arnold Laurier. Alternatively . . . the killer might *be* Arnold Laurier.'

'That is a good point,' he conceded, 'and one I had, of course, considered. We have been told that only five members of the Laurier family went to St Walstan's on 8 September, but what if one more person from Frellingsloe House was also there that day? Do we know for certain that Arnold Laurier was at home, too sick to leave the house?'

'Here's another one for you,' I said. 'What if Vivienne Laurier's fear is real, but the reason she has given for it is a lie? What if she knows it was her husband who killed Niven, and knows, furthermore, that the murder was very probably witnessed by Mr Hurt-His-Head—?'

'Who might still be at St Walstan's when Arnold Laurier arrives there at the start of January!' Poirot looked rather excited by the notion. 'What, Madame Laurier asks herself, will happen when this witness points to her husband and says "Hurt his head, hurt his head" so many times that even Inspector Mackle starts to question his conviction that the killer must be Clarence Niven? This would terrify Madame Laurier, would it not? That her husband might be convicted of murder and live long enough to be hanged? Or have his reputation forever tarnished?'

'It would, but—'

'Naturally, she cannot say this is what frightens her so much, not without revealing her husband as a murderer. Yet she is powerless to hide her fear. It is the hardest emotion to conceal, *la crainte*. It spills out of the eyes, the mouth, even the skin.'

'Arnold Laurier has no earthly reason to have wanted Stanley Niven dead,' I pointed out. 'Unless he particularly wanted Niven's room on Ward 6. I wonder if it was better appointed in some way.'

'Another inspired notion, Catchpool,' Poirot said breathlessly.

'It was a joke.'

'Please, continue in this vein. You inspire me to question everything. Write it down, all of it.'

Feeling extremely foolish, I wrote down my two ridiculous ideas as follows:

1. Arnold Laurier might have gone, secretly, to St Walstan's on 8 September and killed Stanley Niven. (This is why Vivienne is afraid to have him go to the hospital again—in case Mr Hurt-His-Head identifies him as the murderer.)
2. Arnold Laurier's motive for this murder could have been that he wanted Stanley Niven's room on Ward 6, in preference to the adjacent room that is reserved for him.

'And now, Catchpool, I will tell you everything I have been told today about the murder of Stanley Niven, and you will write it all down. Are you ready?'

I was. He started with his visit to the two nurses, Bee Haskins and Zillah Hunt, and their disagreement about whether the door of Arnold Laurier's hospital room was open or closed while the five Lauriers and Nurse Zillah were inside it on the afternoon of 8 September. As he spoke, moving around the room at twice his usual pace, I did my best to keep up. Where there seemed to be connections between different parts, I drew arrows and lines.

There were some things he remembered vividly, and

others he recalled less clearly. Gerald Mackle had furnished him with much of the finer detail—the specifics from witness statements and such like—at the worst possible time: when Poirot was full of dread on account of the alleged disappearance of Arnold Laurier from Frellingsloe House. Still, Poirot's memory was excellent even when he was not at his best, and there was an impressive amount of information to be recorded about people's precise movements on the afternoon of 8 September.

I put down my pencil only when I sensed Poirot leaning over me. He rested his forearm on my shoulder, and made a peculiar, strangled noise. When I turned to look up at him, I saw that he had pulled a handkerchief from his waistcoat pocket and was mopping his brow. 'What is this disordered jumble, Catchpool? How are we supposed to make sense of it? It bears no resemblance to what I have told you. What is this? Is it a word or a . . . a . . . ?'

'It's the word "doctor". I understand every pencil stroke,' I told him. 'And, assuming you have finished your account, I shall now produce a neat version.'

'Thank you.' He sounded relieved. I resisted the temptation to point out that he need only have glanced at the beautifully decorated Christmas tree in the corner of the room in order to be assured of my talent for order.

To spare readers of my narrative the distress that Poirot experienced when confronted by my first scribblings, I have decided not to include my first draft in this account. Instead, I offer the exemplar of clarity that it was soon to become:

Things told to Poirot on 20 December

1. Stanley Niven was murdered between two
    o'clock and ten minutes before three, in his
    hospital room on Ward 6. He was last seen alive
    by Dr Wall and Nurse Bee Haskins at two
    o'clock. They left his room less than a minute
    after two. He was found dead by Dr Robert
    Osgood at ten minutes to three.

2. Several members of the Laurier family were
    present on Ward 6 when Mr Niven was
    murdered. They were in the adjacent room,
    which was empty and will soon be occupied by
    Arnold Laurier.

3. Nurse Zillah Hunt and all five members of the
    Laurier family say that the door of the room
    was closed throughout. This is disputed by Bee
    Haskins, who claims to have looked across the
    courtyard from Professor Burnett's room on
    Ward 7 thirty minutes after two o'clock and
    seen the door to the room that contained Nurse
    Zillah and the Lauriers standing ajar.

4. The Laurier party arrived on Ward 6 that day
    at fifteen minutes past two in the afternoon.
    Their estimate of their arrival time was
    confirmed by Dr Robert Osgood, who was in
    the corridor when they entered the ward. He
    then went to find Nurse Zillah Hunt, who had
    been assigned the task of showing the Lauriers

the room that will be Arnold's from January. Nurse Zillah spent roughly five minutes exchanging words with Dr Osgood and the Lauriers while standing in the corridor outside Arnold's room.

5. Dr Wall and Nurse Bee Haskins, who had been busy checking on other patients on Ward 6 since two o'clock, emerged on to the corridor at twenty minutes after two, having finished their rounds of the Ward 6 patients. They saw Nurse Zillah and Dr Osgood in the corridor and, beyond them, a cluster of others whom they correctly judged to be visitors to the ward; this was the Laurier party.

6. Also in the ward corridor at the same time, twenty minutes past two, was Nurse Olga Woodruff. Bee Haskins, Zillah Hunt and Dr Wall all say she was there. Dr Osgood at first said Nurse Olga was not present at that time, then later amended his statement to say she might have been, but he did not notice her. Nurse Olga herself insists she was there, and burst into tears when Inspector Mackle put it to her that she might not have been; that Dr Osgood had no recollection of her presence. Mackle told Poirot that if he had been less convinced of Clarence Niven's guilt, he might have suspected Nurse Olga, on account of her 'hysterical' reaction when interviewed.

7. Nurse Zillah took the Lauriers into Arnold's room just after twenty minutes past two o'clock. An argument immediately ensued: the courtyard controversy. At the same time, Nurse Bee Haskins and Dr Wall were making their way to Ward 7. When they arrived there, they checked first on a patient with pneumonia and then on Professor Burnett (Mr Hurt-His-Head). The professor's demeanour was markedly different from usual. He did not greet them with his usual salutation: 'Son of man has no place to lay his head.' He was not in bed, where they were accustomed to finding him, but staring out of his window. He might have witnessed the murder of Stanley Niven: Nurse Bee believes that he did, and that this explains his altered manner and the change to his oft-recited saying. Since the afternoon of 8 September, he has only occasionally repeated the phrase in its original biblical form. Far more often, he says 'Son of man has no place to *hurt* his head.' Bee Haskins believes this means he saw the murderer hurting Stanley Niven's head with the vase.

8. Dr Wall was not alarmed by the professor's changed behaviour and thinks it does not necessarily mean the professor must have witnessed Stanley Niven's murder. His contention is that patient behaviour often changes for neurological rather than environmental reasons.

9. My note: if Mr Hurt-His-Head witnessed the killing of Stanley Niven, and that was why he was standing at the window at half past two when Nurse Bee Haskins and Dr Wall checked on him, then the murder must have happened between two and half past two. However, between fifteen and twenty minutes past two, the Lauriers, Dr Osgood, Nurse Zillah Hunt and Nurse Olga Woodruff were in the corridor, as well as Nurse Bee Haskins and Dr Wall from twenty past two until a very short time later, when they left to go to Ward 7. And between two and a quarter past, Dr Osgood was busy in the ward corridor and insists no one went into Stanley Niven's room. Therefore the killer must have entered Niven's room between twenty and thirty minutes past two. (And when did the murderer leave the room? Might he still have been hiding in there at ten minutes to three, when Niven's body was found?)

10. Between twenty past two and ten minutes to three, Dr Osgood and Nurse Olga Woodruff both told police they were 'in and out' of Ward 6. Both said they also spent quite a bit of time during that period on Wards 4 and 5.

11. At five minutes to three, Vivienne Laurier opened the door of Arnold's room so that the party of six, having finished in there, could leave. They emerged on to the Ward corridor to find

Mr Hurt-His-Head standing there. He was extremely distressed and said to Vivienne Laurier, 'Son of man has no place to hurt his head,' then repeated the phrase several times, becoming ever more distressed. Nurse Olga Woodruff took him back to Ward 7 against his will. (Vivienne Laurier said that he seemed terrified and lunged towards her, as if hoping she might pull him back, helping him to escape Nurse Olga Woodruff's clutches.)

12. Once Nurse Olga and Mr Hurt-His-Head had left the ward, Dr Osgood told the Laurier party and Nurse Zillah that Stanley Niven had been murdered and that the police were on their way. All seemed stunned. Vivienne Laurier put her head in her hands and started to weep. She refused to travel back to Frellingsloe House with her sons and their wives, and Dr Osgood had to leave work and take her back there in his car.

'Why a vase?' I asked, looking up from my notes.

'*Pardon?*' Poirot said faintly, mopping his brow again with his grey silk handkerchief. He could not be too hot, surely. I felt a little chilly, and I could think of no previous occasion when I had felt the cold more intensely than he had.

'The vase, as a murder weapon,' I said. 'Wouldn't you think that, in a hospital, medicines might be to hand—substances standing around that, if a chap were to imbibe too much of them, might knock him out not just temporarily but permanently? Poirot, are you all right? You look unwell.'

'I do not feel good. Here.' He moved his hand slowly towards his stomach, then raised it and let it hover in the air. It was as if he could not decide between stomach and chest. 'Wait. Ah, it has subsided. Go on, please. The vase?'

'I think you should sit down, old boy.'

'There is no need. Continue.'

'For some reason, I am suspicious of Dr Osgood. I don't know why. But if he is the murderer, he surely had many easier methods at his disposal. A syringe full of something that would instantly stop the heart—that would be child's play for a doctor.'

'If I were a doctor who wished to commit a murder, I would choose a method to which no doctor would ever need to resort,' said Poirot. 'To divert suspicion from myself.'

It was, I had to admit, a good point.

I heard a banging noise and turned. 'Poirot?'

I did not see him at first. He was not where I expected him to be. Then I looked down and saw him lying on the floor. I gasped. He had collapsed. His face had turned a horrifying shade of pale blue and his eyes bulged. 'Poison, Catchpool,' he whispered.

I cried out for help and started, at the same time, to run.

21 DECEMBER 1931

CHAPTER 23

At St Walstan's

At eleven minutes to three the following morning, Hercule Poirot opened his eyes. 'Thank the heavens,' I murmured, rising to my feet. My bones ached from having sat for hours in an upright chair with a very thin seat cushion. I assumed it was the best that Ward 4 of St Walstan's Hospital had to offer, even if one had a private room, as Poirot did.

'I told you he was going to be all right,' said Nurse Olga Woodruff, who had spent most of the night sitting beside me at my friend's bedside, assuring me that there was every reason to be optimistic. At regular intervals, she had reminded me of the various pieces of good news: his pulse rate, his vital signs, the ruling out of appendicitis, the accuracy of the facts he was able to recite during a brief lucid period. I would not have been entirely surprised to discover that Nurse Olga had somehow willed Poirot's recovery into being with sheer determination; she looked more than equal to such a project.

She was young and vibrant, and both her face and her

figure looked as if they had been designed to advertise robust cheerfulness against the will of the observer: plump pink cheeks, bright blue eyes with long lashes, a wide smile with big white teeth in a perfectly straight row, a tiny waist with huge curves both above and below it. Her hair was the sort of orange one did not often see: carrot-coloured. She had been the principal person attending to Poirot—and, I will admit, to my perhaps excessive exhibitions of distress—since we had arrived by ambulance yesterday.

Poirot had spent almost all of that time either asleep or unconscious; it was not always clear which. I had wondered several times if Nurse Olga was telling me the full story. Each time she had encouraged me to try to get some sleep in my hard, upright chair, I had resisted vigorously, believing against all common sense that if I kept my own eyes open, it would cause Poirot's to open. Finally, it had worked.

'Catchpool?' said my friend in a cracked voice. 'Where are we? What time is it?'

I told him.

'Was I poisoned? These past hours, I have felt worse than ever before in my life. I was not certain that I would see you again, *mon cher*.'

'Well, thankfully, here we both are,' I said.

'It is most likely that you ate something disagreeable to your digestive system, Monsieur Poirot,' said Nurse Olga. 'If you *were* poisoned, it was by someone who knew nothing about how to kill a person.'

'*Non*,' said Poirot. 'I was poisoned. Though the food I am compelled to eat at Frellingsloe House is undoubtedly disagreeable, I do not believe it would have been sufficient, on its own, to cause my sickness.' He groaned. Beneath the bedsheets, his body twisted. 'As you see, it afflicts me still,' he said. 'My throat is as dry as the desert. Also, there is a ringing sound in my ears, like a bell. Every few seconds, a spasm tears through my stomach, so painful I cannot remain still—like a knife gouging the flesh inside me. I am sorry to say that the little grey cells of Poirot are affected too. I am not able to think as clearly as is required—which suits Stanley Niven's murderer very well indeed. *Bien sûr*, I was poisoned. It would be better for this killer if Hercule Poirot were to disappear from the scene!'

'Nonsense,' said Nurse Olga. 'All of the symptoms you describe can be caused by quite ordinary ailments of the stomach—a virus, perhaps, or some bad meat. You have been staying at Frellingsloe House, have you not? There is no one there who would want to poison you, that's for sure. According to my future husband . . .' She raised her left hand and waggled her ring finger, which had no ring on it. 'Oh!' she laughed. 'Of course, I take it off when I'm at work. Never mind. What was I saying? Oh yes: according to Robert, they were all leaping about with excitement at the prospect of your arrival.'

'Robert?' I said aloud. She surely could not mean . . .

'Yes, Dr Robert Osgood.' Nurse Olga smiled. 'My fiancé.'

Immediately, something rose to the surface of my mind. I had given no thought to it at the time, beyond noting that it was an unusual remark to make: Osgood, beside the Christmas tree in Arnold Laurier's study, had said to

231

me of Felix Rawcliffe, disapprovingly: 'He must be your age, or even younger.' Prior to that, he had been talking about the curate in relation to Vivienne Laurier—but what significance was there in the relative ages of Rawcliffe and Vivienne? Had Osgood intended to imply there was a romantic connection between the two of them? And why had he asked me if Vivienne had mentioned Rawcliffe in our conversation of the night before?

Might Osgood and the curate *both* be in love with Vivienne Laurier? Was that why both had taken rooms at Frellingsloe House? It seemed unlikely that a young curate like Rawcliffe would fall for a woman of around twice his own age.

When she had first invited me for Christmas in Norfolk, Mother had told me, as if it were an undisputed fact, that the doctor was in love with Frellingsloe House's matriarch. Perhaps, for once, she was right. If so, then maybe Nurse Olga knew she was not Robert Osgood's first choice.

I then recalled something I had written in my notes immediately before Poirot fell ill: according to Poirot's account, Osgood had initially told Inspector Mackle that Olga Woodruff was not present in the corridor of Ward 6 at twenty past two on the day Stanley Niven was killed. Later, he had amended his account and said it was possible she had been there, but he had not noticed her.

Of course, Olga Woodruff had shed buckets of tears when Inspector Mackle had told her that her fiancé had no recollection of her being there. Could she really matter so little to him that he failed to see her even when she was right in front of him? I could well imagine the unhappiness this thought would have provoked in the poor young woman. And her crying jag made even more sense if she knew, or suspected, that Osgood was in love with Vivienne Laurier, whom he definitely had not failed to notice on Ward 6's corridor at the same time.

The crown notebook I had found in Frellingsloe House's library suggested that perhaps Olga Woodruff would be one of the Lauriers' guests for Christmas. I imagined the possible tension around the table and resolved once more to do everything in my power to ensure Poirot and I were back in London by Christmas Day.

Nurse Olga's voice interrupted my thoughts. 'Robert and I are due to be married at the start of May next year.' She smiled brightly.

'Many congratulations,' I said, trying not to make my pity for her too obvious.

'Please, no more words,' said Poirot. 'I must close my eyes again. It is too noisy to sleep properly here at night: people rushing past my door with fast, heavy footsteps like galloping horses, voices of other patients and doctors.'

'You're quite right. You need rest,' said Nurse Olga. 'Don't worry, Inspector Catchpool is leaving now.'

'Am I?'

'Yes. You are to go back to Frellingsloe House, put yourself to bed at once and sleep for at least eight hours. You look like a ghost.'

'Nurse, *s'il vous plaît* . . .'

'What is it, Monsieur Poirot?'

'I must speak to Catchpool alone for a few moments before he leaves.'

'Very well. I shall give you two minutes. No more.'

Poirot and I agreed to her terms. As soon as she had left the room, closing the door behind her, he said, 'You must contact Scotland Yard, *mon ami*. Who is the person there that you trust most?'

'Sergeant James Wight,' I said without hesitation.

'Then ask him to do this for me as a matter of urgency: ask him to find out what is the thing that connects the Lauriers, or the Surteeses, to the Niven family. For some people living at Frellingsloe House, it might be true that Stanley Niven was a complete stranger—but it cannot be true for all.'

'You could be right,' I said. I reminded him that Vivienne Laurier had told me with great authority that the Nivens were a happy family who all loved each other. She had stated it as a fact, as if she had personal knowledge of them, then claimed to know it only because Dr Osgood had told her.

'Ask Sergeant Wight also to investigate a possible connection between the Niven family and the two lodgers: Osgood and Rawcliffe,' Poirot said. 'And to speak to Stanley Niven's family—his wife, son and daughter, and his brother Clarence. Tell him to ask the Nivens about Dr Osgood. Did they, or did Stanley Niven, encounter any problems at St Walstan's hospital in which Dr Osgood played a part? And have Sergeant Wight check again all of the Nivens' alibis.'

I considered stating the obvious—that James Wight had

a job at Scotland Yard to keep him busy—but decided against it. Wight was a stellar chap; he would manage it all somehow.

'Then I need you to return to Frellingsloe House, Catchpool, to perform a task of equal importance: interview everybody. This time, it will not be the friendly and casual chatter around the Christmas trees—*pas du tout*! This time, they must be in no doubt that each and every one of them is suspected of murder. Ask the five Lauriers who came to the hospital on 8 September what precisely happened from the moment they walked into Arnold Laurier's room until the moment they left it. Then we will compare their accounts—for that is where the answer lies, I think. As for the other residents of Frellingsloe House, the ones not at the hospital that day—Arnold Laurier himself, Felix Rawcliffe, Enid and Terence Surtees—you will ask them where they were between two o'clock and ten minutes before three that afternoon. Was each one of them alone in a different room of Frellingsloe House during those fifty minutes, or were they all together in the same room? This we need to know! I do not believe it is a question Inspector Mackle bothered to ask. He seems happy to assume that them being at Frelly together at the relevant time gives them all alibis—but what does being together in a house mean? If Terence Surtees, Felix Rawcliffe and Arnold Laurier were all in their bedrooms, would any of them have known if Enid Surtees had left the kitchen and gone to St Walstan's to commit a murder?'

'No, they wouldn't,' I said. I certainly assumed Enid

was always in the kitchen; they might well have done the same. 'Is that all, or is there anything else you'd like me to ask?'

'Make Felix Rawcliffe and Vivienne Laurier tell you what their secret conversation was about, the one you overheard on our first night at the house.'

'I think I've worked out the answer to that,' I told him.

The door opened. Nurse Olga Woodruff gave us a stern look. 'I am sure the two of you must be finished your little chat by now.'

'*Oui, oui.* Thank you, nurse.' Poirot closed his eyes. Then he opened them and said, 'Remember, Catchpool: do not be discouraged by lies.'

'Get some proper rest, Poirot. I will root out all the liars—'

'You misunderstand my meaning. I was referring to the biggest liars of all: your own thoughts and assumptions. Do not believe them. Interrogate and doubt them as you would a murder suspect. And never tell yourself you are confused.'

'Even if I am?'

'You need never be in that most unfortunate condition, and it will not help you to believe that you are. Confusion is the mental state of not being able to think in an orderly fashion. It is a different problem from the one you will have: a temporary inability to make all of the apparent facts fit together. Your clarity of thought is what will enable you to see that the pieces you have so far do not yet form a coherent picture. This conclusion will lead you to deduce that there remain other pieces to be found, and you will pursue those missing facts.'

'I shall indeed,' I promised.

Less than five seconds later, Poirot was fast asleep.

'How certain are you that Poirot's sickness is not the result of an attempt on his life?' I asked Nurse Olga as we walked together along the ward corridor a few moments later.

'Quite certain,' she said. 'Put that idea out of your mind.'

'May I ask you a question about 8 September? Where were you, and what were you doing between twenty past and half an hour past two?'

'In and out of this ward,' she said. 'Working. There is no time to do anything else at St Walstan's.'

'Do you happen to recall what Dr Osgood was doing during those ten minutes?'

'Exactly the same as me. Wherever he went, I went. Ward 5, Ward 4, back to Ward 6. If you are asking about those very particular ten minutes—?'

I nodded.

'Robert left Ward 6 a few moments after Dr Wall and Bee had left, and went to Ward 5. I followed him. We both then went to Ward 4, but not before half past two. We stayed on 5 for longer than ten minutes, I should say.'

'You and Dr Osgood were together that whole time, then?'

'Oh, no.' There was unmistakable anger in her voice that seemed to have come from nowhere.

'No?'

'No,' she said firmly. 'Robert was alone, or rather, he was keeping company with Vivienne Laurier in his mind—whispering endearments to her, no doubt. I, meanwhile, was following him around, unnoticed.'

I tried not to look as shocked as I was by her little speech. Why on earth was she still engaged to be married to Osgood if she knew he was in love with another woman?

'Robert must have been delighted that Vivienne was so distraught about Stanley Niven's murder. I found them together a little later, after I had handed Professor Burnett over to the Ward 7 nurses. They were standing by Robert's car, outside, and he had his arm around her shoulders, comforting her. She was sobbing into her hands and mumbling something about the killer having intended to kill her husband Arnold, not Stanley Niven. Silly woman. What killer would make a ridiculous mistake like that?'

Nurse Olga lifted her chin and said defiantly, 'Go on, ask the obvious question: why do I remain engaged to be married to Robert in the circumstances? The answer is simple: because he chooses, every day, to remain engaged to me. That tells me a lot. It means he knows, deep down, that Vivienne Laurier does not love him and never will. He also knows I would do anything for him. I would die for him without a second's hesitation.'

I assumed that 'How foolish of you, when he treats you so poorly' would not be deemed an appropriate response, so I said nothing.

'Deep down, Robert knows he will be better off with a young, strong wife who can bear him children than with

238

a distraught widow older than he is. This great love he believes he has for Vivienne is nothing more than a little emotional tantrum of the sort that vain men like to entertain themselves with. He will soon see sense once we are married. But first Arnold needs to die, Robert needs to propose to Vivienne and she needs to reject him. Only then will he accept the reality of his situation.'

Nurse Olga smiled. 'At that point, I think he will find that he does love me rather a lot after all.'

I had heard enough, and changed the subject. 'When you left Ward 6 just after twenty minutes past two, do you happen to remember if the door of Arnold Laurier's room was open or closed?'

'On the day Mr Niven died?' She frowned. 'I do not think I . . . Wait. Yes, it was closed. Definitely closed. Unless I am thinking of the door to Stanley Niven's room. The two are side by side, you see—only five or six feet between them.'

I translated her words for my own benefit: she didn't know.

'What I can tell you for certain is that I did not take my eyes off Robert for so much as a second between two o'clock and ten to three,' Olga Woodruff announced.

I was thinking to myself that it was unsubtle and possibly counterproductive to emphasize this in the precise way she had, when she took it even further. 'I am not only his fiancée,' she said bluntly, staring at me wide-eyed as if to drive the point home. 'I am also his very solid alibi. There is no way that Robert could have killed Stanley Niven, so if he is on your list of suspects, or Inspector Mackle's, you should strike him off immediately.'

22 DECEMBER 1931

CHAPTER 24

Murder-Solving Oil

Given the number of tasks I had been assigned by Poirot, I had not expected to be back at St Walstan's Hospital quite so soon. Yet here I was at ten the next morning, full of a white, blinding rage that had taken possession of my whole being. At no point before in my life had I ever felt anger like it. When it first took hold of me, I had to sit still with my head bowed and concentrate on nothing more than breathing in and out. I looked at my pocket watch afterwards and saw that it had been nearly forty minutes that I had sat motionless, vibrating with disbelief and fury: *surely this could not be true. Surely not.*

It is a funny thing, anger. Once it has taken root inside you, it affects the way you view everything. As I strode along Ward 4's corridor towards Poirot's room, I wanted to push over the unimaginatively decorated Christmas tree, the chairs, the stupid plant in its pot next to the nurses' station. None of them had done me any harm, but I resented them for being in my field of vision when all I wanted to see was Poirot, sitting upright in his bed, smiling and on his way to a full recovery. I vowed to myself that if by some chance he did not recover, I would abandon all fears for my immortal soul and wreak the most horrible revenge I was capable of inflicting . . .

Of course, any smile would soon be wiped off Poirot's face by what I was about to tell him. No, I corrected myself, not me; the culprit would have to do the telling. Surprisingly, she had declared herself willing and agreed to accompany me to the hospital for that purpose. No doubt her confession would be made in exactly the manner that it had been to me, at the breakfast table at Frellingsloe House this morning: casually, as if such things were to be both expected and quite reasonable in their own way.

Relief diluted my rage a little when we reached at Poirot's room and I saw that he was in far better fettle than he had been yesterday. He was sitting up in bed. There was more colour in his cheeks and I noticed at once that his eyes were that vivid shade of green that I only ever saw when he was in a state of intellectual excitement. He must have made some sort of progress on the investigative front, I thought. I was keen to hear what it was, but first there was the other, disgusting business that needed to be dealt with.

'Catchpool!' Poirot smiled. 'And Madame Catchpool also. What a gratifying surprise. I was not expecting either of you.'

'How are you, Monsieur Poirot?' said Mother. 'On the mend, by the look of it. Well, that's very good news indeed. A lot of fuss about nothing, I dare say.'

'I have never in my life felt worse, madame. Catchpool, what is the matter? You look frightful—like an apparition. Why are you not at Frellingsloe House taking care of the matters we discussed yesterday?'

'I'm afraid I had done no more than speak to Sergeant James Wight and give him his instructions when I made a horrifying discovery that pushed all other thoughts from my mind. Tell him, Mother.'

'Goodness me, the melodrama,' she said. 'Edward is fibbing, Monsieur Poirot. He did not "make a discovery". I told him something. The two are quite different.'

'Tell him,' I said.

'It is thanks to my actions that you are sick, Monsieur Poirot.' Mother smiled at him sweetly. 'I put a little something in your *sirop*. Do you remember—the one I left for you in the library? I knew perfectly well that it would do you no harm whatever in the long term, so it was perfectly safe. I was trying to help you to solve Stanley Niven's murder as efficiently as possible. I asked myself: would Hercule Poirot be in favour of taking unusual and inspired action in order to gain an advantage in a case he was trying to solve? When I put it to myself like that, the answer seemed obvious: of course you would.'

Poirot stared at her in silence.

'I am sorry that my plan resulted in you feeling unwell for a day or two, but I had worked it all out, you see. I knew you would soon visit this hospital in your capacity as detective, and that would have been far from ideal. Everyone you spoke to would have known this was Hercule

Poirot *the renowned murder detective* who was interviewing them. They would have been on their guard and ready to dissemble. I am surprised the same did not occur to you, Monsieur Poirot.'

He said slowly, 'The cup of tea you gave to Maddie Laurier to bring to me when Catchpool and I first arrived at Frellingsloe House—did you also put something into that to make me ill?'

I felt a fresh explosion of rage in my chest. Mother had told me about only one poisoning incident. Surely there could not have been two?

'I took only two sips,' said Poirot. 'It was too cold by the time it reached me—but it tasted peculiar, and soon afterwards, while talking to Arnold Laurier in his study, I felt dizzy and had to go to my room and lie down.'

'Yes, that was my first attempt,' said Mother. 'Unfortunately, you did not imbibe nearly enough of the substance on that occasion to necessitate a stay at St Walstan's.'

I fought the urge to interrupt and tell her that our relationship, such as it was, was finished and done with forever. No more holidays in Great Yarmouth, no more anything from me. I forced myself to remain silent. Poirot was calm and I was not; the sensible thing to do was leave it to him to decide how this abomination should be handled.

'Please do not look at me in that blank and superior way, Monsieur Poirot,' said Mother. 'Or at least, do not look at me like that *yet*. First answer this: are you already, as a result of having spent a mere two nights in this hospital, significantly further on in your investigation into the murder of Stanley Niven? If the answer is yes, and I have no doubt that it is, then you must consider seriously whether you wish to admonish me or thank me.'

'I should like to know more about this . . . substance that you have twice given me,' said Poirot. His voice contained no expression at all. 'What is it?'

'I got it from my friend Daphne,' said Mother. 'She calls it "Freedom Oil". She gives it to her husband when she needs him to be . . . out of circulation for a few days. I have no idea what is in it, but Daphne assured me it would have no lasting adverse effects; it is unpleasant but not dangerous.

'Freedom Oil,' Poirot repeated.

'In your case, a better name for it would be "Murder-Solving Oil",' said Mother. 'I knew that if you were admitted to St Walstan's as a patient, no one would be in the least bit wary of you, which would enable you to find out much more. Tell me: did my plan work?'

'Madame,' said Poirot. 'Listen carefully. I am going to give you an order, and you are going to obey it without a word of complaint. If your response is anything but utmost obedience, I will see to it that you are arrested for the crimes of poisoning and attempted murder. Soon afterwards, your friend who distributes this Freedom Oil will also be arrested for the poisoning and attempted murder of her husband.'

'That seems a little unfair to poor Daphne,' Mother protested. 'She has never used the oil on anybody but her husband. If you had met him, Monsieur Poirot—oh, goodness gracious! He is one of those unbearable know-it-alls who believes he should be in charge of the whole world.'

She might have been describing herself, I thought.

'He is forever writing to his member of parliament and proposing the most lunatic schemes you can imagine. I doubt that even a member of parliament for the Liberal party would be in favour of the enfranchisement of dogs, and I am quite certain that the fifth Baron Brabourne, Michael Knatchbull, would agree with me that it is a preposterous notion. He is the member of parliament for Daphne's constituency.'

'Dogs?' Poirot murmured. His face had lost a little of its colour.

'Dogs,' Mother confirmed. 'Daphne's husband believes they ought to be given the vote. According to him, it is all very clever indeed and the fastest way to solve all the problems of our great nation. There is a long and complicated justification attached to his witless theory—one that Daphne does not entirely understand and neither do I. But her husband seems intent on—'

'*Madame!*' Poirot bellowed. 'Silence!'

Mother looked offended.

The door opened and Nurse Olga Woodruff's carrot-coloured head appeared. 'Is everything all right in here? I heard shouting.'

'All is in order,' Poirot told her. 'Thank you, nurse.'

Once she had gone, he said to Mother, 'Here are your instructions, madame. Follow them scrupulously if you wish to avoid arrest and punishment. You will leave this room and wait outside in the corridor while I speak to Catchpool in private. Afterwards he will take you back to Frellingsloe House, where you will give him your poisonous oil to dispose of. All of it—every last drop.'

Mother sighed.

'You will also communicate with your friend Daphne and see to it that she never again feeds this poison to her husband. Is that clear?'

'If you insist, Monsieur Poirot. Though I must say—'

'Who else knows that you put poison into two of my drinks?' Poirot asked her. 'Did you tell anybody?'

'Of course not,' she said. 'Not until I told Edward this morning. What sort of brilliant secret plan would that have been, if I had told people?'

'Get out my sight,' Poirot said. 'And close the door behind you.'

'I am so terribly sorry, Poirot,' I said once Mother was gone. 'You cannot imagine how ghastly I feel—'

'*Non, non, mon ami.* You are not responsible for the actions of your mother.'

'But if it were not for your friendship with me—'

'Had I known that our friendship would result in a non-fatal poisoning for me, I would still have chosen to embark upon it,' Poirot said solemnly. 'Do you remember I told you that she is an excellent mother for you to have?'

'How wrong you were.'

'*Pas du tout.* I stand by my words. The experience of being her son has not been pleasant for you, I can see, but it has made you uniquely perceptive and instilled in you many fine qualities: sensitivity, resilience.'

I would have much preferred to have a mother who was not a monster.

'You are unique, Catchpool. So am I. It is why we get along so well.' Poirot chuckled. 'How many people, when dealing with something as trivial as Christmas tree decorations, would have come up with your "Now that it's there" theory and given it that name?'

'Lots of people make up all kinds of silly things,' I told him, embarrassed. 'Look, Poirot, you must not be lenient with Mother as any sort of favour to me. She deserves to be—'

'I shall be lenient because her actions, while abhorrent, enabled me to gather much useful information. Last night was noisy and sleepless, but productive. I had a series of fascinating encounters, and there is now a new mystery that we must add to our list of puzzles in need of solutions!'

CHAPTER 25

Poirot's Disturbed Night

The first nocturnal nuisance to disturb Poirot as he had attempted to fall asleep that previous night was Mr Hurt-His-Head, Professor Burnett. A little after midnight, Poirot had heard his heavy, uneven footsteps and then his original refrain line, the one that predated the murder of Stanley Niven: 'Son of man has no place to lay his head.' The professor repeated the line several times in an ordinary speaking voice, then sang it to a tune that at first Poirot did not recognize. ('Monsieur *Mal-de-Tête* is not a talented singer, *mon ami*.')

After listening for a while, Poirot worked out that the tune being butchered was that of the Christmas carol 'Silent Night', which struck him as ironic, given how far from silent his nights on Ward 4 were proving to be. That the words did not fit very well with the tune did not seem to bother the professor in the slightest.

As the voice came closer, Poirot—though he still felt extremely unwell—recognized the opportunity and decided

251

to take it. As quickly as he could, and wincing at the spasms in his stomach, he took off his hospital gown and dressed in his own clothes, which Nurse Olga had hung up for him in the small cupboard by the window. When he was fully dressed, he went out on to the ward and began to follow Mr Hurt-His-Head as he did his strange soporific dance back and forth along the corridor. If Poirot's or the professor's activity was noticed by any of the nurses on duty, they showed no sign of it. None of them looked up in response to the tuneless singing or the trailing up and down.

Eventually the professor made his way out of Ward 4 and hared off, quite unaware of Poirot in pursuit, to another part of the hospital. Soon Poirot found himself in a narrow walkway with only windows and concrete on both sides. In this corridor, there was a blessed and most welcome lowering of the volume: the professor reduced his singing almost to a whisper and also did a much better job of adapting the rhythm of the words so that it better fitted the melody: 'So–on of man, ha–as no place, to–o lay, hi–is head. Son of man has no pla–ace to lay, hi–i–is hea–ea–ead . . .'

The professor loped and staggered, with Poirot behind him, along the connecting corridor until he arrived at Ward 6. He pushed open the door, walked in, and continued at the same pace until he came to a door about halfway along the corridor, the only one with a white sign attached to it. Poirot was too far behind the professor to read what the sign said. Covering it with a hand that made Poirot think of a grey bear's paw, Mr Hurt-His-Head said quietly, 'Son of man has no place to hurt his head.'

'Interesting,' Poirot thought. It had been 'lay his head' every time until this one.

'To hurt his head, to hurt his head.' Professor Burnett was growing more agitated. Two nurses had stood up and were moving towards him. One of them called out in a firm, cheery voice, 'Let's get you back to the right ward, professor.'

Poirot, by now, had almost reached the door with the white sign, and he saw when Mr Hurt-His-Head took his hand away that it was no more than a small square of paper with four words written on it in neat handwriting: *Reserved for Arnold Laurier.*

'Monsieur Poirot.' Bee Haskins had appeared behind him. 'Are you not on Ward 4?'

'Not at present, no. I am here on Ward 6.'

'Well, you are supposed to be on Ward 4,' she said briskly. 'Come on, let's get you back there.'

'To hurt his head! To hurt his head!' Professor Burnett wailed.

'I will return to Ward 4 when I am ready,' said Poirot.

'Oh, no. Oh, dear.' Bee Haskins backed away as the two other nurses grabbed one each of Mr Hurt-His-Head's arms and did their best to move him away from the door to Arnold Laurier's room.

'To hurt his head! To hurt his head!' The wailing got louder. Nurse Bee, who looked more shaken than Poirot would have expected, said, 'I should probably go and help them but I daren't.'

'Are you afraid of the professor?' Poirot asked her.

'Not at all. It is the opposite! He seems afraid of me, and he has no reason to be. I have never done him or anyone else any harm. So why does he . . . ?' She had started to cry and was unable to finish her sentence.

'Please tell me what it is that has so upset you, mademoiselle.'

'To hurt his head! To hurt his head!' Professor Burnett was now pointing his finger squarely at Poirot. Or . . . could it be that he was pointing at Bee Haskins, who was now hurrying towards the exit door of the ward as if she could not escape fast enough?

It took about ten minutes for the two nurses on Ward 6 to calm Mr Hurt-His-Head. Finally, they were able to lead him away, making soothing noises. They planned to take him back to Ward 7, no doubt.

When Poirot returned to his room on Ward 4, he found Bee Haskins sitting in a chair by his bed, drinking a cup of tea. 'I hope you have recovered from the unpleasant incident,' he said, and the word 'recovered' made him aware that he had not had a stomach spasm for some time.

She nodded. 'Can you explain it? You are a detective.'

'Explain what?'

'Why Professor Burnett has so thoroughly taken against me. I have been nothing but kind to the man, but every time he sees me, he does what you saw him do just now: points and yells those words at me: "To hurt his head! To hurt his head!" He does it to no other nurse or doctor here.'

'You entered his room and stood by his side immediately after he had watched through his window as someone killed Stanley Niven,' said Poirot. 'It is possible that the sight of you reminds him of the murder for that reason.'

'I do not believe that is it, and I cannot explain why,' said Nurse Bee. 'Do you know what it seems like to me? It feels as if he is accusing *me* of killing Stanley Niven—and I did no such thing! Professor Burnett of all people ought to know that, if he witnessed the crime. You might not understand this, Monsieur Poirot, but I start to panic and . . . well, it feels a lot like wanting to die. Whenever anything resembling true hostility is aimed at me, that is how my body feels. It is my body more than my mind. As I say: it is nearly impossible to explain. I imagine I must deserve it—that is the worst part. I have been this way ever since—' She broke off abruptly. 'The point is, I am driving myself quietly mad, and trying to make sure no one else notices. I did not kill Stanley Niven, and have dedicated the whole of my working life to saving lives, but the way Professor Burnett is carrying on, I can sometimes almost believe I must be guilty somehow.'

'You have been this way—easily disturbed by hostility— ever since when, mademoiselle?'

Bee Haskins looked uncertain for a second. Then she said, 'Very well, Monsieur Poirot. Though it will be agony to do so, I shall tell you the whole horrible story.'

23 DECEMBER 1931

CHAPTER 26

Deep and Dreamless Sleep

Dr Osgood had news for me when he arrived in the dining room at a quarter past seven the following morning: a nurse from St Walstan's had telephoned to say that Poirot was fully recovered and well enough to leave the hospital.

I don't know what it was that prompted me to ask, 'Which nurse?'

'Why does that matter? It was Nurse Olga Woodruff,' Osgood said with no trace of emotion in his voice.

'Your fiancée,' I said.

The doctor scowled. 'Do you want me to drive you to the hospital to collect your friend, or not?'

'No, thank you,' I made sure to match his offhand and ungracious tone. 'I shall make a different arrangement.'

I stood up, happy to abandon my lumpy, inedible breakfast. Goodness only knew what species of meat Enid had used, or what she imagined she had turned it into. Certainly it was no recognizable dish.

'Take my car, Catchpool,' said Douglas Laurier. 'I'm sure

259

you and Poirot have much to discuss and would rather not have any of us listening in, eh?' Apart from Dr Osgood and me, Douglas was the only other person in the room. I assumed most people were still asleep. I had only risen as early as I had in anticipation of a long walk by the sea, followed by a swim and a hot bath—but I thought no more about these things once I heard that Poirot was fit and healthy again.

I had neither looked at nor spoken to Mother since she had given me her vile 'Freedom Oil' to dispose of yesterday. I had hardly thought about her either; it was as if there was some sort of hazy barrier in my mind that prevented me from thinking in that direction. That is the only way I can describe it: a strange kind of mental numbness that I had not experienced before.

I drove to the hospital in Douglas's car and found Poirot in his room, elegantly dressed and standing to attention, like a visiting dignitary waiting to be taken to his next official engagement. He looked recovered, but preoccupied.

'It is wonderful to see you restored to health,' I told him.

'I slept well,' he said. 'For the first time since arriving in Norfolk I had, to put it in the words of the well-known Christmas carol, the Silent Night.'

'I am delighted to hear it.'

'I did not dream, but I did a lot of thinking in my sleep—about Bee Haskins and the young man to whom she was engaged to be married.'

'Ah, yes. The story you would not tell me yesterday,' I said.

'It is a sad story. The death of Nurse Bee's fiancé was only one part of the tragedy.'

'Died, did he?'

'She was also betrayed by her sister, who was herself in love with the same man, and envious. There was an illegitimate child, who was brought up by a friend.'

'You must have been awake if you were thinking about all of that,' I said.

'*Non*. I slept deeply, as I said. And I did not dream. Instead, I did the sleep-thinking.'

I decided it was not worth arguing with him. '*Above thy deep and dreamless sleep, the silent stars go by*,' I quoted from the carol 'O Little Town of Bethlehem'.

'It made me think, Catchpool, how foolish and unnecessary is the feud between Maddie and Janet Laurier, assuming they have told the truth about its cause. They love two quite different brothers, not the same brother! Why could they not have remained friends?' He shook his head. 'Tragedy, Catchpool—it is an organism with many sub-species.'

'Poirot, now that you are well again—' I began.

'You wish to enquire about our imperilled Christmas plans, *n'est-ce pas*?'

'Today is the twenty-third of December. If we are going to spend Christmas in London, we will need to leave today or tomorrow.'

'Tomorrow,' said Poirot.

'Really?' My heart leapt.

'I think so. I have elevated hopes,' he said seriously.

'Everything points to a particular person. The only trouble is that the person I have in mind has no connection to Stanley Niven that we know of, and therefore no reason to want him dead. Unless Sergeant James Wight has told you otherwise?'

'No. He telephoned yesterday to say he is waiting for one more piece of information which will arrive this morning. As soon as he has it, he will send word.'

'Good,' said Poirot. 'I expect the information he provides to complete the picture.'

We left the hospital and made our way to Douglas Laurier's motorcar. Never had I been so pleased to leave a place behind. It was an unusually bright day for late December, with only a handful of thin, almost translucent clouds that looked like white frost against the chilly blue sky. The weather conditions were perfect for a discussion in which Poirot, for once, told me his thoughts and theories without withholding anything. 'I don't suppose you fancy telling me whom you suspect?' I said as I drove us along the coastal road. The sea was calm and still.

'Of course,' he said. 'I suspect the one person whose untrustworthiness and unreliability is so glaring, it can hardly be missed.'

'Janet Laurier? Jonathan Laurier?' I said. When there was no response, I tried again: 'Dr Osgood? He is my favourite for it, I don't mind telling you. His only alibi for the ten minutes between twenty and thirty minutes past two on 8 September is Nurse Olga Woodruff, his fiancée.'

'The outward appearance of an alibi which turns out,

upon closer examination, not to be an alibi at all,' said Poirot. 'Tell me, Catchpool, what alibis have you been offered by the four residents of Frellingsloe House whom I asked about: Enid and Terence Surtees, Felix Rawcliffe and Arnold Laurier?'

'I am afraid I have not yet had time to attend to all that. Or, to be strictly accurate, I was not in a fit state to do much of anything yesterday. I spent a lot of time walking by the sea, avoiding the house and Mother.' Before Poirot had a chance to admonish me, I said, 'Will you please at least tell me what it was about Stanley Niven being a generally jolly chap that so interested you, when we first learned of his murder?' I managed to phrase the question without mentioning the unpalatable creature who had told us about the crime.

'It is quite simple,' said Poirot. 'I had never before heard that said about a victim, not in all my tens of years of involvement in cases of murder. Oh, I had certainly heard that many victims had no enemies, did no harm to anybody, had no discernible cause of worry or misery in their lives, but I had never been told that a murder victim had been noticeable for his happiness. And what your mother said to us about Stanley Niven was even more than that—significantly more.'

'What do you mean?'

'She did not say merely that Monsieur Niven was happy by nature. He also, according to her, *made others feel happy*. It was impossible not to feel that way in his presence.'

'But Mother didn't know Stanley Niven,' I protested.

'She might have been talking nonsense, as she so often does.'

'It was enough for me that this was what was said about Monsieur Niven. It was how he was known and perceived: as a creator of happiness. I thought of all those other murder victims from my past, and I asked myself: of how many of them had this been said? Of how many might it have been true? The answer was none. *None*, Catchpool. It piqued my interest. People like Stanley Niven, who raise the spirits of others—they do not get murdered. Yet Monsieur Niven did. That is why I was so afraid for Arnold Laurier for so long. I persisted in believing that Madame Vivienne was right to believe her husband was in danger—from a murderer intent on removing happy men from the world, perhaps someone so deeply unhappy himself that he sought to destroy joy wherever he found it. Do you recall that your mother said how difficult it was ever to be angry with Arnold Laurier, because he was so jolly and happy?'

'I vaguely remember something of that sort, yes.'

'I suspected a similarity of character between the two men: Laurier and Niven. Still, if my suspicion as to the identity of Monsieur Niven's killer is correct, then Arnold Laurier will not be the next victim. Indeed, until I discover the connection between Stanley Niven and Frellingsloe House, I have no way of knowing if there will be a second murder. Without motive, Catchpool, it is as if each and every little grey cell has been forced to wear a blindfold.'

We talked no more after that, and I spent the rest of the drive racking my brain to try and work out if Poirot had admitted to me that he too suspected Dr Robert Osgood of Stanley Niven's murder. *The outward appearance of an alibi which turns out, upon closer examination, not to be an alibi at all.* Those words did not amount to a declaration of suspicion of anyone in particular, though in context they might well have meant that Poirot suspected Osgood as much as I did. It was strange to think that the next communication I received from James Wight of Scotland Yard was likely to make the connection to, and motive for, Stanley Niven's death quite clear.

Ten minutes later, I parked Douglas's car on the gravel outside Frellingsloe House. I was about to open the door and get out when the front door of the house was flung open. Felix Rawcliffe staggered outside as if he had been pushed. His face was deathly white and there were purple patches beneath his eyes. 'What on earth . . . ?' I muttered.

'*Mon Dieu!*' Poirot whispered, and I heard in his voice the same anxiety I was feeling.

We alighted from the car and were hurrying towards the curate when another figure appeared behind him: Inspector Gerald Mackle.

'What has occurred, inspector?' said Poirot. 'Tell me at once.'

'Regrettably, Mr Prarrow, there has been another murder.'

'It is Arnold.' Rawcliffe's voice shook. 'Arnold is dead.'

CHAPTER 27

The Deaths of Happy Men

'Arnold has been murdered.' Felix Rawcliffe could barely speak. 'It is too dreadful. Vivienne is . . . We are all . . .' His sentence finished in a strangled moan.

'I'm afraid it is true, Mr Prarrow,' said Mackle. 'The murderer has, unfortunately, struck again. This time the victim is Arnold Laurier.'

Poirot bowed his head and stood completely still. I could almost feel the ache he must have felt at that moment, though he said nothing. He gathered himself, then said to Mackle in a tone of crisp impatience, 'Struck again? How do you know that the same person killed both Stanley Niven and Arnold Laurier?'

'Well—' Mackle began.

'Wait. Do not answer,' said Poirot. 'I do not wish to conduct this conversation outside in the cold. Take me to a room where we can talk in private. The three of us only—you, me and Catchpool.' He turned to Rawcliffe. 'Where is everybody else?'

The curate's eyes darted around, as if uncertain of where to look. 'I . . . I don't know,' he said. 'I have not seen anyone for a while. As soon as I heard what had happened, I went to telephone to the police station, and then I waited in the hall for Inspector Mackle to arrive. I have been by his side since he got here.'

'I asked Dr Osgood to gather everybody together in the drawing room,' Mackle told Poirot. 'We could talk in the study—the scene of the crime—though I am afraid Mr Laurier's body is still there. You might find it an unpleasant sight, Mr Prarrow.'

'I must see it. I must look at it in all its disturbing detail and not turn away. I owe Monsieur Laurier that and more. It is my fault he is dead. If I had worked more quickly—'

'It is absolutely not your fault,' I said firmly as we followed Inspector Mackle through Frellingsloe House. 'You had no way of knowing—'

'But I *did* know, Catchpool. I knew in my bones that Vivienne Laurier's fears for her husband's safety meant something, and the similarity of character between Monsieur Laurier and Monsieur Niven was clear. As for my suspicion as to the culprit . . .' He made a noise of disgust. 'How wrong I was! I could not have been more so.'

'There is nothing to be gained by berating yourself,' I told him.

'I do berate, Catchpool. Forever, I will berate.'

'I have given instructions for Clarence Niven to be questioned,' said Inspector Mackle, coming to a halt outside the closed door of Arnold Laurier's study. 'Though that blackguard will have furnished himself with an even more impressive alibi this time, I'll wager. Fifty people will doubtless swear they were with him when Arnold Laurier was killed, and we will find it impossible to prove otherwise. It will be a travesty, Mr Prarrow. *Another* travesty, I should say.'

'Open the door, please, inspector. And, *je vous en supplie*, do not mention again the name of Clarence Niven. He killed neither his brother nor Arnold Laurier.'

Murder scenes are never a pleasant sight, but I found this one particularly upsetting to behold. Now that his lively soul had departed from his body, Arnold Laurier's frailty was painfully apparent. We sometimes say that people are 'merely skin and bones', but as I stared at the dead body in front of me, I reflected that this was more a case of 'barely' than 'merely'. The bones were so thin they made me wince as I pictured how easily they might be snapped in half. And the skin, particularly, on the face and neck, looked no more resilient than a spider's web.

I wondered what sort of monster could have wished to cause additional pain and harm to a man who was plainly in such an enfeebled state. This led me to a realization: whoever murdered Arnold cannot simply have wanted him dead; they must have wanted him out of the way now, immediately, or else they would surely have waited for his illness to take its course.

Inspector Mackle had started to describe to us the cause of death, which he said Dr Osgood had confirmed—though really no explanation was necessary. It was quite apparent what had happened. The visible details all told the same story: the wound at the back of the head; the body collapsed over the desk; the white vase with an ominous stain on its side, close to the bottom; the pool of water on the floor; the large paper flowers made out of smaller paper snow-flakes, which of course I recognized at once. I had made them myself to hang on a Christmas tree only days earlier.

I noted with interest that Arnold Laurier's lifeless head and upper body were not resting on an empty desk. It seemed that he had been looking at photographs when he was killed; dozens of them were spread out on either side of him and, I guessed, beneath him.

'Exactly the same murder method as for Stanley Niven,' Mackle said. 'Blows to the back of the head, made by that vase which the murderer then dropped or placed on the floor before leaving the room. It is a similar shape to the vase used to commit the first murder.'

'No,' said Poirot. 'It is not the same at all. Catchpool, tell the inspector what is the difference. You cannot have failed to notice, given your recent decorative work in this house.'

'I made those paper-snowflake flowers for the Christmas tree in the library,' I told Mackle. 'That is where they were as recently as yesterday. They certainly were not in a vase full of water. Why would anybody put paper flowers in water?'

'They would not,' said Poirot. 'As you see, inspector, these flowers are dry from top to bottom, the paper unblemished. At no point have they been in water.'

'Which means we have a big difference between murder scenes one and two,' I said. 'At the first murder scene, the flowers and water on the floor had an explanation that made sense: the murderer wanted to use the vase as a weapon, so he or she emptied it of its contents, which would otherwise have got in the way and made a mess. Here, the flowers were never in the vase in the first place. They were on a Christmas tree.'

'And this vase was in my bedroom on the top floor of the house,' said Poirot. 'The killer went up there to fetch it, knowing I was at St Walstan's. He filled the vase with water, brought it here, then went to get the paper flowers from the library . . .' Poirot shook his head. 'Why go to all of that effort when he could have used this brass poker here to achieve the same effect?' He pointed to the fireplace, which boasted a variety of potential murder weapons.

'It is a deliberate reference to the first murder scene,' I stated the obvious. 'Are we supposed to think, "This must be the same person who killed Stanley Niven"? If so . . . well, I am not convinced that I do think that. This strikes me more as . . . as a parody of a murder method, and people rarely parody themselves.'

Poirot turned to Mackle. 'When was Monsieur Laurier murdered? At what time was he found, and by whom?'

'His wife found him this morning, an hour before you and Inspector Catchpool arrived,' said Mackle. 'He did not come down for breakfast, so she went up to look for him after she had eaten hers. He was not in his bedroom, so she came here and discovered this horrible spectacle.'

'She had not seen him earlier in the morning?' asked Poirot.

'No,' said Mackle. 'They did not always sleep in the same room. Their habit was to meet at the breakfast table. According to Dr Osgood, death very likely occurred between midnight and two in the morning, though it might have been as late as three. I am sure I don't need to tell you that the crime was committed here, in this room. Mr Laurier was killed as he sat at his desk looking at old family photographs. There's a broken window in the dining room, which is where the intruder must have got in.'

'The intruder?' Poirot, who had been walking in the direction of Arnold Laurier's desk, stopped and turned round.

'Well . . . yes, Mr Prarrow.' The expression on Mackle's face suggested he would dearly have loved to mention Clarence Niven. Nobly, he resisted the urge.

'How do you know there was an intruder?' Poirot asked him.

'Why, because somebody smashed one of the dining-room windows,' said the policeman, looking more confused by the second. 'How else could they have got into a house that had been locked and bolted for the night?'

'Unless someone who lived here wanted to make the authorities believe that the murderer must have been an outsider,' said Poirot. 'Did anybody hear this window being smashed?'

'No one heard anything at all,' said Mackle. 'Everyone in the house slept soundly—even those who do not normally sleep well. I have spoken to them all, and they were all asleep well before midnight. No noise roused them.'

'Silent night,' Poirot murmured, moving closer to Arnold Laurier's desk. 'Murderous night. All is lies, all is . . .'

'Blight?' I suggested.

'Catchpool, come and look at these photographs. You will see many faces that you recognize.'

Something about the way he said it made me think I was supposed to search for the face of somebody who ought not to be there, which I duly did. I saw no one who did not belong.

'*Mon Dieu!*' Poirot's voice was quiet, but full of new energy. He had seen something that mattered, but I could not for the life of me work out what it was. There were several pictures of Arnold and Vivienne Laurier in their younger, happier days, some of which contained one or both of their two sons. Douglas and Jonathan Laurier, at a variety of ages, were clearly recognizable. There was one much more recent photograph of the Lauriers and the Surteeses together, in front of a bandstand. None of the four adults referred to at Frellingsloe House as 'the children' were smiling. No one was, in fact, except Arnold Laurier.

'Is there anything that strikes you about these pictures, *mon ami*?'

'Only that Arnold Laurier was always painfully thin,' I said. 'And Dr Osgood is right about Vivienne Laurier being half the size she used to be. She is much plumper in these photographs than she is now.'

'But there is something much more significant that you

have not . . .' Poirot stopped suddenly and laughed. 'Of course. *Of course.* Thank you, Catchpool!'

'I have done nothing,' I told him.

'You are incapable of seeing the thing that matters. Do not be offended—I mean it in the best possible way. Inspector Mackle, I wish to speak to several people in the library, all of them together, as soon as it can be arranged: Felix Rawcliffe, Enid Surtees and Terence Surtees. Bring them to me at once.'

CHAPTER 28

Joy and Guilt

As Poirot and I made our way to the library, I asked him about his choice of this particular room. 'Given what happened to you last time you were in there . . .'

'That is why it is so appropriate,' he said as we walked in. 'In this room, I believed I would take my last breath. I clearly recall thinking, "This is the room in which I will die." It would be easy for me to avoid it henceforth. Instead, I shall reinvent this library as the place in which I uncover the truth and put a stop to the wickedness of a murderer!'

'I admire your courage and your ambition,' I told him.

He walked over to the window. 'Observe the Frellingsloe sea,' he said. 'Even on a mild and still day like today, it foams and froths as if possessed by a vengeful spirit.'

'I think the wind is picking up,' I said.

There was a knock at the door and Felix Rawcliffe appeared, looking worse than he had when Poirot had dismissed him half an hour earlier. 'Why have you asked for Terence, Enid and me, but no one else? Do you suspect us of something? I can assure you that—'

'Please sit down, Monsieur Rawcliffe,' said Poirot. 'At the table, please, not in an armchair.'

'I have killed nobody, do you understand? Nobody.' Rawcliffe positioned himself awkwardly on the edge of a chair, almost whimpering. 'I was extremely fond of Arnold Laurier, and I did not know Stanley Niven. I never met him, not once.'

'Why are you so heated in the collar, monsieur? If you are innocent, you have nothing to fear.'

The door opened again and Enid and Terence Surtees walked in. I nearly gasped when I saw that they were both smiling. And there was none of Enid's usual slow trudging— quite the opposite. She trotted into the library in a manner that was positively sprightly.

'Monsieur and Madame Surtees, sit down at the table, please,' said Poirot. He was evidently determined that none of them should get comfortable in an armchair. I wanted very much to sit in one myself—my body and brain both ached from the taxing events of the past few days—but I felt obliged to participate in the communal discomfort, so I too sat on a hard chair at the table.

Poirot walked around the room as he spoke. 'May I ask if you have recently received some good news, madame?' he asked Enid Surtees. 'You seem in a merry humour, in spite of the recent murder in your home of your dear friend Arnold Laurier.'

'I am not sure about the "dear friend" part,' she said,

her smile wavering a little. 'He was our master and we were his supposed-to-be-grateful servants. Frelly has never felt like our home, Monsieur Poirot, even though we live here.'

'That is unfair, Enid,' said her husband. 'Arnold was our friend. He loved us and tried to help us, always. And we readily agreed to the arrangement. Our unhappiness was not Arnold's fault.'

Enid nodded. 'Terence is quite right,' she told Poirot. 'In our moment of joy, I suppose we should be magnanimous. Oh! You think we are . . .' She laughed. 'No, no, not at all. We are not joyful on account of Arnold's death, Monsieur Poirot. A murder at Frelly? That is shocking, and poor Arnold, of course . . . Though one must retain a sense of proportion. He was, after all, about to die imminently—and the terrible pain of a long illness is surely worse than a quick death, I would have thought. And now that Arnold is gone, I might get some grandchildren!' Enid beamed, eyes sparkling.

'We should explain, dear, or Monsieur Poirot will think we are quite mad,' said Terence. 'We are happy because, by some miracle, our daughters no longer hate each other. It happened only this morning: a huge transformation.'

'Thank the Lord!' Enid pressed the palms of her hands together. 'Terence found them in the sitting room earlier with their arms around each other. It is my dream come true at last.'

Terence nodded eagerly. 'They were both in tears, Monsieur Poirot, and both apologizing for their role in the horrible feud that has made them enemies for so long. I told Enid: it was as if they had just found each other again after being forcibly kept apart for years. Which is strange, when you come to think of it, because nothing but their own determination to hate one another was preventing them from being friends. I do worry about the boys, though,' he added a moment later, with a glance at his wife.

'I am worried about nothing!' Enid threw up her hands. 'I feel as if I will never, *could* never, fret about anything again. My wish has been granted. I don't even mind too much about grandchildren now—though of course it would be lovely to have at least one from each daughter.'

'But dear, the boys did not look happy,' said Terence.

'If you mean Douglas and Jonathan Laurier, that might be because their father has just been murdered,' I said.

'Do not worry, dear,' said Enid. 'The two silly boys can continue to dislike each other if they wish, but our girls will never be estranged again. The love that was always there between them has proved itself stronger than any petty grudge. That is a blessing that the murder of Arnold has bestowed upon us—unfortunate though it is in its own right, of course. And I predict that the boys, in time, will fall into line. It is always the women who decide these things, Monsieur Poirot. Jonathan and Douglas will see that Maddie and Janet want to be friends now, and they will jolly well fall into line.'

As Enid spoke, I was watching Felix Rawcliffe. He looked distinctly unhappy, hunched over the table and apparently unable to keep his legs still. Was I being fanciful, or was guilt the emotion that consumed him? That, certainly, was my impression.

'How, precisely, did Arnold Laurier's murder end the rift between your daughters?' Poirot asked Terence Surtees.

'Is the explanation not obvious? They were both very upset by it. It impressed upon them a horrible truth: that it is possible to lose a family member with no warning, in the most brutal way,' said Surtees. 'Maddie and Janet both adored Arnold. The loss of him, in combination with their grief and shock, brought them to their senses.'

'They realized what I have always known,' said Enid. 'Love is life and hate is death. I have hated for so long, and felt dead inside, but now I am so full of love, I might burst.'

'Madame, you said something a moment ago that made no sense to me. Why should the death of Arnold Laurier mean that you are more likely to have a grandchild?'

'Without the stresses and strains of their ridiculous feud, why should either of my girls be unable to conceive a child?'

'There is still the sickly Laurier family constitution to consider,' her husband reminded her. 'Arnold did not come from healthy stock. Wealthy, yes—but not hardy.'

'But, dear, look at Douglas and Jonathan. Look, indeed, at Maddie and Janet—none of them is the sickly type at all, and that should not surprise you. If three quarters of the genes passed down are strong-as-an-ox genes, then surely we will have many grandchildren.'

'Where were you on the afternoon of 8 September,

madame? Specifically, between two and three o'clock in the afternoon.'

'8 September?' Enid frowned. 'I don't see how you expect me to remember that far back, but I dare say I was in the kitchen.'

'He is talking about the day Stanley Niven was murdered,' said her husband. 'You were indeed in the kitchen, dear.'

'How do you know that, Monsieur Surtees?' said Poirot. 'Were you also in the kitchen between two and three?'

'No. I was in the drawing room all afternoon that day. So was Felix—weren't you, Felix? We played chess, then read our books.'

'Is that true, Monsieur Rawcliffe?' said Poirot.

'I . . . I . . .' the curate stammered. 'I'm sorry, what did you ask me?'

Poirot repeated the question.

'Yes, this is right. Everyone else was at the hospital. Terence and I were alone together in the drawing room.'

'Neither of you is able, therefore, to confirm the where-abouts of Madame Surtees during that hour.'

Enid laughed. 'I have told you, Monsieur Poirot, that I was in the kitchen, here at Frelly. It is where I spend every day of my life. Where else would I have been?'

'What about Arnold Laurier?' I asked. 'Where was he that day between two and three?'

'Sick in bed, as I recall,' said Terence Surtees.

'Did any of you see him, or did you merely assume he was in his bedroom?' asked Poirot.

After a short silence, Terence Surtees said, 'We did not

see him with our very own eyes, if that is what you mean.'

'I didn't see him either,' said Enid. 'No doubt he was up there, though. I heard him snoring now and then. Monsieur Poirot, Arnold would no sooner commit an act of terrible violence than he would . . . well, I don't know what!'

'Monsieur Rawcliffe?' said Poirot. 'Do you remember if you saw Arnold Laurier between two and three o'clock on the afternoon of 8 September?'

The curate, agitated, shook his head, then said, 'But . . . I do not remember anything very much from that afternoon. Not really very much at all.'

Poirot thanked them all and dismissed them. They left the room, the Surteeses trotting ahead and Rawcliffe trailing behind them as if weighted down by a thousand invisible burdens. Though I could think of no motive whatsoever that this young curate might have had for killing anybody, his bizarre comportment caused me to wonder if one of the burdens on his conscience might be the murder of Stanley Niven, and if another might be the murder of Arnold Laurier.

CHAPTER 29

Motives and Alibis

'Do you plan to ask Mother where she was on 8 September?' I said to Poirot fifteen minutes later as he and I strolled along the cliff top. The wind had died down, and Poirot had raised only the mildest objection to my idea that we should venture outside.

'*Non*. She was not in Norfolk on 8 September.'

'How do you know?'

'Catchpool, your mother did not murder Stanley Niven. Or Arnold Laurier.'

I repeated my question.

'Because I now know who committed both crimes. At least . . . I am almost certain. The information from Sergeant Wight will confirm it.'

'Let us hope so,' I said. 'It sounds as if you do not need any further contribution from me, but I have been thinking . . .'

'I am always interested in your opinions, Catchpool.'

'Very well then. I believe that the murderer of Arnold

Laurier must be someone who thinks he or she has provided an unshakeable alibi for Stanley Niven's murder. Why go to the trouble of bringing the unnecessary paper flowers, water and vase to the study unless they want us to think it must be the same killer? And why should they need us to think that way, unless they have already been eliminated from suspicion of Niven's murder on account of what seems to be a cast iron alibi? Oh.' I cursed under my breath. 'How stupid of me. If the killer of Arnold Laurier is someone quite different—*not* Niven's killer—then that would be another reason.'

Poirot smiled in the direction of the sea and said nothing.

'Shall I tell you what I would do if I did not have your expert guidance?' I said.

'Please.'

'I would calculate that I could probably solve Laurier's murder far more easily if I separated it from Niven's and considered it as a . . . well, as a quite distinct puzzle. No one, as far as we know, had a reason to want Niven dead, whereas almost everyone had a motive for murdering Arnold Laurier.'

'Do you think so? Tell me more, *mon ami.*'

'Well, his wife, for a start. She might want to spare him the horror of a painful and drawn-out death from his illness. Dr Osgood is in love with Vivienne Laurier according to almost everybody, including his own fiancée. The sooner Arnold dies, the sooner his widow is free and available to marry someone else. Now, Nurse Olga Woodruff thinks Vivienne will send Osgood away with a flea in his ear. She might want that to happen sooner rather than later, so that he can attend properly to loving and marrying her.'

'Nurse Bee Haskins?' said Poirot. 'Nurse Zillah Hunt?'

I frowned. 'Neither of them had a reason to want Arnold Laurier dead, as far as I know.'

He nodded. 'Continue. What about the curate, Monsieur Rawcliffe? He looked most uncomfortable, did he not?'

'We need to get to the bottom of whatever he and Vivienne Laurier were discussing when they didn't know I could hear them. Osgood subtly hinted to me that Rawcliffe is in love with Vivienne Laurier. If that is true, then his and Osgood's motives are one and the same: get the ailing husband out of the way, and marry the widow.'

'And what of Maddie, Douglas, Janet and Jonathan Laurier?' Poirot asked. 'Does each of them also have a motive for the murder of Arnold Laurier?'

'Janet Laurier has an odd one,' I told him. 'She secretly wants—wanted—Arnold to die at Frellingsloe House so that Jonathan would view the place as tarnished and not waste time on the fool's errand of trying to save its life. All four of them—both sons, both wives—stand to gain financially when Douglas and Jonathan each get their half of the family money. Maddie also has the motive of wanting the best for Vivienne, of whom she is very fond. She told me with great conviction that only once Arnold had died could Vivienne begin to recover and find happiness again. Oh—and Jonathan Laurier has an altruistic motive too, in addition to the financial incentive.'

'Which is what?' Poirot asked.

'He believed Arnold would die a happy man if *you* would only promise to save Frellingsloe House from destruction by the forces of natural erosion. I'm afraid I made it plain to him that you were unwilling to lie. When you were taken off to the hospital, Jonathan perhaps saw his chance to spare his father the pain of being told there was nothing you could do to save his beloved Frelly.'

'What about Terence and Enid Surtees?' said Poirot.

'Easy and obvious: they loathed Arnold Laurier, and bitterly resented their status as servants in his household. Enid also blames Arnold's poor genetic legacy for her lack of grandchildren, by the sound of it. Terence blamed him for lobbying in favour of the Jonathan–Janet union and probably most of all for Enid's miserable decline.'

'Note, also, that Monsieur *et* Madame Surtees seem overjoyed today. Observing who is made happier by a murder is an instructive exercise.'

'Quite,' I agreed. 'Though I suppose neither Terence nor Enid could have foreseen that killing Arnold Laurier would lead to the instant healing of the rift between their daughters.'

'Parents know their children,' said Poirot. 'Or at least, it is sometimes true that they do.'

'Well, if you are right, then the Surteeses had a motive so sizeable, it must have had trouble fitting into the county of Norfolk.'

Poirot smiled. 'You have proven your point most adequately, Catchpool. Everybody at Frellingsloe House does indeed have a motive for killing Arnold Laurier, though

some are thinner and less likely than others, *évidemment.*
Let us return to the house and find Monsieur Rawcliffe.
Whether or not he is guilty of murder, I am hopeful that
we can persuade him to tell us whatever it is that is making
him so afraid.'

CHAPTER 30

A Broken Glass Lie
and the Pursuit of Truth

There was no need to seek out Felix Rawcliffe. He was hovering when we arrived back at the house and pounced on us as soon as we entered the hall, pale and perspiring as before, and clutching a yellow envelope.

'This came for you, Inspector Catchpool,' said the curate.

A *telegram*, I thought, and my heart picked up pace.

It was, as I expected, from Sergeant James Wight of Scotland Yard.

Inspector Catchpool,

The alibis of all Niven family members are good. They are all in the clear. I have been able to turn up no link of any sort between any of the people on your list and the family of Stanley Niven. One point of interest: somebody on the list is not who they claim to be. I trust you would prefer me to impart the particulars in person or over the telephone, since written documents can easily fall into the wrong hands.

Yours sincerely,

James Wight (Sergeant).

I handed the telegram to Poirot. His eyebrows shot up as he read it, and his moustaches twitched. At that moment, Inspector Mackle appeared in the hall with two other policemen in uniform by his side and two men in suits following behind them, carrying something large and black. I guessed that this was the container in which Arnold Laurier's body would eventually be placed in order to transport it elsewhere.

Felix Rawcliffe gasped at the sight of this black receptacle. He gripped my arm. 'There is something I must tell you,' he said. 'I have stayed silent for too long.'

A few minutes later, he, Poirot and I were alone in the dining room with the door closed. It was as cold in here as it was outside, thanks to the smashed window.

'Could we not go somewhere warmer?' I said, shivering.

'In my estimation we are still outside,' said Poirot. 'Luckily we have not yet divested ourselves of our coats. Monsieur Rawcliffe, do you wish to fetch a coat, hat and gloves?'

The curate's answer was the most peculiar I have ever heard: 'I am afraid to go anywhere alone,' he said.

I expected Poirot to be as interested as I was in this remark, but he acted as if he had not heard it. He walked over to the smashed window. 'What strikes you about this pile of glass fragments, Catchpool? Come and look at it closely, please.'

'It looks rather like a Christmas decoration,' I said. 'Tiny bits of glass sparkling in sunlight, like beads of frost.'

'Yes, yes, very poetic,' Poirot said impatiently. 'Look again. What is there that should not be?'

'Oh, you mean the little stones? I see what you're driving at. The window was smashed to make it look as if an intruder broke in and killed Arnold Laurier. It was smashed from the *inside*, causing some chips of glass to land in the garden where there are stones. Laurier's murderer must have judged that too much glass landed outside and so shovelled some back in, bringing in a few stones in too.'

'*Précisément*. And there are more than a few stones here—far too many to be brought in accidentally on the soles of an intruder's shoes, for instance. It is the presence and number of these little stones that prove the window was broken from the inside and that, therefore, there was no intruder. Monsieur Laurier was killed by someone under this roof. Was it you, Monsieur Rawcliffe? Did you kill Arnold Laurier and then attempt to build a lie from broken glass in the middle of the night?'

'No. I swear to you, it was not me. I am ready to tell you everything I know, but . . . I am afraid I will be the killer's next victim if I do.'

That, then, explained his reluctance to go anywhere alone.

Poirot settled himself in a chair. 'As I have said to many frightened people over the years, monsieur: you will be safer if you speak up than if you do not. Tell us, please, whatever it is that you can no longer keep to yourself.'

'Dr Robert Osgood is in love with Vivienne Laurier,' said Rawcliffe. 'I believe it is he who killed Arnold. He has been . . . well, almost murderously impatient, waiting for Arnold to die naturally. Time after time I have begged Vivienne to make Dr Osgood leave Frelly. I have even wondered if she might have romantic feelings for him, though she assured me she does not. She said she wanted him close at hand so that he could tend to Arnold more easily.'

At this point, I interrupted and told the curate about the conversation I had overheard.

'Yes, Vivienne and I were discussing the problem then,' he said.

'Who was the stranger you were encouraging her to consider?' I asked.

'Why, poor Olga Woodruff, of course. I suppose she is not quite a stranger, but Vivienne cannot have met her more than once or twice, on the rare occasions that Dr Osgood has brought her here. If Vivienne had told Dr Osgood months ago, clearly and plainly, that she did not love him and would never marry him, he would have left Frellingsloe House immediately, one has to hope, and focused his amorous attention on his fiancée.'

'The Romeo and Rosaline conversation,' said Poirot. 'It was about this same subject?'

Rawcliffe nodded. 'Dr Osgood was at pains to convince me that the destruction of his bond with poor Olga would be no great loss. They were, he argued, more a case of

Romeo and Rosaline than Romeo and Juliet. I don't know why he was so sure that Vivienne would marry him once Arnold was gone. According to her, she had never encouraged him in that expectation. And he is about to find out how wrong he has been.'

'Dr Osgood seems to think you too are in love with Vivienne Laurier,' I said.

'Me?' Rawcliffe looked astonished. 'Goodness, what a preposterous notion. I am deeply fond of her, but not in that way. She is old enough to be my mother. That is how I have always thought of her, in fact: as a maternal figure in my life. I lost my own dear mother some years ago, God rest her soul.'

I remembered that he had mentioned his late mother before, when Poirot and I first met him, at the railway station.

'I might as well tell you the rest of the truth,' said Rawcliffe.

We waited, watching a pinkness creep in from the edges of his face and slowly spread to the centre. Finally, he said, 'If for any reason the marriage plans of Dr Osgood and Olga do not come to fruition, I intend to propose to her myself. No one knows this. You are the first two people I have told.'

'You know Olga Woodruff better than Vivienne Laurier does, then?' I said.

Rawcliffe shook his head. 'I, too, have only met her once or twice. William Shakespeare understood that it only takes a glimpse, sometimes . . .' He broke off, then said, 'What

I cannot understand is why it has not occurred to her that her name would be Olga Osgood, which sounds clumsy and is difficult to say. Olga Rawcliffe sounds perfect.'

'Apart from his romantic attachment to Vivienne Laurier, do you have any other reason to believe Dr Osgood would murder Arnold Laurier, or evidence that he did so?' said Poirot.

'Well, no, but—'

'Do you believe that the doctor also killed Stanley Niven?'

Rawcliffe shook his head. 'No. Why should he?'

'Good question, monsieur, good question. Why should anyone at Frelly wish to kill Stanley Niven? He was a complete stranger to them all. This, we have been told from the start. I thought it could not be true, but I was mistaken. Today we have learned from a trusted associate of Catchpool's that there is no connection of any kind between any member of this household and the Niven family. And with that piece removed from the picture, and given what else Sergeant Wight said in his telegram, I now suspect a new connection. One that does not involve Stanley Niven or any of his relatives. Apart from the fact that he got murdered by the same person who killed Arnold Laurier, Monsieur Niven has nothing to do with anything.'

'But . . . that makes precious little sense,' said Rawcliffe. I was thinking the very same thing.

'Monsieur Rawcliffe, you will please do Poirot a favour. Find Vivienne Laurier and bring her to the library. It is much too cold to stay in this room. Go, *immédiatement*.'

'I have a task for you too, Catchpool,' Poirot said once

we were alone. 'Do not fear—it is not the decoration of yet another tree. There is something far more important that I need you to do for me. It involves going somewhere—to a very specific destination—and lying in wait for somebody.'

'Lying in wait?'

'Yes. When the person appears, when they cross your path, you will not make it obvious that you have been waiting for them. Rather, you will pretend simply to have been standing there, or passing by, perhaps looking at your pocket watch or rubbing your eye.'

'Rubbing my eye? Why would I do that? Poirot, I don't want to set off on some hare-brained long-distance mission. I would then, I suppose, have to come back here, and . . . Have you forgotten that we are supposed to be leaving for London tomorrow? Christmas at Whitehaven Mansions, remember?'

'Do not cavil, Catchpool. Place all of your trust in your friend Hercule. As for the dust in the eye, I have suffered many times in my life from this temporary affliction. It causes great discomfort. But choose something else if you wish—I am happy to leave the irrelevant details of the operation to you. The objective is to look as if you have not contrived to meet your quarry. Your manner must be casual and carefree, *comprends-tu*? Then, once you have looked pleasantly surprised by this chance encounter and once greetings have been exchanged, you are to say these exact words: "I have been meaning to ask you for a while if you would be willing to tell me about the terrible accident." Repeat it, please.'

Had he lost all wit and reason?

'Poirot, I will feel like a fool. May I at least know why I will be asking, and what in heaven's name I am talking about?'

'I am afraid not.'

'Then you will have to do it yourself.'

'Not possible, *mon ami*. I will soon be busy with Vivienne Laurier, and it is better that Hercule Poirot stays still, exerting only the little grey cells and not the rest of the body. Now, repeat your line, please. You must know it by heart.'

I sighed. 'Say it again, then.'

He did so.

I parroted it back to him: 'I have been meaning to ask you for a while if you would be willing to tell me about the terrible accident.'

'Again!'

He made me say it five times. 'Excellent. Now it is etched on your memory.'

'Probably forever,' I muttered. I felt travel-weary already and I had not yet moved an inch.

'One of two things will happen when you say those words,' said Poirot. 'Your quarry will either start to tell you about a terrible accident, or else they will say, "What terrible accident?" If that is their response, you are to say, "The one that happened many years ago. You know which accident I mean." Then you will observe whether they know or do not know what you are talking about. If they appear to be as baffled as you are now, here is what you will say next: "I am sorry. I did not mean to say 'accident'. I meant to say 'crime'. Tell me about the terrible crime that happened many years ago.'"

A shiver ran all the way from the top of my neck to the bottom of my spine. I knew there was little point in asking 'What terrible crime?'

'To whom would you have me say all this?' I said instead. 'And where are you sending me to lie in wait for them, whoever they are?'

He gave me two clear answers: first the person, then the location. It was the very last name I expected to hear, and as for the place where I was to lie in wait . . . I do not mind admitting that I was so surprised, my eyes nearly popped out of my head.

CHAPTER 31

Courtyards Revisited

I was not present for Poirot's conversation with Vivienne Laurier in the library, so I can only recreate the scene from the fulsome report he gave me several days later.

He began with a simple question: 'Who killed Stanley Niven, madame?'

'I . . . Why are you asking me this?' Vivienne said sharply. Her bearing, manner and appearance had not noticeably changed since her husband's murder, Poirot observed. She seemed every inch the grieving widow, with an invisible but tangible pall of despair draped about her person—exactly as she had been on the day we arrived in her home.

'I have not the slightest idea,' she said.

'That is a lie, is it not? I believe you know who killed Monsieur Niven, and why. As soon as you were informed of the murder, you feared—and not without good reason— that the same person would murder your husband. Now that your worst fear has come to pass,' Poirot smiled at her and said as gently as he could, 'will you not tell me the truth, madame?'

'I have. I do not know who killed Arnold, or Mr Niven.'

'So you wish to protect the guilty party, even now. Tell me, then, instead, about the argument that took place in the hospital room reserved for your husband on Ward 6 of St Walstan's Hospital on 8 September.'

'The . . . the argument?'

'About the courtyard.'

'Why?' she said. 'How can a silly argument possibly matter now?'

'Please.'

She sat motionless for a few seconds, then said, 'Jonathan and Janet said that it was quite unacceptable for Arnold's room to be overlooked by the windows of several other patients,' said Vivienne. 'When one is in a hospital room, one is not always in a presentable state and one is rarely fully dressed. Plus, the lack of privacy goes in both directions. That was their opinion. Jonathan told the nurse— Zillah, her name was—that his father would feel as awkward and embarrassed about his own ability to observe other patients in their rooms as he would be uncomfortable about their being able to spy on him in his.'

'Do you agree?' Poirot asked her. 'Is that how your husband would have felt about the matter?'

'I don't know.'

'You did not ask him, when you returned from the hospital?'

'No, I did not. He was very sick that day. I was in a

state of shock, after discovering that a brutal murder had happened in the next room to the one I was standing in.'

'And later?' said Poirot. 'The following week, or month . . . you did not raise the question with him?'

'Douglas had asked him by then, and Arnold had said he was happy to end up wherever they chose to put him, as long as it was at St Walstan's where he could set about solving Stanley Niven's murder.'

'How would you feel if you were the patient?' Poirot asked her. 'About the courtyard?'

'I . . . I don't know.' Vivienne looked utterly perplexed. 'I have not given it any thought.'

'I see. And Douglas and Maddie—did they express an opinion, when you were in the room with the courtyard view that afternoon, 8 September?'

Vivienne nodded. 'They heaped on the ridicule as they always do when Jonathan and Janet are in the firing line. They said it didn't matter a jot what sort of medical care Arnold received, or whether he was well-fed or kept out of pain as much as possible; none of that mattered in the least, as long as his room did not overlook a courtyard. The main thing was not his treatment or the condition of his health—the view was all that mattered. Eventually they ran out of sarcasm and said that for patients to be able to see each other in a hospital was not necessarily a bad thing. Maddie said they might welcome a little companionship and commiseration. And Douglas pointed out that the rooms had curtains, so one could always close one's curtains for moments of privacy.'

'This is, in my estimation, a powerful point,' said Poirot. 'Though of course one cannot then have privacy and daylight at the same time. Which would you choose, madame?'

Vivienne looked at him as if at a madman. 'I have said already: I do not know. Why does it matter what I think?'

'It matters only because I wish to catch and bring to justice your husband's killer.' He smiled. 'Thank you. You have been most helpful while trying as hard as you can to be a hindrance. That will be all for now. You may leave. And madame? I am very sorry about what happened to Monsieur Arnold. You must be heartbroken.'

'Thank you,' she said. 'And no, I am not. My heart died a long time before Arnold did. There was nothing left to break.'

CHAPTER 32

Lying in Wait

I need not have worried about travelling halfway across the country. The location to which Poirot had dispatched me was a recess in the wall next to the door of Frellingsloe House's drawing room. He had laughed like a drunkard at the look of shock that appeared on my face when he told me. 'When I said that the task involved going somewhere, Catchpool, your error was to assume I meant somewhere afar way. I meant only that you would need to leave this room we are in.'

And now here I was, lying in wait and stubbornly determined not to rub either of my eyes, no matter what else came to pass.

The trouble with secretly lying in wait is that no one knows that is what you are doing, so the chance of being left alone is small. I was accosted by four people, one after another, as I stood in that recess like a tall, useless houseplant that had escaped from its pot. The first was Inspector Mackle, who gave me the benefit of his latest theory about that elusive criminal mastermind, Clarence Niven. I nodded along politely, then, when he had finished, said, 'I am sure you are right.' That sent him on his way with a smile on his face.

Next Janet Laurier appeared. Her face was streaked with tears. Seeing me loitering, she ran towards me as if intent on knocking me over. 'Inspector Catchpool,' she said. 'It is all too dreadful. I cannot bear it. Arnold is dead and Jonathan is bereft. I don't think I can make him happy, not after this. None of us will ever be happy again!'

'You have all had a horrible shock,' I said. 'The next few weeks are likely to be verging on unbearable, but you will bear them, and you will find, in time, that life starts to seem worth living again. Jonathan will survive. You all will.'

'I believe my mother has told you that Maddie and I are on friendly terms once more?'

'Yes. I was glad to hear it.'

'I am afraid I might ruin it and make us enemies again. It was all my fault in the first place, the hostility between us. Maddie only ever wanted us to love each other, but I wanted—I *needed*—to defeat her, somehow. I was spiteful and greedy and hypocritical and . . . I must still be all those things, don't you think?'

'Well, I—'

'Once the shock of Arnold's murder wears off, I am likely to forget about the importance of love and find myself consumed by pettiness once again. But . . . I do not want to! I love my sister. What can I do, Inspector? Even Jonathan and Douglas are willing to go along with our new peace agreement. Douglas is calling it "*L'Entente Cordiale*".'

'It sounds like a jolly good arrangement,' I said, looking past her along the corridor for my quarry, who had yet to appear. 'I would make sure not to ruin it if I were you.' I must have sounded impatient and insensitive, but I needed to get rid of her as soon as I could.

I breathed a sigh of relief when she finally gave up on me as a potential source of comfort and left me alone—but I was far from being in the clear. Maddie Laurier came hurtling towards me a few moments later, her eyes red and puffy from weeping. 'Edward!' she cried, throwing her arms around me and squeezing me in a manner that I found thoroughly objectionable. 'I am so glad you and Monsieur Poirot are here. Please, *please*, lead us all out of this utter nightmare. You might not have been able to prevent Arnold's murder, but you can surely solve it. Can you? Do say that you can! Inspector Mackle is about as much use as a square wheel. If he mentions the name of Clarence Niven one more time . . . I must say, it is a huge consolation to me to think of how happy Arnold must be that Janet and I are friends again. I know he is no longer with us in the way that he was, but I feel his presence so strongly. He would never leave his home and family; he loved us all too much. Most people, most souls, would allow themselves to be defeated by death—murder especially—but not Arnold! He is still here, Edward. You do not believe me, I can see that, but it is true.'

I willed her to stop talking and go away. She had never

before reminded me of her mother, but now that Enid was happy and more loquacious, I detected a distinct similarity of manner between the two women.

Eventually Maddie took her ecstatic delusions elsewhere and I groaned in gratitude. Then I heard more footsteps and prepared to look casual and carefree in accordance with Poirot's instructions; this might be my quarry approaching. My heart turned to lead in my chest when I saw Mother striding towards me. 'Edward! There you are!'

I cannot relate what passed between us with any degree of accuracy, so I shall omit a detailed recreation of this scene from my account of the Norfolk murders; it is scarcely relevant. All I can tell you is that, within seconds of Mother staring to speak, I was so angry that I could see only a red blur and all the sounds I heard were reduced to a buzzing noise in my ears, as if someone were drilling into my brain. The distasteful encounter ended with me telling Mother the truth for once in my life and her sobbing and running away. I ought to have been triumphant, but instead I felt (with no justification at all, I might add) as if someone—Mother, come to think of it—had tried to kill me.

Despite this, I remained in place in the wall recess, and finally I was rewarded: I spotted my quarry walking in my direction, and I prepared to play my part in what would doubtless turn out to be a very odd scene indeed.

CHAPTER 33

Mission Accomplished

'Mission successfully accomplished,' I told Poirot when I found him half an hour later on the second-floor landing outside our bedrooms. 'Though Mother nearly ruined everything, as she so often does. She found me lurking and assumed I had nothing important to do and was available to be hectored.'

'Did she hector?' Poirot asked.

I nodded. 'She started on at me about Christmas again—how thrilling it was that we would be able to spend the day together for once, and had I thought of who I was going to nominate for the Morality Game as the worst person ever? "And what about Poirot? Who will he nominate?" she wanted to know, as if there was nothing to think about but fun and games. She said your name quite cheerily, as if she had not poisoned you a mere three days ago. Never mind the fact that anyone in this house on Christmas Day is unlikely to play any games at all. It was as if Mother had forgotten that a murder was committed here last night.

I am afraid I lost the whole of my temper. I cannot remember raising my voice and bellowing at her ever before, but that is what I did.'

'Do you feel better for having done so?' Poirot asked.

'No. Worse. But I am pleased, at least, to have been honest with her, finally. I told her that if by some rotten luck I *did* end up spending Christmas under this roof with her, that would be a side-effect and not something I had chosen on purpose. She started to cry. I have not seen her cry for years. I probably should have left it at that, but I did not.'

'Ah,' said Poirot enigmatically.

'I explained to her my "Now that it's there" theory of Christmas tree decoration and told her that the same applied to this situation. *Now that I am here*—to help you solve two murders, Poirot, and for no other reason—I might have to end up enduring Christmas Day in Mother's company, but only because I would have no alternative, because I would find myself in this house and there would, sadly, be no other choice available to me.'

My friend watched me carefully. He said nothing.

'Oh, damn it all to hell,' I cried. 'I shall have to apologize to her for being unnecessarily cruel, shan't I? Even though she is a poisoner. Still, I should not have said those things. Though they are all quite true.' I felt embarrassed and wished I had not told Poirot about any of it. 'Where have you been, anyway?' I asked him. 'I looked for you in the library, but you had vanished.'

'Moved, *mon ami*, not vanished. I do move occasionally,

you know—sometimes even when not compelled to do so by you.'

I smiled. 'When I couldn't find you, I telephoned Sergeant Wight. As a result, I now know who at Frellingsloe House is claiming to be someone they are not. It is—'

'Silence!' said Poirot. 'Allow me, instead, to tell you. But wait—not here on the landing.' He opened his bedroom door and went in, beckoning for me to follow. Once we were inside, he closed the door, then tested that it was securely shut.

Lowering his voice, he proceeded to explain to me the very same astonishing circumstances that I had been on the point of relaying to him.

'Sergeant Wight did not mention that you had spoken to him already,' I said, peeved to have been deprived of the chance to deliver the news.

'I have spoken to nobody at Scotland Yard.' Poirot sounded offended. 'I discovered the correct answer thanks to my own observations. Now, allow me to tell you what was the reaction to the little speech I made you commit to memory—the terrible accident of many years ago, or perhaps the terrible crime.'

'You have worked that out too? Go on, then—impress me again.'

'Puzzlement was the response, *n'est-ce pas*? A complete and utter lack of comprehension. "What accident? What crime? I do not know what you are talking about!" Am I right?'

'Exactly that.'

'*Bon.*'

'Poirot, please tell me that this means you know who the murderer is. And if you do, please can you pass on the relevant information to Inspector Mackle without delay, so that we can go back to London? I am not asking you to tell me—that can come later; Lord knows I have waited to be enlightened many times before—but please, at the very least, tell Mackle so that we can pack our cases and get out of here today.'

'I shall tell everybody at the same time,' he said. 'It is the most efficient way, and the way I prefer to do it. And, Catchpool, you of all people . . . How is it that you need me to give you the answer? As soon as you had spoken to Sergeant Wight on the telephone, you knew all the same facts that I know. You are in the happy position of being able to solve the puzzle yourself.'

I groaned.

'You can, *mon ami*. All the pieces are now clearly revealed. You need only assemble them in the correct order. Put the little grey cells of Edward Catchpool to work! Though not before you have assembled everybody so that I can speak to them all together—and not only those who live in this house, please. Also Nurses Olga Woodruff, Bee Haskins and Zillah Hunt, and Mademoiselle Verity Hunt, the owner of Duluth Cottage. Not Dr Wall—there is no need for him to be present. Inspector Mackle and his men will want to be there, naturally.'

'Then . . . you are ready?' I said.

'So ready that I have decided to cut off the corner.'

'The corner of what. Oh, I see what you mean.'

'*Oui*. I thought a little while ago that I would speak once more to Zillah Hunt. Then I realized it was unnecessary. I wished only to ask her what happened in that room on 8 September.'

'Arnold Laurier's room? When Nurse Zillah was in there with the five Lauriers?'

Poirot nodded. 'I asked Vivienne Laurier the same question. The account she gave me confirmed all of my suspicions. I do not require further confirmation from Zillah Hunt. I am sure even you could tell me what was said in that room, Catchpool, though you were not there.' He chuckled. 'Entertain your friend Poirot. Imagine that you were there. Describe the scene. Act for me the little play.'

'Poirot, there is no possible way I could—'

'Do not prevaricate, Catchpool.'

Had he always been quite so demanding? Was it likely he would get worse as he got older?

Wanting it over and done with, I gritted my teeth and invented an argument between Douglas and Maddie on one side and Jonathan and Janet on the other, about the merits and drawbacks of a hospital room with a courtyard view. I made every good argument I could think of on both sides.

When I had finished, Poirot said, 'Which side do you imagine Vivienne Laurier was on?'

I considered the question. 'Douglas and Maddie's.'

'Indeed? I am intrigued. Tell me why.'

'Arnold would have liked to see other people, and she

307

would have known that,' I guessed aloud. 'Also, she is fonder of Maddie and Douglas than she is of Jonathan and Janet. Though come to think of it, I only know that because Janet told me. And Maddie said Janet believes Vivienne prefers her and Douglas because they are both eldest siblings and so is she.'

'Janet might be wrong,' said Poirot. 'Let us assume you are right, though: so Vivienne took Maddie and Douglas's side in this argument, you believe?'

'Well, not in public, no. She would have said nothing, apart from maybe begging them all not to fight. She said nothing at dinner, remember, on our first night at Frelly? She sat in agonized silence until she could stand the verbal savaging no longer, and then fled.'

'Very good.' Poirot clapped his hands together. 'You have just proved it, Catchpool: you are more than capable of identifying our elusive murderer all by yourself.'

'Murderer? Only one? Then—'

'Yes, Catchpool: the same person killed both Stanley Niven and Arnold Laurier. And I will offer you a clue to help you on your way: apply your clever "Now that it's there" theory not only to Christmas decorations on trees and your relationship with your mother, but also to this case. If you do that, you will reach the correct conclusion. Trust Poirot!'

CHAPTER 34

Human Objects

Two hours later we were gathered in the library of Frellingsloe House, Poirot having decided once again that he wanted everyone seated around the table. I was sitting with Douglas Laurier on my left and Dr Osgood on my right. To be at the table with the others felt like an accurate representation of my status in relation to the two murders; despite having thought furiously for some time, I had failed to come up with a single viable theory. I was as unenlightened as everyone else here—with the obvious exceptions of Poirot and the murderer.

Poirot had positioned himself by the window, beside the Christmas tree. He had dressed for the occasion; looking at him, one could be forgiven for thinking he was about to make his debut at the Fortune Theatre. Apart from him and me, the following people were present in the library: Inspector Mackle; Mother; Vivienne, Douglas, Jonathan, Maddie and Janet Laurier; Enid and Terence Surtees; Dr Robert Osgood; Felix Rawcliffe; Nurse Olga Woodruff and Nurse Zillah Hunt.

In the sitting room a short distance along the hall were three more people who were not allowed to be seen by the others until Poirot gave permission: Nurse Bee Haskins and Miss Verity Hunt (owner of Duluth Cottage), and one of Inspector Mackle's men, whose name I had been told but forgotten. This young constable's task, as I understood it, was to supervise his charges until he received orders to bring them into the library to join the rest of us.

'*Mesdames et messieurs*,' said Poirot. 'I have been an investigator of serious crimes for many, many years, and I am sorry to say that the business with which we concern ourselves today—the murders of Stanley Niven and Arnold Laurier—are without doubt the two saddest murders I have encountered in my career so far. Why? For two reasons. The first is that these were two truly happy men. Both had a talent for making the most of each day, each moment; both possessed a contagious sort of contentment that spread to those around them. The world was made a better place by their presence in it.'

Vivienne Laurier nodded for several seconds upon hearing these words—rather violently. Enid Surtees had tears in her eyes. She and her husband, Terence, were murmuring their agreement. Had they forgotten, I wondered, that until as recently as yesterday they had been unable to utter Arnold's name without spewing forth a flood of vitriol?

I was pleased when Poirot reminded them of this: 'Of course, even the best people are often disliked,' he said. 'Enid and Terence Surtees felt a deep resentment towards Arnold Laurier, as they told me this morning. And one of

Mr Niven's customers from the post office took against him when he allowed letters to be posted to her that she did not wish to receive. Nevertheless, *mes amis* . . . happy people who have a talent for making others happy rarely become murder victims, because *no one wants them dead*. Day-to-day annoyances, family grievances—these are a quite usual and unavoidable part of life. Taking umbrage is a world away from risking one's liberty and one's soul to cause the death of another human being. And nobody, let me tell you—no one in this room or anywhere in the world hated Stanley Niven or Arnold Laurier enough to want to murder them.'

'Well, then, perhaps no crime has been committed.' Inspector Mackle sounded relieved. 'If what you are saying is that both men were killed accidentally, Mr Prarrow . . .' He frowned. 'Wait. That is impossible.'

'Indeed,' said Poirot. 'Both Mr Niven and Mr Laurier were quite deliberately killed. Neither death was an accident.'

The inspector looked confused. 'But you just said—'

'Listen carefully, please: both men were murdered on purpose *by someone who did not want them dead in the slightest.*'

'In that case, the killer has a serious problem when it comes to matching up his behaviour with his preferred result,' Douglas Laurier said warily.

'Not at all, monsieur. You see, in both cases, the murders delivered results for the killer that were greatly desired. But in neither instance was that result the death of the victim.'

'Are you saying that on both occasions that he committed murder, the killer wanted *something else*?' Maddie Laurier asked. 'The murders were . . . what? An unwanted byproduct of securing for himself this other outcome he wanted?'

'Exactly so,' said Poirot. 'Neither of the desired outcomes could have been achieved if the two murders had not been committed,' Poirot told him.

'I am not finding this guessing game at all congenial,' Jonathan Laurier said. 'Might I remind you, Monsieur Poirot, that everyone in this room apart from you and perhaps Inspectors Catchpool and Mackle is more concerned with seeing the murderer of my father brought to justice than with admiring your cleverness. If you know who the killer is, tell us and have done with it.'

'You wish to know the killer's name? *Bien sûr*. It is someone who is sitting here with us in this room.' Gasps and whispers filled the air, as Poirot must have known they would. 'I would not even need to say their name. I could point at the relevant person and give you your answer, monsieur. But you would not *understand*—and then you would ask me how I came to this conclusion, and what evidence I have to support it. The discussion would end up taking the same length of time that it will take if I tell it in the proper order. Then the story will make perfect sense to everybody.'

Poirot took a step closer to the Christmas tree. 'This tree was not decorated when I arrived here several days ago. Now, thanks to Catchpool's efforts, it is a work of art. Catchpool, please explain to everybody the most insightful

312

"Now that it's there" principle that you developed while decorating the Christmas trees of Frellingsloe House.'

I opened my mouth, then closed it again. I knew what I needed to say, yet somehow I could not seem to gather the requisite words.

'I can explain it perfectly if you would like me to, Edward,' Maddie Laurier said, and then proceeded to do so. Most of the assembled company looked mystified, though she did an excellent job.

'Thank you, madame.' Poirot smiled at her. 'It is fascinating to me that when Catchpool formulated his theory, he did so in relation to *the placing of objects*. But it can be applied with equal relevance to the placing of *human* objects—to the matter of where various people are at particular times. Allow me to illustrate this with an example . . .'

Jonathan Laurier let out a heavy sigh and folded his arms.

'Catchpool and I came to Frellingsloe House to solve the murder of Stanley Niven,' said Poirot. 'That was our only reason for coming. Then Arnold Laurier was murdered. If it had taken me a day or two longer to solve these murders, then we might still have been here on Christmas Day. We would have been *two human objects who were situated here*, still, on 25 December. "Now that we are here," we would have told ourselves, "we must eat the Christmas luncheon and play the Morality Game—assuming the plan were still to play games, which I am sure it is not, but let us pretend it is for a moment. Catchpool and I would have felt duty-bound to participate in whatever festive activities were taking place, as guests in this house. And we would have done so for the very compelling reason of "Now that we are here, it is our best option", even though we would not have chosen to do so, or to be here, if a free choice had been available to us. Do you see, ladies and gentleman? "Now that I find myself here, in this place, this is what I must do. This is the best choice I can now make, given that I am a human object in this particular position."'

'Well, of all the rude, ungrateful—' Jonathan Laurier spluttered.

'I do not see what you mean at all,' said Janet. 'Nor do I see the relevance of any of it to poor Arnold's murder.'

'Oh, you will, madame,' said Poirot. 'You will. Very simply: Stanley Niven was murdered because someone with no knowledge of him or interest in him at all happened to find themselves in his hospital room.' He said all of this so quickly that I had to replay a slower version of it in my head before I could make sense of it.

'This human object, having placed itself quite deliberately in this inconvenient position, then had a grave dilemma: how to explain to Monsieur Niven what it was doing there. There was no good reason to be there. It could think of no excuse! I do not know precisely what occurred, but I can guess. Monsieur Niven must have said something like, "Hello! Who are you?" And the person who was soon to become his killer would not have been able to produce an acceptable explanation, because none existed. To open the door and walk into a stranger's room? Quite inappropriate.

Shocking, even. When Monsieur Niven did not get an answer, and realized that this stranger seemed both distressed and afraid, he probably called out for assistance: "Nurse, nurse!" Or maybe he said only, "Shall I call a nurse?" At that moment, whatever he said, it impressed upon the dangerous human object who had so outrageously entered his room that Monsieur Niven had to be prevented from calling for help. Of course, the murderer could have said to him, "Please be silent. I need to hide in here until the coast is clear." Would they have risked it, though? Would any of you, if you were a patient in a private hospital, respond to a plea like that by saying, "*Bien sûr*, stranger-who-is-shaking-with-fear, you may wait in my room for as long as you wish"? I myself would not.'

'Nobody would,' said Nurse Olga Woodruff. 'Nor should they.'

'A good-natured man like Monsieur Niven would have called for a nurse as much for the sake of the intruder as for his own sake,' said Poirot. 'He would have thought *they* were in trouble and needed help. The intruder knew this was what he was thinking, and knew with the lightning-fast instinct of panic that he needed to be silenced as a matter of urgency, or else doctors and nurses would soon enter the room and come face to face with the person who had no business being there. This cannot be allowed to happen. The killer reaches for the vase on Monsieur Niven's side-table, throws the flowers and water on the floor, and . . .' Poirot raised his hands above his head, then brought them down quickly, twice.

'Now Monsieur Niven is silent, because he is dead. Now his killer can be reasonably hopeful—though by no means certain—that no member of St Walstan's staff will open the closed door and find them in the room.'

'But why did the murderer go into Stanley Niven's room in the first place if he did not know him?' Terence Surtees asked.

'An excellent question, monsieur. To hide.'

'From whom?' asked Vivienne Laurier. 'From the doctors and nurses?'

'From one of the nurses,' said Poirot.

'This is senseless,' snapped Jonathan Laurier. 'Why go to someone's place of work if you do not wish to be seen by them? Is this killer chap a fool?'

'Until the afternoon of 8 September, the killer did not know that this particular nurse worked at St Walstan's Hospital,' Poirot told him. 'Did not know, even, that she had chosen nursing as her profession.'

'Then . . . Stanley Niven's murder had nothing to do with Stanley Niven himself,' said Maddie. 'If his murderer had chanced to open a different door, if he had slipped into some other patient's room to avoid whoever it was that he didn't want to see . . .'

'Correct,' said Poirot. 'Then another patient would now be dead and Monsieur Niven would still be alive.'

'That is horrible,' said Maddie. 'To be killed for a reason that has no connection to you at all. I would far rather be murdered by someone who hated me with a passion.'

'Really?' said her sister. 'I would not. If one must be

killed, surely one would prefer not to be chosen as a victim on purpose.'

'I would prefer my murder to be about me,' said Maddie.

'For pity's sake,' said Jonathan. 'Stop it, both of you.'

'Poor Mr Niven,' Zillah Hunt said. 'He was such a lovely man. I cannot bear it.' She covered her face with her hands.

'Mademoiselle!' Poirot hurried over to her. 'Remain in that exact position, please!'

'Please do not manhandle the young lady, Mr Prarrow,' Inspector Mackle objected.

'This is important, inspector. Everybody, please observe the nurse's posture. How would you describe it?'

'She has her head in her hands,' I said.

'Would anybody describe it any differently?' Poirot asked, looking around the room.

Most people shook their heads. Terence Surtees said, 'I would probably say that she has covered her face with her hands.'

'Excellent. Thank you. Please remember this conversation—I shall refer to it later. It is important. Now, back to Stanley Niven's room . . .'

'Monsieur Poirot, I am sorry to interrupt,' said Vivienne Laurier. 'You seem to know who killed Stanley Niven. Do you also know who killed my husband?'

'I do.'

'Then could you tell me that first, please. Waiting is agony.'

'I am in the process of telling you that very thing,' said Poirot. 'There is only one killer. The same person murdered Monsieur Niven and Arnold Laurier.'

Vivienne's eyes widened. 'But . . . I do not understand. Someone wanted to hide from somebody at the hospital and so they ended up killing Mr Niven—I understand that much—but then why would they later kill Arnold too?'

'It does all sound rather far-fetched,' Mother agreed. 'I hate to say it, Monsieur Poirot, but you are being terribly unfair giving us all these little hints and never getting to the nub of it.'

'The more interruptions there are, the longer it will take me to explain.' Poirot began to move slowly around the library as he spoke. 'Let us picture Ward 6 of St Walstan's Hospital on 8 September. It is twenty minutes after two o'clock. Five members of the Laurier family have come to the hospital to inspect the room that has been reserved for Arnold Laurier. They are standing in the corridor. With them is Nurse Zillah Hunt, for it is she who will show them the room, and she has been summoned for this purpose by Dr Osgood. Before they go inside the room, there is some conversation as they stand in the corridor in a small group. Dr Osgood is present also, and close by stands Nurse Olga Woodruff. Am I correct so far? Please, if you were one of those on Ward 6 that afternoon, tell me if I get anything wrong.'

'Accurate so far,' said Douglas Laurier.

'Good,' Poirot said. 'Then Dr Wall and Nurse Bee Haskins, having finished their rounds on the ward, come out of a patient's room and begin to walk in the direction of the exit door. As they progress along the corridor, but before they reach the spot where Zillah Hunt and the

Lauriers are standing, Zillah Hunt opens the door to Arnold Laurier's room and walks in, leaving the door open for Monsieur Laurier's relatives to follow her in. Is my description of events still accurate?'

Several heads nodded.

What happens next is that the Laurier party and Zillah Hunt remove themselves from the corridor. By the time Dr Wall and Bee Haskins pass Arnold Laurier's room, *none of the five Lauriers remain in the corridor.*'

Zillah Hunt was nodding. 'Aunt Bee and Dr Wall were still a short distance away when we went into Mr Laurier's room.'

'Ah, but you did not *all* go into that room,' said Poirot. 'Only four members of the Laurier family followed you into Arnold Laurier's room, mademoiselle. The fifth went instead into Stanley Niven's.'

'No, that's not right—'

'That is enough!' Dr Osgood barked at her. 'Monsieur Poirot did not ask for your opinion. You are a nurse, not a detective. Remember that, and act accordingly.'

Zillah Hunt looked upset. 'You must have made a mistake, Monsieur Poirot. We were all in that room—I swear it on my life.'

'No, not a mistake, mademoiselle. As I say: one person went into Stanley Niven's room. To hide.'

'That is not true, I am afraid,' said Douglas Laurier. 'All five of us went into Pa's room with Nurse Zillah: me, Maddie, my brother and his wife, and Ma. We all know that to be the truth, because we were all there. You, Poirot, were in London at the time, I dare say. Who is more likely to be right about this: the six people who were there on the scene, or the one who was in a different city more than a hundred miles away?'

'Poirot is more likely to be right,' said my Belgian friend with a smile.

'But you are not,' Janet Laurier insisted. 'You are wrong.'

'One person from the Laurier party went into the room of Stanley Niven,' said Poirot in his most matter-of-fact voice.

'To hide?' said Terence Surtees.

'Yes.'

'From whom?' asked Robert Osgood.

'Ah! I was wondering when one of you would ask that question. From Nurse Bee Haskins,' Poirot told him.

CHAPTER 35

The Hiding

'This is insulting and intolerable.' Jonathan Laurier pushed back his chair and stood up. 'You seem to be suggesting, Monsieur Poirot, that Stanley Niven was murdered by one of us: me or my brother, or one of our wives, or my mother.'

'It is more than a suggestion,' said Poirot. 'It is the truth.'

'You are gravely mistaken,' Janet Laurier said. 'We were all in that room together the whole time.'

Poirot nodded. 'My guess is that some of you—three of you—truly believed that all six of you—five Lauriers and Zillah Hunt—were present throughout.' He looked around the table, searching the faces one by one. 'Of the other three, one, it hardly needs to be said, was Stanley Niven's murderer, and the remaining two, I suspect, knew perfectly well that the fifth family member took a little too long to join the rest of the party. Those two have lied ever since, because they are absolutely convinced that their lies are not protecting a killer. It is difficult to believe that someone we love is capable of doing such evil, and much easier to think, "I do not know why they came into the room later than the rest of us, but I am sure there is a good, innocent reason."

'Now, remember that the murderer had entered Monsieur Niven's room in order to hide from Nurse Bee Haskins,' said Poirot. 'Once Monsieur Niven was dead, what happened next? Probably the killer saw Nurse Bee Haskins on the other side of the courtyard, in the room of Professor Burnett. It cannot have occurred to the killer that there would be a new need to hide from Nurse Bee so soon after the first. Quickly, our murderer must have fled from Monsieur Niven's room and slipped into the adjacent room, Arnold Laurier's, of which the door had been left open. The killer closed it behind them once they had entered. This explains why Bee Haskins said she had seen it open while Zillah Hunt insists it was closed throughout. When Bee Haskins first entered Professor Burnett's room on Ward 7 and noticed that an unpleasant scene was unfolding in a room on Ward 6, the door of Arnold Laurier's room was open. Bee Haskins told me she saw clearly only *some* of the Laurier party—those nearest to the window: Jonathan and Janet Laurier. She was aware of people behind them and Nurse Zillah, but could not see them clearly. When the sixth person, someone who should already have been in the room, finally joined the rest of the party and closed the door, it is hardly surprising that Bee Haskins did not notice. Her concern was for her niece, Zillah, who was being subjected to a series of unpleasant tirades.'

'Mr Prarrow, there is something you have not explained,' said Inspector Mackle. 'Why did this killer want to hide from Nurse Bee not merely once but twice?'

'To be seen and recognized by Bee Haskins would have put an end to a pretence—an escape from intolerable pain—that had lasted for decades,' said Poirot. 'The consequences of such a collision with unpalatable reality . . . psychologically, this would have been a prospect worse than their own death for the killer. It would have been as if they and all they held dear were suddenly obliterated.'

'Well, fancy that,' said Mackle.

'Let us replay the scene in our minds,' Poirot said. 'Bee Haskins was walking along the corridor with Dr Wall. The murderer had spotted her, but Nurse Bee had not yet seen or noticed the murderer—yet that was bound to happen in a matter of seconds if swift action was not taken. In the killer's mind, there were two possibilities only: come face to face with Nurse Bee, or hide in the nearest room—'

'Stanley Niven's room,' said Olga Woodruff.

'*Oui, précisément*. Hide in Monsieur Niven's room until Nurse Bee has walked past and, the killer must have hoped with all their heart, left the ward. Then it would be safe to come out into the corridor, briefly, in order to enter the correct room—the one reserved for Monsieur Laurier. In a state of blind panic, the killer would not have had time to consider that their hiding place might contain a patient, alive and awake, who would demand to know what they were doing there, where they had no business being and who was about to call for help. And Nurse Bee might have been passing Stanley Niven's door when that call for help came. It would have seemed highly likely to the murderer that Nurse Bee would be the one to come to the aid of Monsieur Niven, were he to raise his voice and call for assistance.

'I have described already how this problem was dealt with,' Poirot went on. 'A hastily improvised murder. But still, there is a danger: there is Bee Haskins, standing in a room across the courtyard! The killer must immediately leave Monsieur Niven's room and escape again, this time to the room that contains five other people. In that room, it will be much easier to conceal oneself in the crowd, to be a hardly visible figure at the back of a small group. Remember, Bee Haskins saw Zillah Hunt and Jonathan and Janet Laurier standing at the window. Behind them, she observed not specific faces but only a background of "other bodies".'

'Poirot, you seem to be suggesting that the killer of both Pa and Mr Niven is either me, my wife or my mother,' said Douglas Laurier.

'That is so, monsieur.'

'How ridiculous.' Maddie laughed, tried to stop herself, then started again.

'Wait a minute,' said Jonathan. Turning to Janet, he said, 'I think Monsieur Poirot's theory might be possible.'

'No,' she whispered. 'No, Jonathan.'

He looked at Poirot. 'As soon as I walked into that hospital room, I saw that it was quite unsuitable, because of the courtyard. Immediately, I walked over to the window to inspect the layout more closely. And Janet came to the window a second after I did. The nurse joined us no more than a moment later. Then, for some time and with great zeal, she tried to persuade us that the arrangement of rooms in relation to the courtyard was perfectly all right, that Father would enjoy his view, that such rooms were the best and most sought after—all nonsense of course.'

'It was true,' said Zillah Hunt. 'St Walstan's patients with courtyard views consider themselves lucky.'

'Let us not have the argument again, since it is now immaterial,' Jonathan snapped. 'I brought it up only because the three of us—the nurse, Janet and me—were standing by the window facing the courtyard for at least . . . well, seven to ten minutes, I should say, while this discussion was in progress. I assumed that Mother, Douglas and Madeline were in the room too and standing right behind us, but—'

'They were!' Janet burst into tears. 'We were all in the room the whole time. Why are you saying these things, Jonathan?'

'For pity's sake, woman, I am saying it because it must be true! One of them was in Stanley Niven's room, killing him.'

'Unfortunately, your husband is right, madame,' Poirot told Janet.

'I am afraid your theory has a flaw, Monsieur Poirot,' said Mother. 'If the killer wished to hide from Bee Haskins, why on earth would they not simply dash into the room they had come to see, Arnold's room? They had no reason to think Bee Haskins might walk into that room, did they?'

'It is a good question, madame. My suspicion is that the killer believed that would take too long. If they were standing at the back of the party, for instance, then those standing in front of them, closer to the door of Monsieur Laurier's room, might have been blocking their entrance. Remember, all this time, Bee Haskins is walking towards their little group, getting closer. It would have attracted much attention if the murderer had pushed the others out of the way to get into Monsieur Laurier's room quicker, would it not? That would have turned into the . . . how would you say it? The scufflé.'

'Scuffle,' I corrected him. He had said it as if it rhymed with soufflé.

'Yes, the scuffle, exactly. The only way to vanish from sight and from that corridor *immédiatement* was to open the nearest door to where the killer was standing and slip into that room—Stanley Niven's room.'

'That is pure invention on your part, Monsieur Poirot,' said Mother.

'It is deduction, madame.' His voice had a hard edge. 'In due course, we will receive confirmation from the person in question that I am right.'

'I think I know who killed Mr Niven,' said Jonathan quietly. 'If Monsieur Poirot is certain that it was one of our party . . . I might have been looking out of the window at that damned courtyard, but I recall clearly who joined in the argument and who did not. Douglas and Maddie had plenty to say; they started to harangue Janet and me almost immediately.'

'Jonathan, stop,' his wife begged. 'Monsieur Poirot has said that he already knows who the killer is. If he knows, you do not need to tell him.'

'Please do not ask me anything about who spoke when, Monsieur Poirot.' Zillah Hunt's voice shook.

She knew who the murderer was, I realized. So did Janet Laurier. Both had worked it out by a process of elimination, and so had I—or at least, I thought I had. I recalled something that had not stood out as at all significant at the time, something Poirot had told me that I had written in my notes: according to Inspector Mackle's account of events, it was Vivienne Laurier who had opened the door. If that was accurate, then in all likelihood she had been standing closer to the door than any of the others—because she had been to last to enter the room.

'I doubted your abilities,' she said to Poirot now. 'I was wrong to do so. Perhaps, after this long preamble, you might consent to tell us who the murderer is.' Slowly, a sly smile spread across her face. 'Of course, if you are about to say that it was Vivienne Laurier who killed two kind, innocent men—one of them her beloved husband—then we will all laugh at you, I'm afraid.'

'You, madame, are Vivienne Laurier, are you not?'

'I have been Vivienne Laurier,' she said. 'Sometimes. Monsieur Poirot, surely you are intelligent enough to understand that Vivienne Laurier is not a murderer?'

'That depends on one's point of view,' Poirot told her.

'Please enlighten us: what do you think is the name of this murderer who has killed two people?'

'Her name is Iris Haskins,' said Vivienne.

CHAPTER 36

The Second Murder Explained

'Haskins?' said Zillah Hunt. 'That is Aunt Bee's family name.'

'Iris is your aunt's sister,' Poirot told her. 'Older by ten years.'

'But . . . then if all you have said is true, Iris Haskins must be Vivienne Laurier,' said Zillah. 'They must be one and the same person.'

Poirot nodded.

'Oh, no,' said Vivienne. The eerie smile had not left her face, and I could hardly stand to look at it. 'Two very different people.'

'Ma, be quiet, for pity's sake,' said Douglas. Maddie made a peculiar noise. She bunched her hands into fists and pressed them against her mouth.

'This cannot be true,' Dr Osgood murmured.

'I fear that it is,' said Felix Rawcliffe.

'Of course it is not,' said Mother. 'Balderdash from start to finish, I should say!'

'Vivienne Laurier was the only one who did not speak at all,' said Zillah Hunt. 'Not until much later, at any rate. The two younger couples argued back and forth from the moment we walked into the room, and made nasty remarks to each other, but Mrs Laurier was silent at first, or so I thought. I assumed she was sensibly not saying anything because, really, the whole production was so undignified. No one in their right mind would have wanted to join in. And then . . . when I finally turned round, the door was closed and all six of us were in the room where we were supposed to be. I truly believed that what I told Inspector Mackle about us all being together the whole time was true.'

'Yes, you did,' Poirot agreed. 'So, I think, did Monsieur Jonathan and Madame Janet. As for you two,' he said to Douglas and Maddie, 'you both lied. You knew, did you not, that Vivienne Laurier did not immediately join you in that hospital room? You must have left the door open for her and noticed when she entered not straight away but several minutes later, and closed the door behind her.'

'We noticed no such thing,' said Maddie. 'We were looking ahead, not over our shoulders, and busy squabbling with Janet and Jonathan. I assumed Vivienne was behind me, watching us all bicker and silently disapproving as she always did. She never said anything when the four of us fought. We could scream at each other all day long—often did—and Vivienne would not say a word, she was so afraid of seeming to criticize any of us or take sides.'

'Siblings should love and be kind to one another,' said Vivienne.

I realized this was what Poirot had been thinking of when he had asked me to guess who had said what in Arnold Laurier's hospital room on 8 September. I was meant to work out that Vivienne was the only person whose temporary absence would have gone unnoticed; she was in the habit of staying silent during family arguments, therefore hers was the only voice that would not have been missed.

'I hate to spoil the fun, but I was very aware of Ma's presence at every single moment,' said Douglas. 'She entered Pa's room ahead of me, in fact, and was by my side throughout.'

'That is a lie,' said Poirot.

'Vivienne would never hurt Arnold,' said Maddie. 'I refuse to believe it. She was devoted to him. She would rather have died than harm him.'

'Yet harm him she did,' Poirot said. 'For the same reason that she murdered Stanley Niven.'

'I have told you all: Iris Haskins is the murderer,' said Vivienne, looking at Mother as if in hope of support.

'What rot!' Dr Osgood snapped. 'Look here, Poirot, I have been patient so far, but do not insult our intelligence, please. You have just asked us to accept that Stanley Niven was killed only because the murderer wished to hide from Bee Haskins. Since Bee Haskins was not here at Frellingsloe House when Arnold was killed, there would have been no need to hide from her on that occasion. Therefore, the two men cannot have been killed for the same reason.'

'They can and they were,' Poirot told him. 'Catchpool, please explain to the doctor why it must be so.'

'I . . . don't know,' I said. 'Unless . . .' A jolt of realization shot through me.

'Ah! Light dawns! Go on, *mon ami*.'

Convinced I would turn out to be wrong, I began tentatively, 'Now that Arnold Laurier is dead, he cannot be admitted to St Walstan's Hospital in January. His wife would have been expected to visit him in the hospital every day, until he died—expected to by Arnold himself and by the whole family. Maddie, you said so several times: Vivienne would be at Arnold's bedside day and night. Yet how could she risk going anywhere near the place and coming face to face with Bee Haskins, her sister? The game would have been up: Vivienne Laurier would have been revealed as Iris Haskins. That was an intolerable prospect—as was allowing Arnold to be admitted to the hospital and then never visiting him there.'

Vivienne had started to nod slowly.

'She wanted to be by his side until the end, every second that she could,' I went on. 'The thought of Arnold in hospital, wondering why his beloved wife never came to visit—'

'Dear heavens,' said Mother. I saw from her expression that she was now convinced.

'Excellent, Catchpool.' Poirot beamed at me. 'Most excellent indeed. Quite correct.'

Yes, well, I thought to myself, it was lucky I had tumbled to the explanation at the very moment he expected me to announce it to the room; had I failed to, I would have looked like a prize chump and felt extremely embarrassed.

'This theory is as shaky as one of Enid's disgusting blancmanges,' said Douglas. 'If Ma was so desperate to be able to visit Pa at St Walstan's—desperate enough to commit murder—then why did she not kill this Nurse Bee person instead of Pa?'

'Her own sister?' said Poirot. 'A healthy woman who still has many years left to live, whom she has betrayed once already in the most vicious way? *Non, non*. Besides, it is not easy to kill someone without them catching a glimpse of your face—and that, for Vivienne Laurier, would have meant exposure as Iris Haskins.'

'It was easy for Iris to kill Arnold,' said Vivienne. Everyone stared at her. 'He had fallen asleep on his desk. He didn't know anything about it.'

'What was the vicious betrayal?' Zillah Hunt asked. 'Please may I be allowed to know, Monsieur Poirot? My mother and Aunt Bee have told me so very little, and . . . well, I am not a child any more. All I know is that Aunt Bee had a sweetheart who took his own life, and that her sister had loved him too—the same man.'

Poirot said to Inspector Mackle. 'Please go and fetch Mesdemoiselles Verity Hunt and Bee Haskins, inspector.'

'Oh, no, no,' Vivienne said in a sing-song voice, as if talking to an infant. 'Stay where you are, inspector. We do not want to admit those people to our sanctuary.'

'Douglas, make her stop talking like that.' Maddie blinked back tears. 'She sounds like a madwoman. Vivienne, stop it at once. Remember who you are. I am sure we can sort this out. Can we, Douglas?'

Her husband said nothing. I wondered if he would still insist, if asked again, that his mother had been by his side in the room next door while Stanley Niven was getting murdered. He looked as if he might have been asking himself that very question.

'Inspector. Please.' Poirot gestured at Mackle, who stood up and left the room. I inhaled as much air into my lungs as they would hold. Vivienne Laurier was about to come face to face with Bee Haskins, her estranged sister, and I was not looking forward to witnessing the scene. I found myself hoping that Mackle might return full of apologies and bearing the news that Verity Hunt and Bee Haskins had left unexpectedly.

'That is why you were so frightened,' Robert Osgood said to Vivienne. 'Your terror was sincere, but you lied about its cause. You pretended to be afraid the murderer would kill Arnold next, or had meant to kill him in the first place. That never made any sense—because you were lying.'

'Madame Laurier was frightened because she had just met the sister she had never dreamed she would see again—also, she had just murdered a man,' Poirot told the doctor. 'Both events must have been an enormous shock to her system. And she was afraid of what would happen once her husband was brought to the hospital. As Catchpool has said, she knew she would not be able to visit him there, yet how could she fail to visit him? That would have broken his heart. If only she had been willing to confide in him the guilty secret of her past, her true identity . . . But no.

Iris Haskins had been left behind and could never be thought of again. Her existence had to be denied in the past, the present and the future. Only in this way could Vivienne Laurier continue to exist. There was no place even for a conversation about Iris Haskins in the new life and world of Madame Laurier.'

I forced myself to look at her: the murderer at the table. She gave the impression of not listening at all. It was as if she were (and I appreciated the irony of this observation as I made it to myself) in a different room from the rest of us.

'Earlier, I asked you to describe this gesture made by Zillah Hunt.' Poirot covered his face with his hands. '"Burying the head in the hands" was the consensus. And this, I learned, was what Vivienne Laurier did while standing in the ward corridor after she was told that Stanley Niven had been killed. She was so distraught, she *buried her head in her hands*. In other words, she covered her face. She had no way of knowing when Bee Haskins might reappear on Ward 6, and she had to get herself out of the hospital without being seen or recognized. Dr Osgood, you quickly ushered her out of the hospital and brought her back here. Nurse Olga Woodruff, your fiancée, saw the two of you standing by your car outside the hospital. Then, too, Vivienne Laurier had her face hidden in her hands—still hiding.'

Osgood nodded. 'I wondered why she refused to look at me. I thought, "She must not want me to see that she is crying," though that made no sense. I had seen her cry

335

many times since the day I told her Arnold did not have long to live.' He turned to Nurse Woodruff. 'Olga, dearest, I have been a fool—such a colossal fool.'

She reached over and patted his hand. 'Do not worry, Robert.' The relief on his face was quite something.

'Once safely back at Frellingsloe House after the hospital visit, Vivienne Laurier set to work,' said Poirot. 'She begged her husband to die at home instead of moving to the hospital, using her fear of this roaming murderer as her very convenient reason. Monsieur Laurier, however, could not be persuaded. He insisted he must spend his last days at St Walstan's, for where else was there an intriguing, unsolved murder case just waiting to be solved by him? That was when his wife's fear gave way to resignation. By the time she decided that killing him was the only way she could prevent the exposure of her secret, she had lost all hope of any good outcome. As she said herself, her heart had already died.'

'Where does Mr Hurt-His-Head come into it?' I asked.

'Ah, yes, Professor Burnett,' said Poirot. 'Without the help of his extraordinary behaviour, I should not have been able to put together the pieces as soon as I did. He witnessed the murder of Stanley Niven. Then, moments later, he saw the killer—Vivienne Laurier—appear in the room next door. That is why the professor left his room, walked to Ward 6 and stood outside the door of Arnold Laurier's designated room. For all he knew, the other people in the room were in mortal danger. He did not stretch out his arms to Vivienne Laurier in an appeal for her to rescue him. What he meant to do was *point* to Madame Laurier, while saying the words, "To hurt his head. To hurt his head." He was doing his best to identify Stanley Niven's murderer. He then continued to repeat those same words in an agitated manner—days, weeks, months later—whenever he saw Nurse Bee Haskins. Why? Because before Vivienne Laurier lost a large amount of weight, there was a clear facial resemblance between her and her sister Bee.'

'There was,' Dr Osgood agreed. 'How on earth did I not see it until now? But . . . their voices were so different, and their mannerisms . . .'

'Now Madame Laurier's cheeks are hollow,' said Poirot. 'It has changed the shape of her face entirely—the resemblance is no longer obvious. Before, however, it was unmistakable. When I was in the study, surveying the scene of Arnold Laurier's murder, I caught sight of some photographs on the desk. There were several of Vivienne Laurier as she had once looked. I said to myself *tout de suite*, "Of course: she is a close relation of Bee Haskins. How can she not be, with that face?" You did not notice anything amiss, Catchpool, because you had never met Bee Haskins. You saw nothing suspicious in those old photographs—only a rounder-faced Vivienne Laurier.'

Indeed, I thought. In which case, why had Poirot said to me—admittedly some time later—that I had all the elements I needed in order to work out who the murderer was? I did not. Never having met Bee Haskins, I had not been in a position to deduce that it might have been her facial similarity to Vivienne Laurier in her plumper days that had caused Mr Hurt-His-Head to point and shout at her in an accusatory fashion. No doubt Poirot believed I should have been able to tumble to the truth even without that missing piece; still, there was no doubt that he had benefited, in his attempt to solve this puzzle, from a strong visual clue that I had lacked.

'Iris was clever to think of the vase and the paper flowers,' said Vivienne. 'And the water. She made the scene look as much like Mr Niven's murder as possible. Vivienne had an alibi for Stanley Niven's murder, you see, so everyone would assume she had not killed either of the two victims, if she used the same method. Killers tend to have very distinctive methods, I believe, that they use over and over.'

'*You* are Vivienne.' Maddie took hold of her arm and shook it. 'You are talking about yourself as if it's not you. Stop it!'

'How did you put it all together?' I asked Poirot. 'You knew everything *before* we heard from Scotland Yard that there was no trace of Vivienne Laurier having existed before she married Arnold Laurier at the age of 29, even under her supposed maiden name, Vivienne March.'

'Like the March sisters in *Little Women*,' said Vivienne. 'I loved that book.'

'From the start, Madame Laurier stood out to me as being suspicious,' said Poirot. 'Everybody else in this house, everyone I met, presented, as far as I could tell, a coherent picture of themselves—or at least, not a profoundly incoherent one. Vivienne Laurier was the exception. She seemed to be a strange *mélange* of facts that did not fit together.

She has the strong-as-an-ox constitution, *n'est-ce pas*? The good genes that will cause her to live to be a hundred and fifty? Yet also I am told that she had lost her entire family by the time she married Monsieur Laurier, and she married him at the age of 29. And Monsieur Surtees, did you not tell Catchpool that, like you, she was one of five siblings?'

Terence Surtees nodded.

'I heard, also, that Janet Laurier believed her mother-in-law favoured Maddie, her older sister, because she herself was an eldest child.' Poirot looked around the table, observing our reactions. 'The eldest of five siblings,' he said. 'Good strong genes. And yet all those younger siblings, as well as both of her parents, are dead by the time Madame Laurier is 29? How, then, did they die? Surely not from a range of illnesses—not if she comes from a family of such sound and healthy constitutions. In which case, there must have been a terrible accident. Or else a heinous crime was committed and they were all murdered in their beds one night. Those are the only other possibilities, are they not, once we have ruled out the kind of natural causes that afflict those with poor health and weak constitutions? Of course, sometimes even a strong and healthy person catches a virus and dies—but for this to have happened to all six of Vivienne Laurier's parents and siblings? That I could not believe.'

So that was why he had made me lie in wait for Vivienne Laurier earlier, ready to ambush her with those particular questions as soon as she had finished talking to him in the library. And she had looked baffled and been unable to answer, because there had been no accident all those many years ago, and no crime. Her four younger siblings were all still alive and in good health, no doubt. Perhaps one or both of her parents were too. Come to think of it, Vivienne had not told me that all the members of the family into which she was born were dead, only that she had 'lost' them by the time she met and married Arnold Laurier. Now I understood that she had lost them by ceasing to be Iris Haskins; by leaving her past behind.

Questions pressed in on my mind: what was the vicious betrayal that Poirot had mentioned? What was so unbearable that it had required the abandoning of everything she had known and, presumably, loved, and the creation of a new identity?

Inspector Mackle walked into the room. He appeared to be alone, and stood watching the door as if he expected it to do something. A few seconds later, two women entered: one around fifty years of age and the other much older—perhaps closer to seventy. The younger woman had to be Bee Haskins, I thought. Poirot was right: her face was very similar to that of the less haggard Vivienne Laurier that I had seen in the photographs on Arnold's desk. The older woman had white hair in a peculiar arrangement: curled in parts and straight in parts. She was inappropriately dressed for the occasion, in a red, floor-length evening gown and red shoes with heels high enough to make a person dizzy.

'Mr Prarrow, this is Miss Verity Hunt, whose cottage you visited the other day,' said Inspector Mackle. 'She is Nurse Zillah's mother.'

'Well . . .' said Verity Hunt, as if there was a lot more she could add if she so chose.

'And of course, you know Nurse Bee already,' said the inspector.

Nurse Zillah, the child of this woman in the red dress, with the white hair? I doubted it. Bee Haskins and Zillah Hunt had exactly the same mouth and chin as each other. And Verity Hunt looked nothing like either of them. It was funny the way family resemblances worked. Zillah did not resemble Vivienne Laurier, even when Vivienne was more rotund than she was now, yet both she and Vivienne were strikingly similar to Bee Haskins, though in very different ways.

'Bee.' Vivienne rose to her feet. 'What are you doing here?'

'Iris,' said Bee. She started to cry. 'I have missed you so much, in spite of everything.'

'I am a little confused.' Vivienne looked around. 'Who are all these people? Where is Nicholas? Is he coming to visit today?'

'There is no point in this charade, Vivienne,' Dr Osgood said coldly. 'They will hang you no matter what you say. Pretending to be a lunatic will not save you.'

'She is not pretending,' Bee Haskins said.

Jonathan Laurier was staring at his mother. After a few seconds, he seemed able to bear it no longer and tore his eyes away. Janet was looking down at her lap, crying silently. Maddie kept opening and closing her mouth. The curate, Felix Rawcliffe, was breathing loudly, looking from one

341

face to another. Terence and Enid Surtees were holding hands, muttering to one another every now and then. Olga Woodruff's attention was focused solely on the frowning, hunched Dr Osgood.

There was a frozen quality about the scene. Only Douglas Laurier seemed the same as he had been before the truth about his mother had been revealed. He looked as if he was busy thinking; possibly he was trying to formulate a plan of some kind.

Verity Hunt tottered over to Poirot on her absurdly high heels. 'You have revealed all of Iris's secrets to everybody, I believe? Or you are in the process of doing so. In which case, she has no need to pretend any more. Let me give all of you in this room the best advice you will ever hear from anybody,' she said immodestly, looking sternly at each of us in turn. 'Whatever you most wish to keep hidden, steel yourself for the ordeal ahead, and then tell it to the whole world. At once, you will be free—and that freedom is glorious! It is far more worth having than the approval of others.'

'Bee?' said Vivienne. 'Will you stay with me? You have been gone for a very long time.'

'Of course, dear.' Bee Haskins wiped away a tear. 'I will stay with you until the end.'

24 DECEMBER 1931

CHAPTER 37

A Letter in My Pocket

It was late by the time we arrived back in London on Christmas Eve. I had things to attend to at home, so I took my leave of Poirot at the railway station and told him I would see him at eleven the following morning.

When I opened my suitcase, I saw that there were two items in it that I had not put there. One was a white envelope, sealed, with my name written on the front. I recognized the handwriting, or thought I did, from the Christmas presents list that I had found in the crown notebook at Frellingsloe House. If I was correct, then this was Vivienne Laurier's handwriting. I grimaced. How had she managed to . . . ? Before I could finish asking myself the question, the answer became evident. Sitting on top of the envelope was a small, crumpled piece of paper on which were written a few words:

Dear Edward,
    Vivienne wrote this letter to you yesterday. She gave it to Inspector Mackle who brought it last night and asked

me to give it to you. I did not wish to disturb you, so I put it in your suitcase. Happy Christmas, Darling. I might not be perfect, but I do my best, and I do adore you, you know. I could not be prouder of you than I am. Your father is proud of you too.

All my love, Mother.

I groaned, firmly dismissed the idea that I should probably offer to spend next Christmas with her, and opened Vivienne Laurier's letter. It was dated 23 December 1931: yesterday. I read it once, then again, then a third time. It was without doubt the most extraordinary communication I had ever received.

Finally, I stuffed it back into its envelope and left the house immediately with it in my pocket. Poirot would want to see it straight away, I thought. Unpacking could wait.

As I made my way to Whitehaven Mansions, I found myself replaying Vivienne Laurier's words in my mind . . .

Dear Edward,

I, Vivienne Laurier, am writing this letter. In the shock of everything that happened earlier today, I was, temporarily, not myself. Now I have returned to full mental strength and I wish to make clear that I know exactly who I am. There can be no doubt about it. (Please share this letter with Hercule Poirot, if you would not mind. I should like him to know all this too.)

As a police inspector, you no doubt have a tendency to see and understand things from a legal perspective. In a strictly factual analysis, I have only ever been one person. That person changed her name from Iris Haskins to Vivienne March, and then later, when she married, to Vivienne Laurier. According to the law, therefore, the same person betrayed her sister Beatrice, ran away from home to avoid the guilt and shame caused by her actions, and then later met and fell in love with a man called Arnold and bore him two sons, Douglas and Jonathan, whom she loved with all her heart. According to the law, the same woman who devotedly nurtured and dedicated her life to her new family also destroyed her original family—and then, later still, murdered a stranger in a hospital room and then killed her husband.

I have no desire to claim that I (by which I mean the entity I am for legal and criminal purposes) was not responsible for the two crimes committed. The same hand writing this letter was one of two that lifted those vases and brought them down on the heads of two innocent victims. I am perfectly prepared to pay the price for this.

Now that I have made that clear, I wish to explain something else, something that is equally important to me, and I beg that you and M. Poirot try to understand: Vivienne Laurier did not commit those murders. She never would have done such a thing. What I know to be true, as the only expert, the only person who has lived my life, is that Iris Haskins is the killer. It was Iris who did not want to be recognized by her sister Bee. Iris did not want to exist any more at all, you see. And the moment Bee saw her, she would have no choice but to come back into existence. That would have meant that Vivienne Laurier had nowhere to live—no body to live in. Iris knew she was a loathsome, self-centred monster of a person. She was intelligent and honest enough to find her own existence unbearable, and she willingly disappeared so that Vivienne, a completely different person, could take her place. Iris did not want to come back to life—and, being ruthless and depraved, she was willing to kill to ensure that she did not.

I ask you to consider the following: before 8 September, I, Vivienne Laurier had lived a virtuous life of love and service to my family for many, many years. I had hurt nobody, given as much love as possible, and never even raised my voice in anger, not once. Thanks to Iris's self-sacrifice, I was able to be a good, useful person in the world. If I, Vivienne, were a ruthless, violent character, it would have been impossible for me to hide it for so long. The truth is that I am innocent. Iris is the guilty one. As I say: I am of course willing to pay the price for her terrible crimes in a way that she absolutely would not have been, because I recognize that this is what justice demands. (If Iris were still present, which she absolutely is not, then she would pretend not to be in her right mind in order to dodge the hangman. I, Vivienne, wish to behave as honourably as I can, and so have no intention of trying to escape whatever punishment is coming.)

Iris deserves it, there is no doubt. If only she were here to receive it . . . but I am confident that none of us will see her again. I am pleased, at least, that Vivienne has emerged triumphant, even after the shock of today. That, I intend to believe to the last, represents the triumph of good over evil.

I should like to tell you a little about Iris, if I may: what she did to her sister Bee and, as a result, to Zillah Hunt. As you already know from the scene in the library earlier, Bee is not Zillah's second cousin. She is her mother. Until today, Zillah believed that her parents had both contracted tuberculosis while travelling overseas and died while Zillah was still a tiny baby. Verity Hunt had then taken her in, or so went the tale.

The truth was this: as a young woman of nineteen, Bee Haskins had fallen in love with a man called Nicholas Streeter. He had loved her back, and they soon made plans to marry. Both families were delighted, all except for Iris, Bee's older sister by ten years. Iris, still unmarried at twenty-eight, was, unbeknownst to anyone, in love with Nicholas herself and turned bitter and vindictive towards Bee once the engagement was announced. Then one day, a full year before the date of the wedding, Bee discovered that she was pregnant. Both sets of parents, Haskins and Streeter, were devout Christians who would have been shunned by their social circles if a grandchild had arrived who had been conceived out of wedlock.

Bee turned to her former schoolteacher, Verity Hunt, who was the most creative and unconventional person she knew. Neither Bee nor Nicholas could bear the prospect of parting with their baby as soon as it was born, and nor could they bear the thought of their parents' shame and rage if they were to confess to their predicament. Bee was certain her father would force her to give the child up for adoption, and she knew she would not have the strength of character to stand up to him. There seemed to be no solution, and the couple were filled with despair. How on earth could they have their baby, which they loved already, and keep it without their families finding out?

Verity Hunt came up with the answer: she would take Bee with her to the continent as her paid travelling companion. While abroad, Verity would make sure word reached her friends that the true reason for her trip was to have a baby herself, far away from the prying, judgmental eyes of those who knew her in England. Verity, who was independently wealthy and loved to shock people as much as she possibly could, had never given the slightest damn about what anyone thought of her. Bee could write to her parents expressing her shock at the news of this pregnancy, about which she would say that she had not been told before the travels began. Bee was to express her disapproval of Verity's deceit as well as of her loose morals—for Verity was also an unmarried woman—in a series of letters to her parents. And then, some time later, the plan was for Verity to turn out to be a most unsuitable mother. Bee and Nicholas, who would have married by then, would offer to take in the poor child in order to give it a better start in life. None of their parents would disapprove of this, Verity assured Bee; it was the good and correct thing for a public-spirited Christian married couple to do.

Bee made a fatal mistake, however: a few days before leaving for the continent, she confided in Iris, who had always been her favourite sister until Iris had turned cold towards her after the arrival of Nicholas in their lives. Bee hoped that this appeal for help would cause Iris to remember that she had once loved her little sister Bee very much indeed. Sadly, Iris's soul was so rotten by this time that the opposite happened: Iris saw her chance to cause trouble for the young lovers who, as she saw it, had caused her so much pain, and she seized that chance. She told her and Bee's parents about Verity's plan and the illegitimate child. Her parents told Nicholas's parents, who promptly fired him from the family firm and disowned him. Two weeks later, Nicholas took his own life.

Bee's parents were more forgiving than the Streeters: of Bee, but not of Iris, whom they called cruel, vicious and un-Christian. They said that, while Bee could repent and be forgiven for her sins, she, Iris, would surely burn in hell for what she had done. All of Iris's other sisters seemed to agree, and Iris found herself in the position of pariah in her family. No one spoke to her or looked at her. It was as if she were a ghost in her own house.

Then one day, she walked away from her family and her life forever. She did not see her sister Bee again until 8 September this year, when she glimpsed her at the far end of a hospital ward's corridor.

Wrecked by Nicholas's death, Bee was in no condition to bring up a child, and her parents did not feel able to do so either, so Verity Hunt took over. She adopted Zillah, and then seven years later, when Bee was finally well enough to look after herself again and live a normal life, Verity invented the 'second cousin' story so that Bee could become a regular presence in Zillah's life and have a close relationship with her daughter. Regularly in the years that followed, Verity advised Bee to tell Zillah the truth, but Bee refused. She feared Zillah would reject her altogether if she knew that, for seven years, Bee had neglected her motherly duties—that was how Bee put it to herself, at any rate. No matter how often Verity told her to stop being ashamed of herself when she had done nothing wrong, Bee chose to remain the unsullied aunt in Zillah's life rather than risking presenting herself as the mother who abandoned, however involuntarily, her daughter.

Verity, Bee and Zillah all lived together in South Devon until about two years ago. It was only in November 1929 that Verity visited a friend in Norfolk, saw Duluth Cottage with a 'For Sale' sign outside it, and fell in love. She and Zillah had soon moved to their new home, and of course Bee followed them a few weeks later. Bee and Zillah, both nurses, found work at St Walstan's hospital. None of them had the slightest idea that Iris, the monstrous sister who disappeared all those years ago, had become Vivienne Laurier and lived only a short distance away, in Frellingsloe House.

One thing I would like you to know, Edward, is that Bee can see that I am no longer the Iris she knew. She has a new sister now: me, Vivienne. She loves me, and I love her. It is a wonderful blessing to have this happen at the end of my life, and it is a great comfort to Bee to know that I was so shocked by Iris's behaviour towards her that I took the steps I did to ensure that wicked creature would cause no harm to others in the future.

I am glad, in spite of everything, that your mother persuaded me to invite you and M. Poirot to Frellingsloe House. My darling late husband, with whom I am constantly in communication (no, I do not expect you to believe it, but it is true nonetheless), is tickled pink that his murder was solved by the great Hercule Poirot.

Yours sincerely

Vivienne Laurier

25 DECEMBER 1931

CHAPTER 38

Righter Than Thou

Poirot and I had a delightful Christmas Day in London, and refrained from discussing the Norfolk murders apart from for a few brief minutes after lunch. 'We are lucky indeed to have arrived home in time for Christmas,' Poirot said.

'I cannot believe we managed it,' I said. 'With only hours to spare, too. Good old George—he rustled up a proper feast for us at very short notice.' Poirot's valet was something of a wonder. I raised my glass. 'Merry Christmas, Poirot.'

'And to you, *mon ami*. Your poor mother, though. How disappointed she was not to be able to spend Christmas with you.'

'Good! Let her be disappointed. Father Christmas has far too keen a sense of right and wrong to reward mothers who poison their sons' friends.'

Poirot chuckled. 'To think: we might at this very moment be playing the Morality Game, if things had turned out differently.'

Incidentally, this remark of his on Christmas Day was what gave me the idea on New Year's Eve, six days later, of developing my own version of the Morality Game for Poirot and me to play. The sheet of paper I had squashed into a ball and hurled at the fireplace, after deciding it was in dreadfully bad taste, had contained the names of my five nominees for Very Worst Person at Frellingsloe House, and abbreviated notes about why each deserved to hold that title.

In case anyone is interested, my list was as follows:

Mother—for poisoning Poirot.
Vivienne Laurier—for killing Stanley Niven and Arnold Laurier, not to mention all the misdeeds of Iris Haskins.
Jonathan Laurier—for being the nastiest, most uncongenial person in the house.
Janet Laurier—for her grossly unfair treatment of her sister for many years.
Robert Osgood—for his appalling treatment of his fiancée, Olga Woodruff.

Since I seem to have jumped forward to New Year's Eve already—the same place I started this tale—I might as well return to what I began with: the discussion of the thing that surprised me most of all and caused me to want to pick up my pen in the first place: Poirot's apparent wrongness about Vivienne Laurier's motive for committing two murders.

Careful readers will recall that, very close to the beginning of this story, he declared that she had killed Stanley Niven and her husband to prevent her secret from being discovered: that she was, or had once been, the cruel and destructive Iris Haskins.

I told him he was quite mistaken. 'It is not that she wanted to prevent others from finding out,' I said, 'though she knew that was necessary if she was to achieve her main objective.'

'Which was what?' he asked.

'She wanted *not to be, in any way at all or ever again, Iris Haskins.*'

Poirot started at me in puzzlement.

I tried to explain. 'When she walked out of her life, leaving behind her family, her past, and all of her relationships, she did not merely start to *pretend* to be someone else. She became, in her mind, a completely new person. Her continued existence only felt possible to her if she ceased altogether to be Iris, the jealous sister who caused so much harm. She became Vivienne: a new person. She feared people finding out, naturally, but it was not other people knowing that was the most unbearable prospect for her. What she was most afraid of was having to face the truth herself. She knew that if she and Bee Haskins were to come face to face, as might so easily have happened on Ward 6 on 8 September, she would be recognized as Iris Haskins. That would make her, in her own consciousness for that moment, undeniably Iris Haskins and not Vivienne Laurier.'

Poirot was shaking his head. 'Sorry, *mon ami*. You are wrong. Vivienne Laurier knew always, deep down, that she was Iris Haskins. When she told you that she had lost all of her family by the age of 29, it was Iris's family she meant. Therefore, she knew she was Iris.'

'Yes, but—'

'I understand your argument, Catchpool. As well as wanting to conceal her secret from the world, she did not wish to perceive herself as Iris Haskins, or to feel the guilt of Iris Haskins.' Poirot smiled. 'Shall we agree that on this occasion we are both correct?'

'Well, all right, but—'

'*Bien.* We are both right. Nobody is wrong.'

I decided not to pursue it further.

After a silence of a few seconds, Poirot looked up from his book and said, 'Though I do believe that you are a little more wrong than I am, Catchpool.'

THE END

THE AGATHA CHRISTIE COLLECTION

Mysteries
The Man in the Brown Suit
The Secret of Chimneys
The Seven Dials Mystery
The Mysterious Mr Quin
The Sittaford Mystery
The Hound of Death
The Listerdale Mystery
Why Didn't They Ask Evans?
Parker Pyne Investigates
Murder Is Easy
And Then There Were None
Towards Zero
Death Comes as the End
Sparkling Cyanide
Crooked House
They Came to Baghdad
Destination Unknown
Spider's Web*
The Unexpected Guest*
Ordeal by Innocence
The Pale Horse
Endless Night
Passenger To Frankfurt
Problem at Pollensa Bay
While the Light Lasts

Poirot
The Mysterious Affair at Styles
The Murder on the Links
Poirot Investigates
The Murder of Roger Ackroyd
The Big Four
The Mystery of the Blue Train
Black Coffee*
Peril at End House
Lord Edgware Dies

Murder on the Orient Express
Three Act Tragedy
Death in the Clouds
The ABC Murders
Murder in Mesopotamia
Cards on the Table
Murder in the Mews
Dumb Witness
Death on the Nile
Appointment With Death
Hercule Poirot's Christmas
Sad Cypress
One, Two, Buckle My Shoe
Evil Under the Sun
Five Little Pigs
The Hollow
The Labours of Hercules
Taken at the Flood
Mrs McGinty's Dead
After the Funeral
Hickory Dickory Dock
Dead Man's Folly
Cat Among the Pigeons
The Adventure of the Christmas Pudding
The Clocks
Third Girl
Hallowe'en Party
Elephants Can Remember
Poirot's Early Cases
Curtain: Poirot's Last Case

Marple
The Murder at the Vicarage
The Thirteen Problems
The Body in the Library
The Moving Finger

A Murder Is Announced
They Do It With Mirrors
A Pocket Full of Rye
4.50 from Paddington
The Mirror Crack'd from Side to Side
A Caribbean Mystery
At Bertram's Hotel
Nemesis
Sleeping Murder
Miss Marple's Final Cases

Tommy & Tuppence
The Secret Adversary
Partners in Crime
N or M?
By the Pricking of My Thumbs
Postern of Fate

Published as Mary Westmacott
Giant's Bread
Unfinished Portrait
Absent in the Spring
The Rose and the Yew Tree
A Daughter's a Daughter
The Burden

Memoirs
An Autobiography
Come, Tell Me How You Live
The Grand Tour

Plays and Stories
Akhnaton
Little Grey Cells
Murder, She Said
The Floating Admiral†
Star Over Bethlehem
Hercule Poirot and the Greenshore Folly

* novelized by Charles Osborne
† contributor

ALSO BY SOPHIE HANNAH

The Monogram Murders

'*It is hate that makes people kill . . . not love.*'

Hercule Poirot's quiet supper in a London coffee house is interrupted when a young woman confides to him that she is about to be murdered. She is terrified, but begs Poirot not to find and punish her killer. Once she is dead, she insists, justice will have been done.

Later that night, Poirot learns that three guests at the fashionable Bloxham Hotel have been murdered, and a cufflink has been placed in each one's mouth. Could there be a connection with the frightened woman? While Poirot struggles to connect the bizarre pieces of the puzzle, the murderer prepares a hotel bedroom for a fourth victim . . .

'*Grips from the very start. Hannah gets it right in every particular.*'
THE TIMES

'*Immensely satisfying—an ingenious ending*'
INDEPENDENT

'*A highly readable locked-room mystery with a delectable twist.*'
MAIL ON SUNDAY

'*Superbly orchestrated . . . as exhilaratingly complicated as anything by Christie.*'
SUNDAY TIMES

ALSO BY SOPHIE HANNAH

Closed Casket

'What I intend to say to you will come as a shock . . .'

Lady Athelinda Playford has planned a house party at her mansion, but it is no ordinary gathering. She announces that she has decided to change her will, cutting off her children and leaving her fortune to someone who has only weeks to live . . .

Among Lady Playford's guests are Belgian detective Hercule Poirot and Inspector Edward Catchpool of Scotland Yard, who have no idea why they have been invited . . . until Poirot starts to wonder if Lady Playford expects a murderer to strike. When the crime is committed, and the victim is not who Poirot thought it would be, will he be able to solve the mystery?

'Sparkling second outing for Hannah's reimagined Poirot'
SUNDAY TIMES

'Offers a clever twist which the Queen of Crime would have applauded'
DAILY EXPRESS

'Another satisfying addition to the Agatha Christie canon'
IRISH TIMES

'A novel fizzing with ideas and spikey dialogue'
SUNDAY EXPRESS

ALSO BY SOPHIE HANNAH

The Mystery of Three Quarters

'Murder! Me? How dare you!'

Hercule Poirot's tranquil afternoon is ruined when an angry woman accosts him outside his front door. She threatens to report the famous detective to Scotland Yard for falsely accusing her of murder. Seeking sanctuary inside, Poirot is startled to find that he has a visitor—another stranger claiming to have received a letter from Poirot accusing him of killing the same man.

How many more innocent people have been sent letters? If Poirot didn't send them, who did? And who is Barnabas Pandy, the alleged victim—is he dead or alive? Poirot has answers to find, and quickly, or more lives may be put in danger . . .

'What Sophie and Agatha have in common is a rare talent for fiendish unpredictability. They make you see how the impossible might be possible after all.'
SUNDAY TELEGRAPH

'A literary marriage made in heaven!'
THE TIMES

'Sophie does justice to the Belgian brainiac, both in terms of bringing his character to life and giving him a mystery to solve that is worthy of his talents. It's her best Poirot novel so far.'
SUNDAY EXPRESS

ALSO BY SOPHIE HANNAH

The Killings at Kingfisher Hill

'You sat in the seat you should never have sat in,
now here comes a poker to batter your hat in.'

Hercule Poirot has been invited to the exclusive Kingfisher Hill
estate to help defend someone who has already confessed to
murdering Frank Devonport. To get there, he must endure a
journey by coach, which is interrupted by a woman who is
convinced that another death is imminent. Later a body is
discovered with a macabre note attached . . .

Could this new murder and the incident on the coach be clues
to who really killed Frank Devonport? And can Poirot solve the
mystery in time to save an innocent person from the gallows?

'Perfect . . . a pure treat for Agatha Christie fans.'
TANA FRENCH

'I was thrilled to see Poirot in such very, very good hands.'
GILLIAN FLYNN

'The latest in Sophie Hannah's series of mysteries featuring
Agatha Christie's beloved detective is a magnificently intricate
puzzle for Poirot's famous little grey cells.'
DAILY MAIL

MARPLE: Twelve New Stories

'Never Underestimate Miss Marple.'

Whoever you are, wherever you live, we all have our
own 'village', and Miss Marple knows only too well what
wickedness can lie under the most innocuous surface.

Reacquaint yourself with one of Christie's finest creations
as twelve of the world's best writers weave brand new stories
that take you from St Mary Mead to New York, the South
Downs to Hong Kong, the Italian Riviera to Cape Cod . . .

Here, for the first time, Naomi Alderman, Leigh Bardugo,
Alyssa Cole, Lucy Foley, Elly Griffiths, Natalie Haynes, Jean
Kwok, Val McDermid, Karen M. McManus, Dreda Say Mitchell,
Kate Mosse and Ruth Ware—all of them dedicated Agatha
Christie fans and Marple aficionados—have breathed
new life into Christie's much-loved detective.

'All reimagine Miss Marple from a fresh perspective,
while remaining true to her role as a shrewd observer
of human nature and social change.'
GUARDIAN

'Each author captures Christie—and Marple—perfectly,
while also displaying just a bit of her own unique touch.'
WASHINGTON POST

ALSO AVAILABLE

Agatha Christie's Poirot: The Greatest Detective in the World

Hercule Poirot has had near-permanent presence in the public eye ever since the publication of Agatha Christie's very first book, *The Mysterious Affair at Styles* in 1920. And the story of Poirot is as fascinating as it is enduring.

Investigating the phenomenon of probably the world's favourite fictional detective, Mark Aldridge tells this story decade-by-decade, exploring and analysing Poirot's many and varied appearances, not only in Agatha Christie's original novels and short stories but also across stage, screen and radio productions.

Based on extensive research and previously unpublished correspondence, *Agatha Christie's Poirot: The Greatest Detective in the World* is essential reading for any Christie fan, tracing Poirot's footsteps through the literary canon and behind the scenes of nearly a century on screen.

'Delightful, detailed and compulsively readable.'
MARK GATISS

'Exhaustively and entertainingly surveys the book, stage, radio, magazine and film appearances of that fussy little Belgian.'
MICHAEL DIRDA, *WASHINGTON POST*

'What a magnificent book! An essential component of every Poirot fan's book collection. I couldn't put it down.'
SOPHIE HANNAH

ALSO AVAILABLE

Hallowe'en Party

'You want beauty. Beauty at any price.
For me, it is truth I want. Always truth.'

At a Hallowe'en party, Joyce Reynolds—a hostile
thirteen-year-old—boasts that she once witnessed a
murder. When no one believes her, she storms off home.
But within hours her body is found, still in the house,
drowned in an apple-bobbing tub.

Set against a night of trickery and the occult, Hercule Poirot
and Ariadne Oliver must race to uncover the real evil
responsible for this ghastly murder.

Hallowe'en Party is the sensational Agatha Christie novel that
inspired the brand new feature film *A Haunting in Venice*,
directed by and starring Kenneth Branagh.

'A thundering success . . . a triumph for Hercule Poirot.'
DAILY MIRROR

'Complex and sinister, with echoes of old legends
and no flagging of the accustomed verve.'
SUNDAY TELEGRAPH

About the Authors

SOPHIE HANNAH is an internationally bestselling writer of crime fiction, published in more than 50 languages. Her novel *The Carrier* won Crime Thriller of the Year at the 2013 Specsavers National Book Awards. She lives in Cambridge, where she is a Fellow of Lucy Cavendish College, and as a poet has been shortlisted for the TS Eliot Prize. Sophie was awarded the CWA Dagger in the Library in 2023.

AGATHA CHRISTIE is known throughout the world as the Queen of Crime. Her books have sold over a billion copies in English with another billion in foreign languages. She is the most widely published author of all time, outsold only by the Bible and Shakespeare. She is the author of 80 crime novels and short story collections, more than 20 plays, and six novels written under the name Mary Westmacott.